CW00430390

WATCHERS OF THE DARK

LLOYD BIGGLE, JR.

Wildside Press
Berkeley Heights, NJ · 1999

Other Great Titles from Wildside Press!

WATCHERS OF THE DARK

WATCHERS OF THE DARK

ISBN: 1-880448-75-0

Published by:

Wildside Press
PO Box 45
Gillette, NJ 07933-0045

www.wildsidepress.com

To my most faithful readers
Ethel C. Biggle
and
Lloyd Biggle, Sr.

WATCHERS OF THE DARK

1

Whistling gusts of wind drove swirling snow against the glass with a hard, rattling sound. Jan Darzek, watching from his office window, thought that New York City had never experienced a more unlovely snowstorm. The powdery granules ricocheted from the window, performed looping acrobatics at the wind's whimsy, and dove to a moist and grimy doom in the slush churned up by crawling traffic.

Ed Rucks, staring moodily from the next window, demanded, "Why *do* people insist on driving automobiles into Manhattan?"

Darzek grinned at him. "If taxicabs weren't extinct, I'd say you were talking like a cabdriver."

"I'm serious. In this enlightened year of 1988, when our fair city is peppered with trans-locals, and a person can go from anywhere to anywhere at the drop of a half dollar—"

"You're thinking of the automobile as a means of transportation," Darzek told him. "It isn't, except incidentally. Its chief function is play. People drive cars because they like to drive them."

"In Manhattan, in a snowstorm?"

"Automobiles fulfill a very important psychological need. In an age when man is completely at the mercy of the machine, he must have one machine all his own that he can pretend he's the master of. His ego demands it. So he drives a car."

Rucks said doubtfully, "Well, maybe."

"I take it that you think we're stumped."

"I *know* we're stumped. I've never seen an accumulation of facts that added up to less."

"I have," Darzek said, "but I didn't solve those cases, either."

"Look," Rucks said earnestly, "if you really want to identify these snoops, just turn Miss Schlupe loose on them. If she can't find out who they are, they don't exist."

Darzek shook his head. "She's a dear, and I don't want anything to happen to her. If we get close to these people they may decide to play rough."

"It's them you should worry about. Honestly—Schluppy is the deadliest person I ever met. It's her little-old-lady innocence that makes her so dangerous. People don't believe it, even after it happens to them. Like on that Morris case. She gives the guy her cute little smile and says, 'Excuse me, *please.*' Then she breaks his arm. Anyway, these jerks don't play rough. They're darned curious about Jan Darzek, but in a very gentlemanly way."

"Perhaps. But I'm keeping Schluppy out of it. Couldn't you get anything more from Jake Ennoff?"

Rucks shook his head. "It was just a routine inquiry, and he gave it the routine treatment. He thought maybe you'd applied for a loan, or credit, or something."

"Credit! I'll buy that crummy building where he has his office and throw him out!"

"Well, he didn't know you were a rich Universal Trans stockholder until his men turned in their reports. He was paid to investigate you; he investigated you. It didn't occur to him to check on the guy that ordered the investigation. Jake would investigate his own mother, no questions asked, if anyone was willing to pay cash in advance for it. I'll carry on if you want me to, but as far as I'm concerned it's obtaining money under false pretenses. I've done everything I could think of, and everything you could think of, and we don't know any more than we did the day I started."

"All right, Ed. Give Miss Schlupe your time, and she'll write you a check. When I need you again I'll call you."

Miss Schlupe came in a few minutes later. She carefully rearranged an unruly lock of graying hair while she peered at him doubtfully over her spectacles. "Couldn't they find out anything at all?"

Darzek shook his head. "They narrowed the field a little. Three of our unknowns were men from out-of-town detective agencies. Someone paid a lot of money for a full-scale blitz on Jan Darzek. I wonder if he got what he wanted."

"What about Able-Baker-Charlie-Dog?"

"Those four are as anonymous as they were the day we first spotted them. It seems incredible that a dozen good men could investigate them for two weeks without learning a thing, but that's what happened. Maybe they're supernatural. They never go home; they just vanish."

"They may have been lucky."

"I doubt it. Not for two weeks. The fact is that the trans-locals make it almost impossible to tail anyone in New York City. Well, I have two choices left. Either I hire a private army and go after them in a big way, or I ignore them."

"You might try to kidnap one of them. I know a museum custodian. He'd loan us a thumbscrew overnight."

Darzek smiled. "They really haven't done anything except spend a lot of time and money investigating me. Maybe I should be flattered." He turned to the window and looked dreamily at the wind-whipped snow. "Is there a Universal Trans terminal in Tahiti?"

Miss Schlupe sniffed. "You vacation more than you work. Sometimes I think you vacation *when* you work."

"That's because you don't leave anything for me to do."

"Mrs. Arnold called. She wants you for dinner on Sunday."

"I already have an engagement."

"Oh, dear! Have I goofed again? There wasn't anything on the calendar."

"I just thought of it. A friend in Samarkand has misplaced his toupee. He wants me to help him look for it."

Miss Schlupe giggled. "Is Mrs. Arnold matchmaking again?"

"Her cousin is visiting her," Darzek said gloomily. "The Arnolds had me over to meet her, without any warning to either of us, before the poor girl had time to unpack her bags. The way married people keep trying to marry off their friends is incontrovertible proof of the venerable adage that misery loves company.

"It isn't Mrs. Arnold's fault. A man who's as handsome as you are has no business being a bachelor. Blame your blue eyes and your curly blond hair and your broad shoulders. Any woman who doesn't try to marry you off is a traitress to her sex. Anyway, you shouldn't talk like that. I know lots of people who are happily married."

"You do not. You know lots of people who *seem* happily married, but mere histrionics can't disguise the fact that the state of matrimony has two basic flaws: husbands and wives. Every male has an innate talent for being a deplorable husband. Females match this with a truly astonishing aptitude for being wretched wives. What the human race needs is a third sex, neuter, with a boundless domestic capacity. Then either of the present sexes could marry it and be happy. If you think so highly of matrimony, why is it that you never married?"

"A Mr. Smith telephoned for an appointment. He wouldn't say what he wanted."

"Don't change the subject. Why is it that you never married?"

"Nobody ever asked me," Miss Schlupe said sadly. "Mr. Smith is on his way now."

"From where?"

"He didn't say."

Darzek smiled. "John Smith?"

"I didn't think to ask."

"If his business brings him out in this weather, it must be urgent. Did he sound urgent?"

"He sounded like a dead fish."

"I may not see him. If he was using a really original pseudonym, such as Rzeczywistość—"

"Smith may be his name."

"Mmm—I suppose it *is* possible. There must be someone somewhere whose real name is Smith, but the Smiths I meet professionally invariably turn out to be Joneses. Does Universal Trans have a terminal in Tahiti? I think I asked you that."

"I'll inquire."

"Please do."

Miss Schlupe closed the door quietly, leaving Darzek to commune with the storm.

He inventoried his detective agency's current commitments. The poison pen letter writer would take at least another week. The employee who'd been tampering with the Arnado Company's bookkeeping apparatus had been identified, and would be nabbed when he tried it again. The Murray Hill vending machine pirates were a problem for an engineer, but a boresome millionaire had insisted that Darzek take the job. He did, and turned it over to an engineer, who promised to have an answer for him shortly.

The other matters were trivial. With some help from Ed Rucks he could easily be free in two weeks. He stood looking out at the snow and thinking of Tahiti. He had never been to Tahiti. He wondered how he'd managed to overlook it.

Miss Schlupe knocked once and entered quickly, closing the door behind her. "There is no Universal Trans terminal in the South Sea Islands," she announced. "The company confidently expects to establish one there no later than the fall of 1990."

"Fine state of affairs," Darzek grumbled. "The terminal on the moon starts operating next year and they're making noises about putting one on Mars. How could they overlook Tahiti?"

"The nearest terminal is Honolulu."

"All right. I'm going to Tahiti if I have to swim. What are you smirking about?"

"Mr. Smith is waiting."

"I won't see him. I'm not taking on any more work."

Miss Schlupe straightened her spectacles and frowned disapprovingly. "Really! And he walked all the way over here in the snow!"

"I don't care if he skated over on his—what *are* you smirking about?"

"It's *Dog!*"

"Ah!"

"He looks as dead-fishy as he sounds."

"Or dead-doggy?" Darzek went to his desk, seated himself, and announced grimly, "It's cost me two thousand, seven hundred and forty-two dollars, plus whatever you paid Ed today, to not find out who this guy is and what he wants. It better be good. Send him in."

Miss Schlupe smiled Smith-Dog into the room. He shuffled forward awkwardly, reached back to close the door, and seemed discomfited to find that Miss Schlupe had already done so. Darzek remained seated and coldly indicated a chair by his desk. He had seen Smith seven times previously, but never from closer than thirty feet. He watched narrowly while the man got himself settled on the edge of the chair.

Miss Schlupe was right. He looked like a dead fish.

"I understand," Smith said, his eyes fixed unblinkingly on Darzek's face, "that you undertake dangerous commissions for hire."

"I suppose you could put it that way," Darzek said peacefully. "*I* wouldn't, but you may if you like." He thought he had seen mounted fish with more expressive faces. The fish Smith resembled was not merely dead, it was petrified.

"Then—you *don't* undertake dangerous commissions for hire?"

"Certainly not."

Without displaying a ripple of emotion Smith managed to convey the impression that he was dumbfounded.

"Occasionally one of my commissions turns out to be dangerous," Darzek said. "When that happens I place it in the hands of the police at the earliest opportunity."

Smith said slowly, "I was reliably informed that you undertook dangerous commissions for hire. I have such a commission for you, and I wanted to inquire as to your stipend, or fee."

"I don't undertake any kind of a commission without first knowing what it involves," Darzek said. He had been trying to identify Smith's accent, and he realized with a start that the man had none. His pronunciation was so precise that it sounded odd.

"Could you not at least give me some indication of your customary charges?"

Darzek shook his head. "They depend on the expenses I incur, on the time required, and to a considerable extent on the degree of ingenuity that I have to exert. I charge heavily for wear and tear on my brain. Without knowing what it is that you want, I can only say that I am an extremely expensive private detective."

"I do not think that you would incur expenses," Smith said. "The time required might be considerable."

"What do you mean by 'considerable'? Weeks, months—"

"Years," Smith said flatly.

"With extensive travel, I suppose," Darzek suggested with a smile.

"Yes, indeed. Very extensive travel."

"And the commission would be dangerous?"

"Exceedingly dangerous. The odds would be overwhelmingly in favor of your losing your life."

Darzek tilted back comfortably. "On the basis of that information I believe I can tentatively establish a fee, or stipend. I would require an advance payment of one million dollars. I would prefer small bills, ones, fives, and tens, though I wouldn't mind a few twenties and an occasional fifty. When the job was finished to your entire satisfaction, I would then bill you for the balance of my fee. I couldn't tell you ahead of time how much that would be, but I doubt that it would exceed another million."

He had hoped to spark a glimmer of emotion in that disgustingly blank face, but he could detect none. Smith seemed to ponder the matter for a moment. Then he asked, "Isn't that rather excessive?"

"Not to my way of thinking. I don't know what your life is worth, but I value mine highly, and I think I have the right to set that valuation myself."

"I was not questioning your right to your own valuation," Smith said apologetically. "I fear, however, that the fee would vastly exceed my available resources. Is there any possibility that you could accept less? I can assure you that your services are urgently needed. Individuals with your qualifications are exceedingly difficult to find."

"That's why we're so expensive," Darzek said dryly.

"Yes. A million dollars in advance." Smith nodded, then shook his head. He got unsteadily to his feet and turned to offer Darzek a limp, dry hand.

"One question, if you don't mind," Darzek said. "Who sent you to see me?"

"I am not at liberty to disclose that."

"I am not at liberty to accept any commission, at any price, without knowing whom I'm working for."

"To be sure. If we are able to engage you, you will of course be informed fully. However, a million dollars is, I fear—"

"Excessive."

"Precisely. Thank you, Mr. Darzek."

Smith nodded jerkily, pivoted, shuffled from the office. Darzek looked out a moment later and found the outer office empty. He sat down in Miss Schlupe's rocking chair to await her return.

She came in swinging her purse disgustedly, cheeks reddened from the stinging snow, glasses fogged, her protruding gray locks encrusted with white.

"I followed him to the trans-local," she announced. "I thought he pressed the Central Park West button, but he wasn't there, and by the time I got to Central Park East—"

"Never mind," Darzek said. "It wasn't worth the trouble. Someone with money to throw away and a perverted sense of humor is pulling a gag on me. I played it wrong, and Smith got cold feet. Too bad. It might have been good for a laugh, and I could use one on a day like this. I wonder which of my alleged friends are involved."

He took his overcoat from the closet.

"Where are you going?" Miss Schlupe asked.

"To Tahiti," Darzek said dreamily. "Just as quickly as possible."

2

Dawn routed the rioters and sent them scurrying for home.

Biag-n crept from his hiding place to watch them go. Few were wearing light shields, and as the swiftly rising sun streaked the pink sky with glowing orange, they fled from shadow to shadow in a stumbling, groping panic, cupping long, rooty fingers to protect their great, lidless eyes.

An uneasy, smoldering silence settled in their wake. The smoke of a hundred fires choked the horizon; plunder from twice a hundred looted warehouses and dwellings was scattered from one end of Biag-n's oval to the other. Proctors had marched away the foreign traders and their families, and the mobs had moved in behind them to smash and loot and burn. Even the traders' prized personal possessions had been carried off, only to be abandoned at whim. A jeweled dinner paten worth a lifetime's solvency had been casually dropped at Biag-n's door.

Throughout the flame-flecked night, mob after demented mob had raged unseeing past the humble abode of Biag-n the peddler. He accepted that night's miracle gratefully, but he had no illusions as to what the next night would bring. As soon as he dared he crept anxiously from his dwelling dome, sample case under his arm.

Already the hot, hushing cloak of day lay limply across the inert city. Large, luminous blossoms, torn from beds of nocturnal flowers by the trampling mobs, sparkled gemlike amidst the abandoned plunder that littered the black pavement. Sadly Biag-n picked his way around them. The sun had shriveled and curled their petals and flecked the glossy surfaces with a darkening blight. Even their delicate, lingering scent carried the taint of death.

However cautiously Biag-n moved, the sharp click of his tiny feet on indurated silica rang out alarmingly. He winced with every footstep. All of his instinct of self-preservation demanded flight, but he forced himself to walk, to swing one arm nonchalantly while the other crushed his sample case in a tightening grip of terror, to keep his gaze at street level when he knew that the huge, glowing eyes of the natives regarded him with hatred from behind the tinted transparency of their bulging cupolas.

He slowed his pace as he approached the neighborhood *jramp* and squinted into the gloomy interior, but he could make out nothing in that melange of shadows and filter-stained dimness. With a deep, sobbing breath he lunged forward blindly. He had actually reached a destination board, and was haltingly touching off numbers when a proctor sprang out of the shadows with a hoarse cry. "Grilf! Grilf!"

Biag-n ducked under one knobby arm, wrenched free from the grasping, rootlike fingers of another with a rending of cloth, and fled.

Three proctors chased him the full length of the oval, light shields flapping in the breeze, long, segmented legs rattling as they hurdled their way over the riot's ungainly leavings. Biag-n scrambled through a hedge of sleeping night flowers and plunged into the tall vegetation of an herb garden. He clawed his way forward for a short distance and sank panting to the ground. The proctors ranged along the hedge shrilly mouthing vituperations, but they made no attempt to follow him. Even with their shields the full light of day was painful to them, and they soon returned to the cool dimness of the *jramp*.

When Biag-n finally mastered his fright and pushed free of the pungent herbs, the abbreviated Quarmian day had passed its high noon. The sun hung low overhead in a ruddy, cloudless sky. Biag-n turned his back on the *jramp* and resignedly set out to walk. He followed a widely circuitous route about the city's perimeter, carefully avoiding the elliptical clusters of dwelling domes. Afternoon was already waning when he cautiously stepped out of the protective shadow of an orchard to look down on the small, weather-scoured domes of the Old City.

He glanced anxiously at the setting sun and broke into a run. Soon the short Quarmer day would make its abrupt, orange-tinted plunge into darkness, and his last opportunity would be gone forever. He rushed frantically down the slope and had almost reached the congestion of tiny shops and crude factories when a sudden twist of wind brought him to a shuddering halt. Faintly he heard the slobbering clamor of the mobs: "Grilf! Grilf!"

"They're out in daylight!" he gasped.

The narrow ovals of the Old City were still peaceful, deserted. Biag-n hurried toward them, seeking illusive concealment in the domes' humped shadows.

He darted to the first shop and stepped heavily on its call slab. Through the air vents he could see the swirl of colored light. Finally the clumsy door slid open, and the tall proprietor loomed in the doorway. Peering uncertainly through his light shield, at first he did not see Biag-n's short, rotund figure. Then his body bent forward with a snapping of segments. His large eyes glowered behind the tinted shield.

"Go away!"

Biag-n plucked a circle of cloth from his sample case and offered it with a ceremonious sweep of his arm. "I have something to show you."

"Go away!"

The proprietor stepped back; the door closed with a crash. Sadly Biag-n turned away.

Even in normal times they would have resented his calling on them in daylight. On this day they hated him for it, but it could not be helped. They hated him anyway, and he did not dare to wait for darkness.

He sprinted from dome to dome. The few proprietors who responded snapped low to snarl into his face, and then slammed their doors. He wondered how long it would be before one of them summoned the proctors.

He had worked three-quarters of the way around the oval before he thought to vary his approach. As the next door opened he said breathlessly, "Cown, I need your help!"

And pushed inside.

For a moment the Quarmer was too thunderstruck to protest. Biag-n faced him desperately. "I'll have to leave soon. You know that?"

Cown grunted.

"Look at this," Biag-n said, offering the sample.

Cown's rooty fingers moved forward, touched, jerked back. "What do you want?"

"I have a hundred *gios* of this in limited-time storage. If I don't sell it before I leave Quarm, I'll lose it all. It's one of the best bargains I ever happened onto, and you can have it for half what it cost me."

"Get out!" Cown snarled.

Biag-n regarded him steadily. "Cown, have I ever done you an unkindness?"

The Quarmer looked away.

"The order means a big profit for you," Biag-n urged, "and it lets me salvage something from a certain loss."

He searched Cown's face uneasily. The Quarmer must have been aware that ships already at the transfer stations were not unloading, and that no merchandise ordered from Quarm on this day would ever be consigned.

Cown continued to avoid Biag-n's eyes. He said nothing.

"I'll write it up," Biag-n said tremulously, and fed a message strip into his pocket inditer.

He was rather long about it. He had to make the message look like an ordinary order for textiles, and still code as much information into it as possible. He muttered numbers to himself, concentrating fiercely.

Cown continued to look away, but when Biag-n had finished he handed over his seal without a murmur. Biag-n marked the order with a sigh of relief.

"May you prosper," he said gravely.

Cown did not reply.

Biag-n turned to the door, which was still open, and gasped with dismay. The abrupt Quarmian dusk was upon them; the yapping of the mobs was closer, and terrifyingly distinct. "Grilf! Grilf!"

He was too late. There had never been more than a wisp of a chance that he could get a message off, that the clerks would accept it from a despised foreigner. Now there was no chance at all. He could never reach a *jramp* safely.

He took a step toward the door, head bent under the bitter burden of a near-success that had ended in total failure. Suddenly he whirled. "Cown! *You* send the order!"

Cown stared at him.

"I'll pay, of course. It's already coded for my solvency credential. They'll accept it from you. They might even send it." He added softly, "It's the last thing I'll ever ask of you. I pledge that."

Cown's rooty fingers closed on the message strip. He gazed at it dazedly. Behind the tinted hood his face was an expressionless mask of scaly tissue. From somewhere in the circular room came the steady drip, drip, drip of the clepsydra. Biag-n shuddered. He needed no reminder that the fast-moving Quarmer time was running out on him.

Without a word Cown turned and strode toward the door. Biag-n drifted back into the shadows, away from the open doorway and the menace of prying eyes. He counted the clepsydra's drips and cursed this primitive world where one could not dispatch a message, or travel from one place to another, without walking to the nearest *jramp*.

The dusk hardened quickly and became night. The mobs were close by, now, and full-throated. Natives were stirring in the neighboring domes.

Finally Cown returned. "You sent it?" Biag-n demanded. "Was it accepted? Was it really transmitted?"

"Of course," Cown said tonelessly. "I waited for a confirmation. That was what took so long. It also cost you extra."

"May you prosper," Biag-n murmured, with a sweeping genuflection. He clutched his sample case and darted into the night. The one way he could show his gratitude was to leave immediately.

Cown's door crashed shut behind him, and he hunched his shoulders against hostile stares from the neighboring domes as he stumbled off through the thick darkness. He could hear the mobs yapping on all sides of him, and the polished tips of the cupolas dimly reflected the flicker of fires that burned beyond the horizon. More warehouses had been touched off; one was an oil storage, and suddenly it exploded long tongues of flame into the night sky.

None of it mattered now. His message had been transmitted. He could begin his wearisome trek home with a light step, humming triumphantly to himself.

He knew that he would never get there, but he had nowhere else to go.

*　　*　　*

In its first month of operation the Universal Transmitting Company killed the commercial airlines. Railroads and bus companies lasted longer, but both were doomed. Subways were doomed. A few taxicabs still prowled the streets of New York City in search of those rare individuals who were unwilling to walk a block to a trans-local; but an overwhelming majority of travelers, whether their destinations were the other side of Manhattan or the other side of the planet, preferred the step through a transmitter frame to a tedious and in varying degrees dangerous ride on plane, ship, train, bus, subway, or taxi.

Jan Darzek's fortunate investment in Universal Transmitting Company stock ruined his private detective business by making him independently wealthy. His reaction to affluence was the one long-practiced by doctors, lawyers, and other professional men: he raised his prices. A stampede of customers followed. They seemed to think that a man who charged so exorbitantly must be very good—which of course he was—but he found to his chagrin that the clients who could afford his new fees were no more likely to have really interesting problems than those who could not.

He learned something about the detective business that had not been apparent to him while he was earning his living at it. Very few jobs held out much promise at the beginning. The obstruse complications that so delighted him rarely became evident until he had methodically cleared away dead wood and underbrush and probed the problem's root system. He had to accept ten cases to find one that genuinely interested him; and the tediousness of laboring through nine routine cases he did not care about, for fees that he did not need, destroyed his savor of that exceptional tenth.

He loved his work too much to retire, but he found it impossible to keep occupied with the sort of work he loved. He planned exotic vacations to escape the boredom of unwanted cases, and his vacations were invariably ruined by his impatience to get back to his office in quest of the elusive exception.

He was just beginning to realize that he was an unhappy man.

But Tahiti, now. He wondered how he had managed to overlook Tahiti.

Returning from an extended lunch hour during which he had devised three new ways to say no to prospective clients, he jerked open the door of his office and halted dumbfounded. Miss Schlupe, looking flustered for the first time since he'd known her, leaped from her rocking chair with fluttering hands.

"I told the man there was some mistake," she wailed. "But he insisted—"

"*What—in—the—world—is—this?*" Darzek demanded weakly.

Cardboard cartons filled the office, each of them new and neatly taped shut. A narrow alley had been left leading to Darzek's private office. He opened that door and saw more cartons.

"Your name is on every box," Miss Schlupe said defensively. She fluttered her hands again. "What could they be?"

"I don't know. Time bombs, perhaps, though one would think that a dozen or two would satisfy the most bloodthirsty intent. Whatever it is, there must be a couple of hundred of them. Which of my current enemies has no sense of moderation?"

"Are you sure you didn't order something for your trip, and hit the wrong number on your typewriter?"

"It takes more than a typing error to produce a deluge like this one. Anyway, I haven't ordered anything. Go down and have your lunch while I open one."

"Nonsense!"

"Miss Schlupe!" Darzek said sternly. "Your loyalty is not in question here—just your common sense. Go!"

"Nonsense!" She stood on tiptoe to joggle a carton from the top of a pile, caught it deftly, and placed it on her desk. "Open it. It isn't heavy enough to be a very big bomb."

"Then we'll die together, in a small way," Darzek said cheerfully. He slit the tape with his penknife, peered inside, closed the flap.

"You didn't even let me see," Miss Schlupe complained. "What is it?"

"Money."

"Money? You mean all of these boxes—but that's ridiculous!"

"It's more than that. It's outrageous." He handed her the penknife. "Try one yourself."

She lifted down another box and slit the tape. "Money!" she whispered. "Wait'll Internal Revenue hears about this!"

"I don't suppose there's a return address."

"I don't see any."

"Pity. Then I can't send it back. Do we know anyone who has a room-sized vault?"

"Aren't you going to count it?"

Darzek perched frowning on the edge of her desk. "It would take hours. Anyway, I know how much it is. It's a million dollars. Did you see the truck that delivered it?"

She shook her head.

"Pity. If you'd gotten the license number—"

"You never left any instructions about getting license numbers."

"I never thought the occasion would arise. From now on, let's make it standard procedure. Any time a million dollars is delivered here, get the license number."

"Have you any idea at all who sent it?" she asked.

"Certainly. Mr. Smith sent it. I knew as soon as I saw him that he was trying to pull some kind of gag."

"Gag!" she exclaimed indignantly. "Why, there must be hundreds of dollars in every box!"

"Thousands, I think. Who besides the U.S. Treasury would have this much ready cash for a practical joke? Several New York banks, I suppose, but financial institutions have notoriously bad senses of humor. The government has none at all. It has to be Smith."

"You ought to find out if it's real. I could take some of it down to the bank and ask."

"Quiet. I want to think."

Obediently she returned to her rocking chair, and Darzek remained seated on her desk. "Smith offered me a job," he said slowly. "I named my price, and he seems to have met it. I think that constitutes a contract."

"What sort of a job?"

"Quiet. First I'll have to figure out how to get the money to a bank. Then I'll cancel the Tahiti trip, and see a lawyer—"

"You need a whole law firm. Internal Revenue—"

"I'm not worried about the taxes. I want to make a will. Smith said the job might take years, with extensive travel, so there's no point in keeping the office open. It's a shame."

"What's a shame?"

"I've never had to do anything that I liked less."

"What do you have to do?"

"Schluppy," Darzek said sadly, "I never thought it would come to this, but here it is. You're fired."

"Mr. Darzek!"

"I'll pay you two years' salary in lieu of a month's notice. Make that five years. No objections, now—it won't scratch the surface of that million. You can set up your own detective agency. Or retire, and take my trip to Tahiti."

Miss Schlupe blew a blast into her handkerchief. "I don't want to retire," she blubbered. "I want to work for you."

"It's nothing to cry about. There wouldn't be anything for you to do if I kept you on."

"I'm not crying about that."

"Then why are you crying?"

"That's the first time you ever called me Schluppy!"

Darzek picked up a box of money, hefted it thoughtfully, and put it down again. "I don't like this at all. But I made a bad joke, and Smith called me on it, and I feel obligated to take his job. I wonder what it is."

3

There were seventeen new passengers in the ship's day lounge and three in the night lounge, and none of them possessed a time segment's worth of solvency. The captain alternately cursed the world of Quarm and all of its workings for inflicting these unwanted passengers on him and pleaded with those who occupied compartments to make room for them.

"They can't live in the lounges," the captain said.

"Why not?" asked Gul Brokefa, a wealthy trader whose family was occupying two compartments.

"Because," the captain said gloomily, "the Quarmers say I have to take at least a hundred more passengers before they'll release the ship. And if these stay in the lounges, where will I put a hundred more?"

Gul Brokefa rudely suggested a place, and the captain snarled back. There was a spirited exchange before Gul Brokefa flounced away disdainfully.

Biag-n, settled unobtrusively in a remote corner, enjoyed the altercation tremendously. So did the other passengers. They had little enough to occupy themselves. The viewing screen had been turned off at their request; there was nothing to see except the looming silhouette of the transfer station and Quarm's distant, silvery crescent. The one was uninteresting and none of the refugees wanted to look at the other.

Biag-n was sharing a small compartment with four factors and their families. He considered himself fortunate, but this did not prevent him from finding the factors boring, their wives and mates disgusting, and their children an infernal nuisance. Eventually he would have to move in with them; in the meantime, *he* was living in the lounge. He liked it there.

He liked being alive. He had fully expected the rabid mob to tear him to pieces, but the proctors had marched him off to the Interstellar Trade Building, held him captive with other foreigners for three suspenseful days and nights, and finally transmitted the lot of them to a transfer station, where they were assigned to ships.

All cargos had been jettisoned and the ships' hulls packed with passenger compartments, and these now held four times their planned capacity. No one knew how much longer the Quarmers would hold the ship in the paralyzing safety field of the transfer station. The captain, worried about his reserves of air and water and food, had imposed strict rationing.

Biag-n was hungry, but he made no complaint. Eventually they would reach safety, and he liked being alive. He even enjoyed the crowded lounge, where occasionally he could eavesdrop on the conversation of a colossus of interstellar trade, or watch his wife carelessly squandering solvency at a game of *jwur*. In normal circumstances he was not even privileged to glimpse such fabulous animates from afar. The warp of fortune was indeed crossed with both good and bad.

Biag-n quietly got to his feet and trailed after the captain, who was carrying the vain appeal for accommodations to the other end of the lounge. Gul E-Wusk, an enormous old trader and a giant even among the colossuses, sprawled near the entrance to the night lounge in a complicated ooze of arms and legs, proboscis dangling limply in a long-necked goblet of clear liquid. Common gossip had it that he drank water; Biag-n was curious, but lacked the temerity to ask him. The door to the night lounge lay open, and E-Wusk was conversing with a nocturnal invisible in the darkness beyond. An awed group of young undertraders stood nearby, listening with polite fascination.

The captain stated his problem, and E-Wusk quivered with laughter. "Oh, ho ho! A *hundred* more? I didn't even know there *were* so many foreigners on Quarm! Where were they hiding?"

"Under rocks, with the rest of the slime," the captain said gloomily.

"Oh, ho ho! Take my compartment. There's room for twenty there if *I* stay out of it. Take Gul Meszk's, too, and send him back to Quarm. He's a Quarmer at heart—they didn't even burn his warehouses!"

Gul Meszk, an angular sexrumane, was shuffling past with a look of constrained boredom on his pebbly face. He said resentfully, "Is it my fault that I don't stock combustibles? Anyway, they did burn them. They burned all of them. You just didn't happen to see it."

E-Wusk delivered a long, gargling laugh. "You saw *my* warehouse burn. I hope the rascals singed their knobs."

Meszk looked at him slyly. "Now that you mention it, your warehouse *did* produce an unusual smudge."

"Smudge! You saw the flames. The Quarmers had to run home for their light shields. Oh, ho ho!" Rippling waves of laughter encircled his body. "I saw it coming. You can't say I didn't warn you. I cleared out my warehouse ten days ago. I told you then—"

"You told me," Meszk agreed resignedly. "I thought it was another of your jokes."

"Oh, ho ho!" E-Wusk flopped out supinely, gasping for breath. "Thought it was a joke!" He gurgled helplessly. "Oh, ho ho! That *is* a joke!"

"I hadn't forgotten that gag of yours about the *frunl*," Meszk grumbled. "I dumped my whole stock at a loss. So did everyone else."

"That wasn't my gag," E-Wusk said. "It was Gul Rhinzl's. I saw what he was doing and cut myself in on it."

"Anyway, the two of you cornered every scrap on Quarm, and then you doubled the price. With operators like you fleecing them at every turn, no wonder the Quarmers revolted."

E-Wusk shook with merriment.

"So when you came around with that tale of doom and disaster, naturally I didn't believe it. All I did was check through my inventory to try to figure out what items you were after *that* time. Tell me something. If you cleared out your warehouse ten days ago, what made it burn so spectacularly?"

"I leased my warehouse—oh, ho ho—to a *native!* He just got it filled with *mron* oil in time for the fire!"

The undertraders laughed uproariously; Meszk seemed puzzled. "If it was native oil, why did the Quarmers burn it?"

"Quarmer reasoning," E-Wusk gasped. "It was a foreigner's warehouse, don't you see, so they had to burn it. But they were careful to set fire only to the building. They didn't disturb the contents at all!"

The joke spread through the lounge in widening circles. Meszk laughed and moved away, and Biag-n edged closer to E-Wusk. He was smitten with a severe palpitation of the conscience. He had his full report indited and ready to send at the earliest opportunity, and he suddenly realized that he knew nothing at all about the critical question, the only one he had been specifically instructed to investigate. He had forgotten the Weapon.

The wealth of detail provided by a world in revolt had overburdened his senses. He had eagerly inventoried every aspect of the Quarmers' behavior except the one that mattered. He had not once asked himself *why.*

He said timorously, "Excuse me, Excellency, but you—you say that you—*saw it coming?*"

E-Wusk regarded him curiously. "I don't believe that we've met."

"Biag-n, at Your Excellency's service," Biag-n said, with a sweeping genuflection.

"Biag-n. I don't seem to recall—what is your line?"

"Textiles, Sire," Biag-n said humbly.

"Textiles? I still can't place you. Where was your office?"

"I—I sold direct," Biag-n stammered, face suffused with humiliation.

"Ah! But you needn't be apologetic about it. One must start somewhere. I, too, have 'sold direct.' Don't look so startled. I sold direct on Jorund. I had to. I arrived there completely destitute of solvency, after having been evicted from Utuk. The natives took everything. I was also evicted from Jorund, but that didn't cost me much. I may be old, but I haven't forgotten how to learn. After Utuk, I had the good sense to record my surplus solvency in a safe place."

"You've experienced the Dark *three times?*" Biag-n asked breathlessly.

"Four. After Jorund I went to Suur, with distressingly similar results. Now it's Quarm. The Blight, or Dark, or whatever you choose to call it, seems to be pursuing me. But as I said, I've learned. On Quarm I lost almost nothing."

"Excellency, what *is* it?"

"Who knows? Not I, certainly, but I don't think it's any *thing.* It's merely a state of mind."

"Ah! Mind!"

"It's a form of madness, as any fool should be able to see. And it's sweeping the galaxy. These idiots think they're going to transfer to a nice safe world where it'll never bother them again. Nonsense. Intelligent beings can lose their reason any time and anywhere. The Dark, if you want to call it that, will move again. And again. There's no point in trying to run away from it. I'm going only as far as the first world that will let me in. When the Dark next moves, I'll be moving just ahead of it."

"But if it's madness, why didn't we catch it? Why did it affect only the natives?"

E-Wusk delivered himself of a monumental shrug. "As a trader, I deal exclusively in inanimate objects. I've never had occasion to regret that. As long as I know *what,* and I can make a reasonably accurate guess as to *when,* I'll leave the *why* to others. Did you lose much?"

"I didn't have much to lose. Just a few personal effects and my sample case—and they let me keep my sample case!"

"Congratulations! You'll be ready for business the moment you land."

Biag-n withdrew discreetly. He had a new line for his report, and he wanted to think about it. The Weapon, whatever it was, induced a state of madness. That much was obvious—was already known and accepted. And for some inexplicable and highly complicated reason, it worked only on the natives. That, too, was known and accepted.

But a foreigner who had experienced the Dark several times might become aware of the Weapon, might even be able to predict the Dark's coming. Biag-n felt certain that Supreme would find this very interesting.

* * *

Miss Effie Schlupe was indeed a dear. She was over twenty-one and under seventy; a year before she'd had to stop saying she was over twenty-one and under sixty, for she refused to tell a lie except for money. She typed 130 words per minute from her office rocking chair, though when her rocking got too rambunctious her accuracy suffered somewhat. She could peer innocently over her old-fashioned, rimless spectacles at a policeman while picking the pocket of the man behind her. If the subject she was tailing sought solace in a bar, she could drink him under the table while he sobbed out his troubles to her. Three purse snatchers who thought her a likely victim had regained consciousness in hospitals with broken bones. Darzek loved her as he would have loved his own mother if she'd been a jujitsu expert and owned an unsurpassed secret recipe for rhubarb beer. He paid her more money than she had ever earned before, and she retaliated by trying to do all of his work for him.

But now he had fired her. Her pride was hurt. She felt that her employer was unjustly casting aspersions on both her loyalty and her competence, and she resented it.

He was also underestimating her stubbornness, and she resented that, too.

With binoculars she watched from a curtained window across the street while Jan Darzek packed his suitcase.

She knew the suitcase. It had been made to Darzek's specifications, and it would thwart forcible entry by any device less potent than an acetylene torch. Once when Darzek temporarily mislaid his keys an expert locksmith had toiled for five hours trying to open it—unsuccessfully.

Miss Schlupe watched openmouthed as Darzek methodically fitted equipment into the suitcase. "Isn't he taking any clothing at all?" she wondered.

He always carried extra ammunition on a trip—but so much? And were those the gas grenades he'd told her about? And could that be a submachine gun?

"Gracious!" she murmured awesomely. "He's going to start a war!"

* * *

In the basement of a house in an old, eminently respectable section of Nashville, Tennessee, Jan Darzek stepped through an oddly designed transmitter frame.

He emerged in a small circular room, bare except for the transmitting receiver. Through two arched openings could be seen a larger circular room that surrounded it. Curiously he released his heavy suitcase, watched it settle slowly toward the floor, caught it again.

He turned to greet Smith, who emerged from the transmitter on his heels.

"So here we are," he said.

Smith reached for the instrument panel. "Yes—"

A third party shot out of the transmitter and crashed into Smith. The momentum carried both of them through an arch and into the room beyond. Smith lay dazed, too bewildered for speech. Miss Effie Schlupe picked herself up and primly smoothed down her skirt.

"Where are we?" she asked innocently.

"Schluppy!" Darzek exclaimed. His suitcase floated away as he collapsed in laughter. "You followed us—" He wiped his eyes. "You followed us to Nashville?"

Miss Schlupe perched on the wide ledge that ran around the circumference of the outer room. "A hell of a chase you gave me," she complained.

"How'd you get into the house?"

"I picked the lock. You didn't really think you could get away with it, did you? Firing me from the only job I ever had that I really liked. The idea!"

Smith got slowly to his feet and tried unsuccessfully to speak.

"It's my fault," Darzek told him. "I should have expected something like this. Miss Schlupe has a certain bulldog tenacity— female bulldog tenacity, which is the worst kind. Just what were you trying to do, Schluppy?"

"I'm coming along," Miss Schlupe said. "Isn't that obvious?"

"Obviously you've come along, but this is where you get off. Sorry, Schluppy. I'm going to be gone a long time, and Smith thinks the odds are decidedly against my ever coming back. Even when I allow for his naturally pessimistic disposition, I have to admit that the outlook isn't good. There will be dangers the likes of which neither of us have ever imagined. I won't have you mixed up in it. Do your stuff with the controls, Smith, and we'll send Miss Schlupe back to Nashville. Then you'd better throw the switch fast. She has an uncanny sense of timing. Another two seconds, Schluppy, and your dive through the transmitter would have brought you nothing more than an embarrassing familiarity with the basement wall."

"Poo!" Miss Schlupe said. "I'd have made it with plenty of time to spare if you hadn't kept me waiting on those creaky basement stairs until my leg went to sleep. Don't think you can scare me. If there are dangers the likes of which I've never imagined, I want to see them."

Smith spoke for the first time. "Impossible. I could not permit it."

Darzek turned slowly. "What do you have to say about it?"

"My instructions are precise on that point. Supreme requested yourself only."

"Our agreement," Darzek said coldly, "was that I accept your commission and its general objectives, but that I am to have complete freedom in accomplishing these. Did I misunderstand you?"

"No. That arrangement should be fully satisfactory to Supreme."

"Surely that freedom includes the right to select an assistant."

Smith did not answer.

"Miss Schlupe and I wish to converse privately," Darzek said.

"No, just stay where you are." He led Miss Schlupe to the far side of the circular room.

"Where are we?" she asked.

"According to Smith, we're on a spaceship somewhere beyond the orbit of the planet Pluto."

"That's nice," Miss Schlupe said cheerfully. "Is there a view?"

"Be serious."

"What do you expect when you make silly statements like that?"

"Miss Schlupe," Darzek said sternly. "If I weren't an abnormally sane man, the events of the past few days would have reduced me to gibbering idiocy. They still may do so if I have to argue with you about them."

"All right. We're on a spaceship. What are we doing here?"

"Our Able-Baker-Charlie-Dog tandem hails from outer space. That's why they had all of us running in circles. They know tricks I don't even believe after seeing, and they have gadgets I never will believe. How did you ever manage to get a line on that Nashville headquarters?"

"I didn't follow Smith-Dog. I followed *you*. But—outer space?"

"It's true. They wear a synthetic epidermis to make them look human, and it succeeds remarkably, in a dead-fish sort of way. I made Smith remove his, and I have never seen more convincing proof of anything. They really are from outer space."

"What do they want with you?"

"It seems that I once did some work for them. *I* don't remember it, but I must have given satisfaction. Now they've hired me again."

"And me," Miss Schlupe said confidently. "I never had any fun in my life until I went to work for you. You're not firing me now. What did they hire us to do?"

"That's where things start getting complicated. It seems that this galaxy of ours, which we vulgarly call the Milky Way, has habitable worlds without number, with equally numerous intelligent life forms whose appearances would tax the imagination if it weren't for the fact that any healthy imagination would reject them out of hand. Our galaxy also has something that might be loosely referred to as a government, with most of the burdensome appurtenances that this implies. One outstanding exception is a military establishment, which has never been needed. Our galaxy is made up of maybe millions of worlds existing peacefully in free association with each other."

"I don't believe it."

"It is not only beyond comprehension, but also beyond knowledge," Darzek agreed. "One has to accept it on faith. These worlds get along together under one loosely organized galactic government in a peace that defies the laws of nature. So Smith describes it, and if he's capable of either mendacity or subterfuge I haven't been able to catch him at it. The main reason for this halcyon condition is that any world that might upset it is kept isolated and not permitted to play with the others until it's demonstrated that it can be trusted to observe the rules. Which is why we humans don't know anything about it. We have a well-documented predilection for making up our own rules. Earth is what they call an *uncertified world*. Smith's cohorts belong to a certification group that takes our temperatures at regular intervals and seeks to stuff medicine into us without our knowing about it. When they decide that we've been cured of our disposition for foul play, they'll certify us. That doesn't seem likely to happen in the foreseeable future."

"You haven't answered my question. What did they hire us to do?"

"Well—their system worked very well until, as their time goes, recently. Now they're afraid that this galaxy—don't laugh—is being invaded from outer space. A neighboring galaxy, known to us as the Large Magellanic Cloud, is suspect. It has arms trailing in our direction, and several expeditions sent in that direction vanished from the ken of mortal men, if it is correct to refer to the galaxy's collective populations as 'men.' A logical inference would be that whoever or whatever resides in the Large Magellanic Cloud got curious as to where the unwelcome expeditions were coming from, and decided to investigate. Hence our Milky Way galaxy is being invaded from outer space. Now what's the matter?"

Miss Schlupe had burst into wild, uncontrolled laughter. "Excuse me," she said, raising her spectacles to dab at her eyes. "But it's so *silly!* The galaxy is being invaded. That sounds like a military operation on a scale that would make World War II look like a fracas in a flowerpot. So what do they do about it? They call in a private detective!"

"Smith couldn't explain it, so don't ask me to. Supreme, whoever that may be, asked for me by name, and what Supreme asks for Supreme gets. Look. Some menace from outer space, which they refer to as the Dark, is gobbling up worlds in huge gulps. They haven't been able to figure out what it is, or how it manages to do the gobbling. That's the job they're handing to me. I'll be a spy, with a very good chance of being shot at the dawning of some sun I never knew existed."

"Then I'll be shot with you. It'll be better than rusting away in my rocking chair."

Darzek smiled at her. "This will be a grim sort of business. I'm tempted to take you along for the laughs. I may need a few."

"Ha ha. I'm coming along to *work.*"

"You will," Darzek promised. "And you may not like it. We start by going to school. Before we can move freely in a strange civilization we'll have to learn everything from the language to how to hold our teacups. It won't be easy."

"Can I go back to New York before we leave?"

"You'll have to. If you don't do something about your apartment, Missing Persons will be looking for you. If you don't pack a suitcase—carefully—you may be doing some looking yourself. Macy's won't have any branches where we're going."

"I gave up my apartment before I left, and I have a suitcase packed. Carefully. It's in Nashville."

"Then why do you want to go to New York?"

"My sister has what was left of my rhubarb beer. I want to take some along."

Darzek threw up his hands despairingly. "Smith, our departure will be delayed while Miss Schlupe inventories her beer."

Smith stepped into view and said blankly, "I don't understand."

"Miss Schlupe comes with us. Her suitcase is in Nashville and her beer is in New York. A deplorable state of affairs. Get her to both places, so we can leave."

Smith stoically turned toward the transmitter.

4

They lost track of time.

Day and *night* were meaningless in the unending light of the softly glowing walls that enclosed them. *Hours* became a dubious subdivision of a temporal reference that no longer existed. Their watches ran down and were packed away.

They slept when tired. They ate perfunctorily when hungry from an enormous stock of canned goods that Smith had brought from Earth.

They studied.

Smith, displaying qualities that would have made him a creditable success as Simon Legree in a small-time stage production, tirelessly kept them at their lessons. He lashed them with words when they faltered, and, on the rare occasions when they pleased him, damned them with faint praise. ("You learn well—but so *slowly!*")

First they learned a basic interstellar language that Smith called, in all seriousness, *small-talk.* It was so wonderfully concise, so amazingly logical, that they would have mastered its rudiments in a sitting had it not been for the pronunciation, which was fraught with fiendish traps for the human vocal apparatus.

They quickly achieved a measure of fluency in *small-talk,* though they continued to massacre its pronunciation. Then Smith introduced *large-talk,* and the words they already knew were revealed to them as abbreviated clues to an incredibly rich, dazzlingly vast panorama of expression.

They arrived—somewhere—and transmitted from the spaceship

to a sealed suite of rooms in Smith's Certification Group Headquarters. They studied. They learned to talk, read, and write *large-talk*. They learned a supplementary universal alphabet whose characters turned out to be numbers, allegedly capable of arrangement in combinations that could depict the sounds of any of the uncounted spoken languages of the galaxy. There was also a universal *touch* alphabet, for species of intelligent life incapable of phonation, and special modifications for species with sundry other handicaps. Darzek found himself gloomily contemplating the problem of communicating with a species that possessed no senses whatsoever.

"I know of none," Smith said, with a slight gurgle that Darzek had begun to suspect was a laugh. "But anything is possible. It takes all kinds to make a galaxy."

"I believe you," Darzek said fervently.

Smith was one of them. He had shed his epidermis as soon as they shed Earth's Solar System, and he appeared vaguely human in the way a human might look after he'd been run over by a steamroller: flattened out. Immensely broad when viewed from the front, but unbelievably thin in profile. His face was caved in, its features weirdly inverted. The enormous eyes were widely separated and almost on a line with the single, gaping nostril. The mouth was a puckered gash in the chin, the neck a slender pipe. There were no ears or hair. The flesh was of a distinctive hue that Miss Schlupe at once labeled *oxygen-starvation blue*.

"If he wants to remove *that* epidermis, too, it's all right with me," she had confided to Darzek.

Smith added absently, "There are even species that have rather involved communication systems based upon odors, but no one has ever been able to reduce these to symbols."

"Thank God!" Darzek exclaimed.

"You must have a fair mastery of *large-talk*, and if you remain long on a world you may want to learn the local languages, assuming that you are physiologically capable of doing so. You needn't worry about the more complicated forms of communication, but you should know about them. For example, a strange male who approaches and touches a female on your world would be guilty of criminal misconduct. In interstellar society the action would be recognized as a search for someone with an understanding of touch speech."

"There'd be the same understanding on Earth," Darzek said, "but the woman probably wouldn't like what was being said."

"I mention this so that if it should happen to Miss Schlupe she would not react in the accepted manner of your Earth women."

Miss Schlupe blinked innocently. "I'd take it as a compliment—on Earth or anywhere else."

"If all we need to know is *large-talk*, let's get on with it," Darzek said.

"*Large-talk*," Smith agreed gloomily. "And manners and customs and finance and business and practical technology and—and the Council of Supreme is becoming impatient. There is so little time, and you learn so *slowly*."

Finally there was a brief farewell ceremony with Smith, and Darzek and Miss Schlupe drank a toast with the last of Miss Schlupe's rhubarb beer, which Smith refused to touch. They stepped through a special transmitter hookup to a passenger compartment of a commercial space liner. With that step they crossed their Rubicon. They knew, now, that they could not turn back. They did not even know how to get back.

While Miss Schlupe curiously explored the compartment's five compact rooms, Darzek opened his suitcase and took out a thick throw rug. He carefully arranged it in front of the transmitter.

"What's it for?" Miss Schlupe asked.

"It's a little thing I rigged up before I left. I got to thinking about the implications of life in a transmitter-orientated society, and I decided that I didn't like some of them. Step on it."

Miss Schlupe did so and leaped off hurriedly when a buzzer rasped.

"I couldn't sleep if I thought anyone or anything could step into my room without knocking," Darzek said.

"Is that possible?"

"It shouldn't be, but I'm taking no chances."

"What if they jump over it?"

"A person sneaking into a room is more likely to tiptoe than to jump."

Miss Schlupe winced as a thump sounded over their heads and the compartment shuddered. "What was that?"

"Probably they're loading another compartment. These space-ships are hollow hulks, except for their operation and service sections. The transmitter eliminates the need for corridors and stairs and elevators and such paraphernalia. Passenger compartments are taken aboard as they are engaged, and hooked up to power and ventilation connections. They load freight compartments the same way. We may have tons of freight above us, but that doesn't matter in weightless space—and a spaceship never ventures where there's significant gravity. We can be buried in the tail of the ship and still be only a step from the passenger lounge by transmitter."

"How long does it take them to get us out of here if the transmitter doesn't work?"

Darzek shook his head and dropped onto a chair. It gently shifted to accommodate him, thrust up a protrusion to support his back, spread out to provide a footrest. "Lovely," he murmured. "I wonder if they call it 'Interspacial Modern.'"

Every piece of furniture looked like a monstrous hassock, and certainly contained enough electronic gadgetry to stock a TV repair shop. The chairs could accommodate the posterior or anterior contours of any conceivable life form, at any desired height, and were probably adjustable in ways a human wouldn't think either necessary or possible. The larger cylinders served as tables or desks, and kept records, recorded financial transactions, sent and received anything from a message to a full-course meal. Darzek would not have been surprised to learn that in private homes they also did the laundry and cared for the children.

Miss Schlupe seated herself beside him. "I miss my rocking chair," she grumbled.

They followed the routine they had become inured to: they studied. Occasionally they practiced ordering food with the service transmitter, but they took most of their meals from the dwindling stock of Earth food. When they tired of study Darzek paced the floor, grappling futilely with the many questions Smith had left unanswered, and resisting the temptation to deplete his stock of cigarettes. Miss Schlupe got out her knitting, and read and reread the stack of confession magazines she'd brought along, accompanying her clicking needles with disapproving clucks of her tongue.

Smith had recommended that they remain in their compartment, but Darzek, to satisfy his curiosity, made one trip to the ship's lounge. Several of the life forms he encountered there could not be believed even when seen, and this fact convinced him that galactic civilization was best taken in a long series of extremely small doses until one had built up an immunity to it.

They experienced no sensation of motion. A transmitter that transmitted itself, the ship moved through space on a series of enormous transmitting leaps, each laboriously calculated. *Area-transmitting*, Smith called it: it involved a leap to a destination area, carefully selected to avoid suns; as distinguished from *point-transmitting*, which was used only for limited distances within a solar system, and even then was rarely attempted without a transmitting receiver. The ship's final transmitting leap would be to the general area of its destination. There it would revert to the clumsy status of an atomic-powered rocket in order to reach its assigned transfer station.

They were only an Earth day from Primores, the central sun of the galaxy, when Miss Schlupe finally spoke the thought that had been on both their minds since they started.

"I don't like it," she said. "I wish Smith had come along."

"Smith was scared silly. Didn't you notice?"

She stared at him. "How could you tell?"

"Various things. He was afraid of the Dark, no pun intended. He was afraid the Dark would somehow locate us and polish us off right under his indented nose. That's why we were spirited away from Earth in a sealed compartment, and why we were then held incommunicado in sealed quarters, and why Smith made elaborate arrangements to put us on this ship without our passing through a transfer station. The crew on Smith's ship didn't know we were aboard. No one at Certification Group Headquarters—except Smith—knew we were there. And no one on this ship knows anything about us except that we're here. Smith was scared silly that the Dark would find us."

"It doesn't make sense," Miss Schlupe said.

"It makes a great deal of sense. It shows us how omnipotent this menace is. What it's done is so utterly unbelievable that rational people like Smith are convinced it can do anything."

"It doesn't make sense to me. If Smith feared for our safety, why did he kick us out on our own? Why didn't he come with us?"

"He's a prominent certification official. He was afraid it would compromise our mission if he were seen with us. He was afraid to take steps to protect us, because they would only attract attention to us, and the omnipotent Dark would promptly finish us off. An escort would attract attention. A special ship would attract attention, because nobody travels on special ships. A disguise might be recognized as such, and make the Dark's agents wonder what we were trying to hide. Our only chance of safety is to be so inconspicuous as to be beneath suspicion."

"All right. So we arrive at Primores, and this Biag-n, or whatever his name is, meets us, and everything is hunky-dory. But what if he doesn't show?"

"He's an agent of Supreme, so he's probably a highly capable person. He knows the ship we're on. He knows what we look like. We know what he looks like. Nothing has been left to chance. At least, I hope not. I'm looking forward to meeting this Mr. Biag-n. If he really knows the Dark from personal experience, I want some long overdue answers to about a thousand questions."

"I still think Smith should have come with us."

"I think so, too, but there was no arguing with him. Like I said, he was scared silly."

They cleared away all traces of their occupancy, dumping the last of their Earth food into the disposal, and they were packed and waiting when the signal came to disembark. Each of them clutching a suitcase, they stepped through to Primores Transfer Station Twelve, Arrival Level.

And into a surrealist's private zoo.

For all of Smith's talk about the galaxy's divergent life forms, nothing he said had quite prepared them for this. Long before their minds had decided to accept what their astonished eyes saw, the sounds and odors had overwhelmed them. Several ships were unloading simultaneously, and from the curving row of transmitters came striding things, leaping things, scurrying things, crawling things, slithering things, even *bouncing* things, all pouring nonchalantly into the milling press of the Arrival Level. Some carried luggage, some towed it floating above them or rolling along the floor. A few were carried by it, riding haughtily on purring, streamlined valises.

Darzek, keeping a firm grip on his own suitcase, nudged Miss Schlupe out of the central flow of passengers and into a quiet eddy, where they both stood staring.

"The mere thought of it would have driven Noah nuts," Darzek observed. "I never realized what a relative thing beauty is. Take that snail, for example. Not that one, the one with legs and no shell. Its shape is unimaginably ugly and its colors are indescribably beautiful. Smith was right. We didn't need a disguise. I couldn't even imagine a shape that would be conspicuous in this melange. Is that an octopus with wings?"

"How will this Biag-n character locate us in this mob?"

"We'll be conspicuous enough to anyone who knows what we look like. No chance of confusing us with that insect, for example —are the flowers part of its head, or is it wearing a hat? Biag-n should be conspicuous, too. Just keep an eye open for Tweedledum in skirts."

They drifted in widening circles, adroitly dodging through the main currents of traffic and pausing frequently. The room began to thin out.

"Somebody goofed," Miss Schlupe announced firmly.

"It would seem so. However, we must allow for the inevitable mix-up and the unavoidable delay. This is Transfer Station Twelve; our friend may be dashing from station to station looking for us. Let's keep circulating."

They began another circuit of the room. More ships had docked, and the arrival gates debouched a fresh surge of passengers. "It may be that he's here, but doesn't think the moment propitious," Darzek said. "He may want to check carefully to see if anyone is spying on him."

"Spying with what?" Miss Schlupe demanded irritably. "Some of these things don't have eyes. Some are even luckier—they don't have noses."

Darzek looked at her quickly and thought he detected a tinge of green in her normally ruddy complexion.

"I don't mind the way they look," she went on, "and I could probably get used to all this hissing and squealing and honking, but the *smells!*"

"It does seem that we've stumbled upon an unlimited market for perfumes and deodorants," Darzek agreed. "We can't be certain, though. Maybe what we smell *is* perfume and deodorant!"

They joined the newcomers and again drifted slowly across the room toward the numbered transmitter gates that linked the transfer station with the planets of the Primores system. Before they reached them they turned aside, made a half-circuit of the room, and began the trip anew.

"Somebody goofed," Miss Schlupe said again.

"I was wondering if for some reason or other they might have found it necessary to send a substitute, but none of these hallucinations seems to be looking for us. They're all intent on going somewhere else, and it's just occurred to me that we'd better do the same, before someone gets the idea that we're behaving abnormally."

"Sure. Where will we go?"

"Schluppy, you have a remarkable gift for placing your finger on the precise nub of the problem. Let's give it one more try."

They joined another surge of newcomers, but Darzek felt certain, now, that they were wasting their time. They were not going to be met—by anyone.

5

Darzek nudged Miss Schlupe, and they turned away from the transmitter gates and followed a trickle of passengers toward the only other exit. Beyond the flat arch of a wide doorway were the moving conveyors that connected the passenger levels of the transfer station.

"Where are we going?" Miss Schlupe asked.

"To the dining room. It's the one place where we'll have a reasonable excuse for waiting, and we can do it sitting down."

"Good idea. What are we waiting for?"

"I don't know. If Biag-n does show up, he'll certainly look for us there. In the meantime, we can be thinking about what we're going to do if he doesn't come at all."

They rode the conveyor, and on the upper level they passed through a small lobby flanked with more transmitters and entered the enormous, transparent-domed dining room.

The light rose mistily from the floor, and they unconsciously tiptoed as they crossed to an empty table. Darzek set down his suitcase and dropped onto a hassock with a sigh of relief. Even in the light gravity of the transfer station his arsenal quickly became uncomfortably heavy. Sitting sidewise—for the cylindrical table provided no place for his feet—he turned to face Miss Schlupe.

"I wish I'd brought a camera," she said. "I could have taken enough monster magazine snapshots to make me independently wealthy."

"You couldn't sell them. There are limits to the credulity of even a monster magazine editor."

As he spoke a huge ball bounced past, landed on a chair at an unoccupied table, and deflated noisily into an untidy heap. Darzek blinked and rubbed his eyes.

Miss Schlupe snickered. "That looked like fun." Then she glanced behind her and blanched. Seated at the next table was something that resembled a large sausage, with arms and legs. It was eating, with reverberating gusto, something that looked like small sausages.

There were *almost* humans everywhere, creatures whom some distorting mirror trick of evolution had left with blurred features or gruesomely unbalanced proportions. There were also incomprehensibly hideous monsters with disconcertingly human features.

"Do we look just as odd to them?" Miss Schlupe asked.

"I doubt it. If they've been participating in scenes like this all their lives, I don't see how anything could look odd to them. Shall we order?"

"How can anyone eat, with all these smells?"

"If we sit here very long without ordering, we'll start being conspicuous again."

"All right. I just hope we don't get sausages. I'd feel guilty eating them, with one sitting next to me."

Darzek opened a service panel and carefully touched out his order on the rows of numbered and colored slides, mumbling the formula that Smith had taught to them: All food well cooked (neither raw, half raw, nor burned); meat moderately aged (neither fresh nor spoiled) and of the third type (which was vaguely similar to beef—Smith had discouraged him from trying anything else); vegetables of the first type; all food prepared in chewable form, in pieces no larger than human mouth-size; a small portion of each (they seemed huge, to Darzek) with service of the second type. The dishes would be shallow rectangular bowls, and there would be a small ladle, modified on one side to facilitate pouring liquids into mouths of various shapes, and a set of automated tongs for the solid food. Darzek had been unable to find a drink that appealed to him, so he ordered water. That, too, would be served in a shallow bowl.

Darzek turned to Miss Schlupe, who was mumbling over her own service panel. "Ready?"

"I suppose."

They offered their solvency credentials for the table's scrutiny, placing the palms of their right hands over the unblinking crystalline eyes of the service panels. It accepted the two orders with a purr and a click.

"Marvelous invention, the solvency credential," Darzek murmured.

It was an invisible tattoo, an artificial fingerprint that served as legal signature and all-purpose identification card. It was the key that enabled them to use their monetary reserves, or solvency, which had been registered with the spaceship's passenger service for automatic transfer to the Primores Credit Central on arrival. It also ensured that private transmitters would not admit unauthorized persons, but in that respect Darzek was not fully prepared to trust it.

"I'm afraid I did something wrong," Miss Schlupe said.

"Even if you did everything right, you're due for a surprise. Smith said that foods will vary drastically from place to place. Each world will have its own type three meat, for example, no two of them alike."

"Oh, dear. I'm afraid I didn't order type three." She sighed. "I'd just like to have a waitress walk in and take my order for a hamburger. I suppose when they have all of these monsters to feed, and each kind needing a different food, prepared and served in a different way, they can't possibly worry about satisfying individual tastes."

"True. It must be quite a problem just to provide something that every life form can eat."

"Anyway, it's a lovely dining room."

Darzek nodded. "Many of the customers have little or no sense of taste anyway. The atmosphere in which they eat is more important to them than the food."

The table clicked; the service panels opened. Darzek's food was approximately what he expected; Miss Schlupe had made several small errors. Her meat dish looked like a segment of dinosaur bone, stuffed with what was obviously large insects and covered with a rubbery-looking sauce. Her vegetable dish was grass in an advanced stage of decomposition. She hurriedly slid the dishes into the disposal slot.

"Try again," Darzek suggested.

"No, thank you. You eat. I'll watch the stars."

Darzek chewed ruminatively, indulging in an occasional sidelong glance at the nearby tables. On his right, a human-sized insect was imbibing some unmentionable liquid from a tall, narrow-necked container into which it had unreeled a proboscis. At the next table a feather-flecked snake was crunching something that looked like tree bark.

"How's the food?" Miss Schlupe asked.

"The meat is tough and the vegetables are cooked to a pulp, but it's edible."

She turned her attention to the sky, where a multitude of dazzlingly bright stars wheeled in a breathtaking panorama. The view was magnificent, but Darzek could not enjoy it with her. He was more worried than he cared to admit. At any moment she would be asking what he intended to do next, and he did not know.

There had been too much secrecy and too much haste, and no provision for unexpected contingencies. The missed contact wouldn't matter if they'd been properly prepared to find their way about on a strange world. They hadn't been. They had no idea of where the illusive textile merchant planned to take them, or how to get in touch with the mysterious Council of Supreme. They could not even retrace their steps and try again. Smith would have left his headquarters, and none of his subordinates knew that they existed.

"What are we going to do?" Miss Schlupe asked.

Darzek shook his head.

"We're in trouble," she said flatly.

"We'll muddle through somehow. The important thing is not to panic. We haven't been here much more than an hour, and we don't know whether punctuality means anything in this society. Maybe our errant Biag-n is busy elsewhere. We'll wait awhile longer, and then—what's the matter?"

Miss Schlupe gasped. Darzek followed her upward, transfixed gaze and saw a body floating across the transparent dome, just outside the station. It differed in two important respects from the other life forms they'd seen: in its small, rotund shape, and in the fact that it was quite spectacularly dead. The sudden thrust into vacuum had caused certain of its internal organs to explode through its mouth. It turned slowly, head over heels, entrails trailing gracefully, and with a myriad of frozen droplets of purplish blood fanned out in its wake.

The room's cacophony of weird sounds suddenly subsided to horrified silence. Those with vision stared hypnotically upward; the sightless stirred uneasily. Miss Schlupe, who possessed an iron stomach, was struggling valiantly not to be sick.

"Wait here!" Darzek snapped, and leaped to his feet. He glanced once more at the orbiting corpse as he left the dining room; it had reached the apex of the dome, still performing in slow motion its ghastly acrobatics.

He cursed himself for an inexcusable blunder. He had learned long since that one could not control events while sitting around waiting for them to happen; and yet he had wasted time in leisurely dining and gawking like an innocent tourist while his contact was being brutally and horribly murdered.

He rode the descending conveyor down to the Arrival Level and thoughtfully looked about him. "He was here to meet us," he muttered. "If he was conscientious—and a person who takes his job seriously enough to give his life for it is likely to be conscientious—he was here early. He was waiting on this level. Then what?"

Beyond the conveyors a corridor curved out of sight. Darzek followed it, forcing himself to walk normally. Instantly he scented danger. The passageway was curving, curving, curving to the point where it would intersect the inevitable orbit of Biag-n's death flight. Doors were spaced irregularly along either side: here, there, and there again; then, unexpectedly, two facing each other like the jaws of a trap. Darzek placed his hand on the automatic in his shoulder holster as he passed them, and tried to remember if these strange collapsing doors could be opened silently. He kept looking back even after the doors had vanished around the curve. As often as not sudden death was compounded of minutiae such as that; which was perhaps something that Biag-n had not known or had forgotten.

Then Darzek was at the end of the passageway, standing between two more facing doors and thinking it unaccountably strange that he could walk halfway around this bustling transportation exchange without meeting either body or—to whatever extent the expression was applicable—soul. He turned to the doorway on the right, pressed the release and held it, and let the door drop slowly.

His apprehension had been correct; it made no noise.

Beyond it was an office, with a few workers bent over cylindrical desks. A row of elliptical windows looked out into space. Darzek stepped back and silently rippled the door closed.

He turned to the opposite doorway, opened it, and stepped inside.

The room had some kind of maintenance function, but Darzek dismissed the complex of strange machines with a glance. On the floor lay a small circular container, dented as if from a blow. Nearby was a broad stain that looked black in the tinted light, and a trail of black droplets that led to the transparent double doors of an air lock.

Darzek picked up the container and opened it. The neat compartments were filled with circles of fabric, each with an identifying mark.

He gave the room a final, searching look and turned away. He retreated cautiously, watching the doorways, and relaxed only when he reached the conveyors. Grimly he rode back to the upper level.

Miss Schlupe was waiting expectantly; several nearby tables were empty. The corpse was no longer visible.

"What's been happening?" Darzek asked.

"Three giraffe's uncles came charging in just after you left. They took one look at the thing and charged out again. Several diners lost their appetites and left hurriedly. Otherwise, nothing."

"They'll probably intercept it before it makes another orbit."

"After all that talk about remaining inconspicuous, you picked a fine moment to dash out."

"It couldn't be helped."

"What's that?"

"Our textile merchant's sample case."

Her eyes widened, and she clapped a hand to her mouth. "Then—" She gestured at the dome. "Then that was—"

"Biag-n. Of course. Didn't you recognize him?"

"I suppose I was too shocked to really see him. What's in the sample case?"

"Samples. I didn't dare take time for more than a quick look."

"What did you find out?"

"That he was dead when he was pushed into space. Stabbed, maybe, except that there was an unusual amount of blood for a stab wound. His kind may bleed easily."

"We're in trouble."

Darzek nodded. "The Dark has been infiltrating even more successfully than Smith realized. A few guesses: The Dark knew we were coming. It knew Biag-n was going to meet us. It *didn't* know who we are, or where we were coming from."

"How can you be sure?"

"If it had known, we'd have been met—by agents of the Dark." She shuddered.

"It isn't too difficult to reconstruct what happened," Darzek said slowly. "Biag-n was waiting for us on the Arrival Level. A friend, an associate, perhaps a stranger pretending to be an associate, came to him and said, 'I have important last minute instructions. Let's go where we can talk.' He led Biag-n to an empty room. There was a struggle—the sample case had been stepped on—and then a murder. The murderer didn't want to leave the body where it was, and the clerks in the next room could have seen it at once if he'd pushed it out into space. So he sent it slowly upward to orbit the station, and he had time to transmit elsewhere or lose himself in the crowds before it became visible up here."

Miss Schlupe shuddered again.

"Put it down that our textile merchant was, in his small way, a considerable hero. I'm betting that they used persuasion, threats, bribery, maybe even torture to make him betray us. He wouldn't have any of it, so he died. That's worth remembering. It isn't just a job that we're working on. It's a cause, and some of these creatures are loyal enough to die for it."

"*One* of them was loyal enough," Miss Schlupe said. "He's dead. Who else can we trust?"

"No one on this transfer station," Darzek said. "So let's leave it."

Back on the Arrival Level, Darzek studied the transmitter gates for a moment and chose the longest line. "The heaviest traffic should be going to the capital city of the capital world," he said. "And that's where we want to go. At least, I think it is."

"We could ask someone."

"Who—the assassin? Take the sample case, will you? I'd like to have one hand free."

"No one seems to be paying anything," she observed.

"Not for my solvency credential," Darzek said dryly. "For my automatic."

The line moved steadily. Several times Darzek looked about him suspiciously, but none of the fantastic arrays of eyes in his immediate vicinity seemed to be focused on him.

They approached the transmitters. Miss Schlupe called over her shoulder, "Stay close behind me. If we don't come out in the same place, all I'll be able to do is sit down on my suitcase and look lost."

She stepped through.

Darzek followed on her heels, and they emerged a stride apart in the staggering drag of full gravity. They were in an enormous dome, but they saw little of it because it enclosed another dome almost as large.

Around the base of the inner dome were the transmitter receivers out of which the arriving passengers emerged. Opposite, around the base of the outer dome, were three-sided alcoves lined with transmitters. They drifted uncertainly, moving at right angles to the flow of traffic; the other passengers walked directly to the nearest alcove, touched out destinations on do-it-yourself transmitter controls, and disappeared.

"Are we being followed?" Darzek asked.

"No," Miss Schlupe said.

"Let's go back. We're as likely to figure out this setup where we came in as any other place, and we're being highly conspicuous."

They retraced their steps and stood with the traffic flowing around them, studying an alcove. "Obviously this is the main transmitting exchange," Darzek said. "Each of these alcoves should be equipped to handle all the likely destinations for anyone arriving here."

"Did you notice the floor?" Miss Schlupe asked.

Darzek nodded. "Three banks of transmitters, and a different floor pattern in front of each: wavy lines, straight lines, and checkerboard. Meaning—"

"Different cities?"

"*All* the likely destinations," Darzek said meditatively. "One pattern would be for other planets of this solar system, or the moons and transfer stations. That would be the one with the fewest transmitters. Another would be for other destinations on this world. The third—"

"Destinations in this city?"

Darzek nodded. "And since the greatest volume of traffic will be local traffic, that pattern should have the most transmitters. So we'll use one of those."

"And we'll end up on a street corner. Or in a Turkish bath."

"Good idea. One of these characters with tentacles could be the masseur I've always wanted to find."

They had moved slowly toward the alcove; again they stopped to scrutinize it, letting the traffic flow around them. Miss Schlupe said nervously, "Are you about to be brilliant? If so, hurry it up. We're conspicuous again."

"Say a businessman arrives by plane at Kennedy International Airport. Where is he likely to go first?"

"Maybe to his hotel, but he'll have a reservation, or he'll telephone for one from the airport. We haven't, and can't. At least, I haven't seen any phone booths."

"Nor any Travelers' Aid," Darzek said thoughtfully. "And yet there must be some way for a stranger to engage a hotel room or its equivalent. I just noticed that the transmitter on the end has no destination board. Anyone using it just presents his solvency credential. Watch."

"Do you think—"

"I think it's possible. All the other transmitters are free. Shall we try?"

They approached the transmitter. Miss Schlupe tucked Biag-n's sample case under her left arm and placed her right hand over the solvency credential scanner. "It clicked," she said.

"Try it again. We both want to go to the same place."

"It clicked again."

"Good. I'll go first." He unbuttoned his coat. "Wait two minutes. If the trouble is still going on when you arrive, just hit the floor and leave it to me."

He stepped through the transmitter. When she joined him, two minutes later, he was calmly relaxing on a hassock and smoking one of his dwindling supply of cigarettes.

She looked about her in amazement. "Are we back on the ship?"

"No. The layout is the same, but the gravity is normal and the rooms are larger."

"Then it *is* a hotel!" She darted excitedly to ripple open doors.

"A hotel compartment on the same order as our ship compartment."

"The ultimate in standardization," Darzek agreed. "The glorified average—the arrangement that will satisfy the needs of the most people."

"I'd feel better about it if there was a fire escape. Or at least a window."

"You are enjoying the hotel of the future. A honeycomb hotel. With perfect lighting and air conditioning, no windows are needed. With a transmitter in every suite, every inch of space can be used for rooms. When travelers want accommodations, they pay with their solvency credentials, and a computer assigns them to a vacancy. They can transmit directly to their rooms from the transmitting exchange, or from the corner drugstore, or even the hotel lobby, if there is one. Neat, don't you think? There's a service transmitter in the table, so we can eat as long as our solvency lasts."

"I'd still like it better if there was a fire escape."

"So would I. I'm wondering how long it will take our friends to trace us."

"I didn't know we had any friends!"

"But we do," Darzek said confidently. "We must have. The Council of Supreme is expecting us. Supreme himself is expecting us. Eventually someone will think to put a tracer on our solvency credentials, and find out where the computer put us."

"If our friends can trace us, what's to prevent our enemies from doing the same?"

"That's another thing I've been wondering about. When someone finally shows up, how will we know which it is? While I'm watching the transmitter, why don't you look through our ex-friend's sample case."

She sorted through dozens of circles of cloth, clucking her tongue softly over the superb quality of the fabrics, but she found nothing but samples. She returned them to the sample case and got out her knitting. They waited, Darzek watching the transmitter steadily, automatic in hand, and Miss Schlupe directing wary glances toward it as she knitted.

Time passed.

They came so suddenly that Darzek was startled into momentary inaction. There were three of them, and they loomed hugely in the small room: creatures of a kind they had not yet seen— gaunt, segmented stalks with a multiplicity of knobby limbs, looking like weirdly animated flowers because their angular bodies terminated in tinted, transparent hoods that covered their heads.

Darzek murmured, "Who goes there friend or foe," and rose slowly, automatic leveled. He could not discern whether the oval that gleamed faintly behind the hood was a face or a huge, searching eye, but he had the sensation of being scrutinized calculatingly, as an entomologist might examine an insect while deciding whether it would do for a vacant pin in a collection. He tightened his finger on the trigger.

He never quite perceived where the weapon came from. One of the creature's numerous arms moved with incredible speed, and a short tube was leveling on him.

He dove to the floor as he fired. There was a sickening crackle, a whiff of ozone, a scream of pain. The weapon thumped onto the polished floor and rolled. Darzek kicked at it, missed, twisted away as the second creature leaped toward him. He shot another weapon from a hand of the third and tried to get to his feet.

The second pounced upon him. The multiple arms whipped around him like ropes. As they constricted they forced his hand upward, and he pulled the trigger again and shot his assailant through the head. The arms lashed once and went limp. Darzek pulled free, leaving the creature lying in a thickening, gelatinous ooze.

He turned quickly and saw Miss Schlupe coolly impale the first creature with a knitting needle. It collapsed with a soft, squishy moan. The third creature, one arm dangling uselessly, had pursued one of the rolling weapons. Miss Schlupe was there before it, trailing strands of yarn. She planted her foot on the tube and brandished her needles. Darzek pointed his automatic. The creature hesitated. Suddenly a jerky tremor seized its body. Without uttering a sound it collapsed in an ungainly pile of segments that shook violently for a moment and then subsided. Darzek bent over it warily. "Schluppy," he announced, "you are a terror. You've frightened it to death."

"Serves it right," she said indignantly, pulling her half-finished scarf from a puddle of ooze. "They've ruined my knitting."

Darzek was examining a hole high up on the wall. "If that had hit me, you'd have had to knit me a new shirt. See if it goes through the opposite bedroom wall. If our neighbors are going to be complaining, we might as well be forewarned."

She returned shaking her head. "There's just a pinprick up by the ceiling. What is it?"

"Some kind of a ray gun. What do we do now—ask Room Service to clean up the mess?"

"We pack up and get out of here before their friends arrive."

"There's nothing to pack except your knitting."

"I'm not packing that!"

"You'd better," Darzek said. "I don't know how efficient their police are, but let's not go out of our way to leave clues. Wash it off and wrap it in something. I'll watch the transmitter."

She hurried away, pulling the knitting along the floor.

Darzek pocketed the spent cartridges and took up a position in the shelter of a bedroom door. He could survive only by learning quickly, and the first lesson was not to be sitting within plain sight and easy reach when a group of enemies came through a transmitter.

Miss Schlupe reappeared, her wet knitting enfolded in handkerchiefs. "I'm ready."

Darzek walked over to contemplate the transmitter's enormously complicated destination board. "I just remembered. We can't leave. We don't know how to operate this thing."

6

Miss Schlupe said bitterly, "If Smith were here, I'd turn his nose right-side-out and tweak it. Why didn't he explain this?"

"Either he had so much to teach us that he forgot, or he left transmitters for Biag-n to explain. What are you mumbling about?"

"I was counting. There are just seventy-one possibilities. If we had a couple of days, we might figure the thing out."

"You're thinking of trying one slide at a time," Darzek said. "They probably work in combination, too, which would make thousands of possibilities. Or maybe they're used successively, like on a dial telephone. Our problem isn't the number of destinations, but the fact that we have only one choice. Wherever we end up, we're stuck there because we don't know how to come back and try again."

"Any place would be better than this," Miss Schlupe said distastefully, tiptoeing around a puddle of ooze and touching her fingers to her nose.

"Not necessarily. The dead bodies in the next place could be our own. But I agree. We should get out of here." He turned for another look at the destination board. "These lower slides are arranged differently. If we knew why, it would probably be important."

Miss Schlupe gasped and leaped aside. Darzek whirled, leveling his automatic. A strange creature stood beside them, a blurred image of Smith, with wider body and an extra three feet of height. Darzek backed away slowly, but the creature paid no attention to him. He was staring at the three dead bodies, and on his inhuman face was a very human look of horror.

He bent over one of the tubular weapons and spoke in *large-talk*. "The Eye of Death!" he moaned.

"Poetic," Darzek said agreeably. "In spite of which it might be a highly effective gadget if used properly."

"It is forbidden!"

"Too bad we didn't know. We could have spanked their hands."

The creature turned his attention to Darzek. He said wonderingly, "You were attacked by three, with Eyes of Death—and you live?"

"My mother always said I was stubborn, but my father blamed it on meanness."

The huge, hideous face became contorted with an expression not remotely unlike astonishment. The mouth shaped a whisper. "*Now* I understand why you were chosen. Praise Supreme!"

"I'm glad someone understands. Look, friend—normally I don't stand on formality, but under the circumstances I think you should tell us who you are."

The other delivered a genuflection, a curious circular movement of the arm. "I am EIGHT."

"Eight what?" Darzek demanded.

"I am the eighth member of the Council of Supreme."

"Congratulations. Would you mind proving that?"

The other stared.

"I have a nasty, suspicious disposition," Darzek went on, "and it wasn't improved by what happened a short time ago." He gestured at the three bodies. "Who are they?"

"Agents of the Dark. Where is Biag-n? Why didn't he bring you to me?"

"Biag-n died before he could meet us, which left us in a situation I would call a pretty pickle if that weren't so aptly descriptive of some of the local citizens." He said in English, "Does he look honest, Schluppy?"

"He looks scared to death."

"It may amount to the same thing. Look, EIGHT," he said, changing to *large-talk*, "we're allergic to rooms containing dead bodies, and we don't know how to work the transmitter. Would you mind getting us out of here?"

EIGHT had sunk onto a chair, where he sat with arms encircling his head despairingly. "It is as I feared," he moaned. "The Dark has agents everywhere. Biag-n—"

"Died a hero's death—I think. But let's eulogize him some other time."

EIGHT got to his feet. "Did you personalize the transmitter?"

"I don't think so. Not unless I could have done it without knowing how."

"I am not thinking. I *can't* think. Of course you didn't, or I could not have entered. The agents of the Dark could not have entered. You should have personalized the transmitter. You really don't know how? I'll show you."

"Not with this transmitter, you won't. Not if 'personalize' means what I think it does. The less evidence we leave here, the better I'll like it."

"How could the Dark have learned that you were coming to Primores?" EIGHT demanded. "And that Biag-n was an agent of Supreme? No one knew. No one except—how could the Dark—"

"Let's play Twenty Questions some other time. Get us out of here."

EIGHT strode to the transmitter, thought for a moment, touched out a destination. "Follow me," he said, and was gone.

Miss Schlupe gestured disgustedly. "Damn! And we *still* don't know how to work the transmitter!"

"He set it for three passages. Take the sample case. Maybe these people know about fingerprints. Have we touched anything?"

"I don't think so. The doors?"

"Go ahead. I'll wipe the latches."

He rubbed quickly with his handkerchief, snatched his suitcase, and leaped into the transmitter. Miss Schlupe stood waiting for him; EIGHT was already hurrying away.

They were in a public garden. Above a transparent dome the night sky blazed with stars. The walks were faintly luminous, and huge, glowing flowers gave off a soft effusion of light that bathed the park in a ghostly halo. Their pungent perfume hung heavily in the motionless air. Miss Schlupe sniffed gingerly, sneezed, and muttered, "Vicks Vaporub."

EIGHT chose a route that avoided the strange-looking figures who walked the paths. At the opposite side of the park he halted at a transmitter station and waited for them impatiently.

He touched out another destination. They stepped through and found themselves in the main transmitting exchange.

Darzek murmured approvingly. "I don't think any police science could trace us through this place."

"I don't think he's worried about the police," Miss Schlupe said. "He's just like Smith—afraid of the Dark. I'm beginning to be a little afraid of it myself."

EIGHT had paused for thought again. Darzek turned an anxious eye on the stream of unlikely shaped passengers that flowed around them. He said softly, "Can't we go somewhere, and then think about it?"

EIGHT started. "I was wondering—yes. Of course."

He led them to the alcove and offered his hand for a transmitter's scrutiny, a large, puffy, hairless hand with a vast row of short, stubby, hairy fingers. EIGHT motioned to Miss Schlupe. "Quickly!" he said.

"I'll go first," Darzek told him, and stepped through the transmitter. He inventoried the room with a glance and leaped to investigate the adjoining rooms. Miss Schlupe and EIGHT were waiting when he emerged from the last one, EIGHT looking about for him bewilderedly.

"Are we safe here?" Darzek demanded.

"I am EIGHT! I am a member of the Council of Supreme! The transmitter admits no one without my seal."

"How many people have your seal?"

"This is my official residence," EIGHT protested. "There are few places in the galaxy where we could be safe if we were not safe here."

"I'll take his word for it," Miss Schlupe said wearily. She dropped onto a hassock and kicked off her shoes.

"The Council will meet soon," EIGHT said. "I have already convoked it. I did so as soon as I learned that you were coming."

"You look tired, Schluppy," Darzek said. "Are you up to a meeting with the Council?"

EIGHT said protestingly, "But only *you* are to meet with the Council."

"Is that so? Supposing I were to tell your Council to go soak its collective heads, of which it probably has a surplus."

"We did not know you would bring an assistant. No one can be present at a Council meeting without a pass certified by all of the members, and I obtained only one."

"Then obtain another one."

"Never mind," Miss Schlupe said. "If it's like other council meetings I've attended, I won't be missing anything."

"How long will this meeting take?" Darzek asked.

"I do not know. Perhaps a long time. Perhaps several days. There may be much planning to do."

"Can she stay here? Is there a service transmitter?"

"Of course."

"All right. I'll meet with your Council. But first I'd like to remedy certain deficiencies in my education, and before that I'd like all of the official information about the Dark."

EIGHT moved over to the table and opened a panel. The ceiling glowed softly, and a pattern emerged. "This," EIGHT said, "is the galaxy."

Darzek glanced indifferently at the spiraling haze of light. Then he started. This was no theoretical projection, but a map.

"And this," EIGHT whispered, "is what the Dark has done."

A tiny crescent of blackness appeared at the edge of the glowing disk. Suddenly it widened and plunged inward to form a sinister finger that lay across the galaxy's remote perimeter, pointed unerringly at its heart.

It continued to grow. It bulged unevenly, filled in hollows, bulged again. Its base oozed outward, and it began to lengthen. Then the tip darted forward, leaving a widening emptiness in its wake, and when the movement finally stopped the finger had become a muscular arm with incongruous bulges and indentations, a vast corridor of cancerous Dark.

No stars shone there. No lines of commerce or communication crossed it. Stars there had been, and habitable worlds with prosperous societies and intricate networks of trade and travel, but the Dark had consumed them.

"So that's the Dark," Darzek mused. "But what happened to the suns that were there? Are they just—*gone?*"

"Gone," EIGHT agreed.

"How could a sun vanish?" Darzek demanded.

"Vanish?" EIGHT repeated, puzzled. "They are there, but they are lost to us, to the galaxy. The Dark has taken them. The native populations have been afflicted with madness—the madness of the Dark. They have evicted all foreigners and confiscated their property. They have terminated all trade and communication with the rest of the galaxy. What the Dark does with them we do not know."

"Then it's some kind of revolution," Darzek mused. "The Dark doesn't literally consume the worlds. It merely enslaves them—which could be worse. All right. I understand that much. Now tell me what is known about the Dark. Everything."

EIGHT darkened the ceiling screen, and Darzek and Miss Schlupe composed themselves to listen attentively.

Darzek's certified pass looked like a blank strip of plastic. It first admitted him to a special transmitter built into a room-sized closet just off EIGHT's reception room. He emerged in a narrow corridor, and EIGHT, stepping out of the transmitter behind him, remarked, "This is the Hall of Deliberations."

Darzek looked about him and announced, "There doesn't seem to be room for much deliberation."

"That is merely what it is called. The Council does not meet here."

They walked past other transmitters. Darzek counted eight and asked, "One for each member of the Council?"

"Yes. These connect only with the official residences."

They turned abruptly into a large room, or what had been a large room. The arching ceiling could just be glimpsed above the enormous structure that filled it. Darzek squinted uncertainly into the dim red light of a tunnel that opened before him.

"You must enter here," EIGHT said. "Walk slowly, and do not be alarmed at anything you hear—or feel. Supreme has been notified that you are coming. It will simply verify your pass and confirm that you are yourself."

"Where do I show the pass?"

"Hold it flat on your hand. There. Now walk slowly."

Darzek took a firm grip on his suitcase and held his other hand out in front of him, palm upward. He had the foolish illusion of being a small boy entering a House of Horrors in an amusement park. He took a step forward. And another.

A blast of warm air whipped past him, and incongruously he felt cold. His skin began to prickle, as if gently probed by icy needles. Already he regretted the suitcase. He had left his arsenal with Miss Schlupe and brought little more than a change of clothing against the possible several days that the conference might last; but after a few steps the almost-empty suitcase became staggeringly heavy, and he had the sensation of a tremendous weight crushing down on him. Each footstep commenced with an agonizing struggle against gravity and ended with intense relief and a reluctance to take another. His limbs became numb, and dizziness swept over him. He had a sudden apprehension about his automatic. Would Supreme admit an *armed* visitor to a meeting of the Council of Supreme? He should have asked.

Perspiration was streaking his face and burning his eyes. Behind him, EIGHT called out something. He stopped and looked back, and EIGHT called again, "Keep going!" He staggered forward. A few feet ahead of him he could make out the blank end of the tunnel.

A high-pitched vibration had been with him from the beginning, like a dull ache just above the threshold of pain. Suddenly it crescendoed to a piercing shriek that ended in a whir and a loud click. His weight was normal. He opened his eyes, found himself in a circular alcove off a curving corridor. His skin continued to tingle painfully.

EIGHT stood beside him. Darzek glanced down at the pass that still lay on his perspiring hand. It was shriveled and blackened.

"Great!" he exclaimed. "Now how do I get out of here?"

"No pass is necessary to leave a meeting of the Council, but once you leave you cannot return without another pass. Now I'll show you to your accommodation."

On one side of the corridor regularly spaced arches led into a large, circular room. Opposite each arch was a door. They passed four doors, and EIGHT rippled open the fifth and led him into a suite of rooms. There were elliptical glassless windows in a curving outer wall, and an open arch that led out onto an attractive terrace.

Darzek dropped his suitcase, made himself comfortable on a chair, and remarked companionably to EIGHT, "The Dark isn't the first crisis that's threatened the Council."

"Why do you say that?"

"These security arrangements weren't devised for the fun of it. Obviously the Council once met in the Hall of Deliberations. Either its secrets were vulnerable there, or it feared for its physical safety, or both. That room was converted into a massive transmitter, tamper-proof to the nth degree, and made a security check on the route to the real meeting place, whose location is probably the best-kept secret in the galaxy. Exactly where are we?"

"It has no name," EIGHT said.

"But *where* is it? Where in relation to the Hall of Deliberations?"

"I do not know," EIGHT confessed.

"You see? So secret that not even the members of the Council know where they meet. It would have required a crisis of monumental proportions to inspire such elaborate precautions."

"And yet I have never heard of such a crisis," EIGHT said politely.

"It happened before your time. The architecture of this building is proof of that. I recommend that you read up on it. It should be consoling to know that Supreme has already weathered one severe threat."

EIGHT gaped at him bewilderedly. "I'll tell the others that you have arrived," he said.

As soon as he was alone Darzek went to look at the terrace. It was flooded with sunlight. Spacious lawns stretched to a shallow horizon. Exotic flowers lined the walks and ringed the terrace. Curious, he touched one of them, touched it again, bent over it. It was artificial. The horizon was artificial. The sun was artificial, and so was the sky.

"All of it under a dome," Darzek told himself. "At a guess, a bombproof dome. Any kind of bomb. That really was a first-rate crisis, and if I were a member of the Council I'd be grateful. The Dark won't be breaking in here very soon."

He examined the circular building and quickly confirmed that the crisis was, indeed, ancient history. The meeting place of the Council of Supreme was built of—wood!

"There must have been better materials available," he mused. "Probably this was an architectural fad at the time. With the temperature and humidity controlled, and with no exposure to the elements, I suppose wood will last forever. The whole setup seems ancient. A meeting place built of wood, the eight transmitters for eight Councillors—now they would design one that could do the same job—and that chamber of horrors, which probably is something out of their equivalent of the Middle Ages. It must have happened millenniums ago."

EIGHT returned and joined him on the terrace. "The others have arrived," he said. "The Council awaits you."

They sat around the huge cylindrical table in numerical order: eight monsters and, located between ONE and EIGHT, Jan Darzek. After his initial shock Darzek did not look at them directly. His mind refused to assimilate the details that his senses provided. He saw them as eight grotesque blurs, each with a characteristic or two that overlapped into stark reality: the long, tapering tentacles that bristled out of the SIX blur; the three protruding antennae of TWO that blossomed into large eyes at their tips; the two faceless heads of THREE. SEVEN was a bundle of sticks behind a tinted, vaguely transparent light shield, and his stringy body pulsated with ceaseless internal grindings. FOUR was a detached voice emitted by a box that he placed on the table in front of him. FIVE was a collapsed ball, almost indistinguishable from the hassock it perched upon. Chameleon-like, his leathery body had assumed the hassock's dull-brown color as soon as he landed upon it with a dull *plop*. ONE was a double row of appendages, each equipped with suckerlike discs.

They were eight animates, of contrasting and contradictory form and tissue, and their origins were eight widely separated, contrasting and contradictory worlds. They held in common only their galaxy, their Councillorships, their presence around the Council table, their fluency in *large-talk*, and, in relative degree, their consternation. Darzek hesitated to call them frightened—he would more readily have assigned emotions to the chair he sat on—but as the meeting progressed all showed signs of agitation.

They were severely divided upon the subject of the Dark and what should be done about it. More specifically, they held sharply conflicting opinions as to the role to be played by Jan Darzek.

SIX waved his tentacles despairingly. "I disapproved of this when it was proposed. I still disapprove. How can one uncertified creature thwart the Dark?"

"Supreme knows," EIGHT intoned.

"Supreme knows!" SIX hissed scornfully. "Supreme knows nothing about the Dark! It admits that!"

EIGHT turned on him angrily and half rose from his hassock. "Supreme expects us to make some feeble use of that inert cell tissue we choose to call our brains. The uncertified creature's mission is not to thwart the Dark, but to learn about it, to identify it, above all to discover what weapon it uses. That was our question: by what means, or through what medium, can we find out these things, and Supreme named this uncertified creature. Why I have no more idea than you. Supreme never explains. Until now no Councillor has ever questioned its judgment."

"Until now it has never had the Dark to contend with," SIX muttered.

TWO leaned forward to point his remote eyes at Darzek. "The Dark's weapon is almost certainly mental. Does the uncertified creature possess a defense against mental weapons?"

"He says that he does not," EIGHT said.

"Does his kind embrace death eagerly?" SEVEN asked. "Desperate our need is, but we cannot send him to what I consider certain death unless he knows the risk he assumes and goes willingly."

"He asked for payment according to the standards of his kind, and the certification group responsible for his world has tendered the requested solvency. He knows the risk he assumes, and he goes willingly."

"We're wasting time," SIX rumbled gloomily. "With each movement the Dark digests what it has consumed more quickly. And with each movement it consumes more."

They fell silent, all of them looking at Darzek—all except FIVE, the eyeless one, who remained collapsed in his headless mound of folded membrane. SIX braided and unbraided his long, sinewy tentacles. TWO—Darzek could not decide whether he wore lightly fitting garments or loosely fitting skin—hunched an enormous, pulsating abdomen over the edge of the table and wheezed mournfully with each jerky breath. THREE parted an absurdly fashioned smock, activated a liquid spray, and inhaled greedily through nostrils located far down on his chest. SEVEN nervously gulped food and masticated with noisy constrictions of his stomach.

"But what can it *do?*" SIX demanded, with eyes fixed on Darzek.

"That is what we are here to decide," EIGHT said.

"Doomed!" SIX muttered. "The galaxy is doomed. Even if we knew the weapon we could do nothing. What defense is there against a weapon that plunges an entire world into madness?"

SEVEN nervously gulped more food. FOUR's voice box emitted static. The others said nothing.

"Will the creature report to us, or directly to Supreme?" THREE demanded suddenly.

"That is not yet decided," EIGHT said.

"If it reports to Supreme, Supreme will reveal only what it wants us to know—and that only if we ask," THREE grumbled.

"What can it *do?*" SIX demanded again, eyes still fixed on Darzek. "And if such a creature *can* thwart the Dark, might it not possess a dangerous mental weapon of its own? Might we not be replacing one menace with another?"

"I place my trust in Supreme," EIGHT said simply. "Supreme selected him. Supreme does not err."

Darzek decided that he had heard enough. The longer he listened, the more puzzled he became. Obviously his business was with Supreme, rather than the Council. There was no real necessity for this meeting, except to satisfy the Councillors' curiosity. They wanted to see him; they had seen him. They wanted to know his plans, but as yet he had none, and he would have been disposed to keep them to himself if he had.

He got to his feet. Somewhere there was work for him to do, even if he did not know precisely where, or what the work was. It was time that he brought this farce to a close.

But as he faced the Council he had another idea. He said bluntly, "What help can you give me?"

He could only guess that they were startled, for he still could not look at them individually. He repeated his question. "What help can you give me?"

FOUR's voice box squawked protestingly. "Supreme has already given you unlimited solvency!"

"Am I supposed to *buy* the Dark?" Darzek demanded.

It was disconcerting just to listen to them breathe. They whistled and fluttered and puffed and gargled. One of them rasped horribly with each breath, as though his respiratory system had to tear the air apart with brute force to get at the life-giving oxygen. There were odors, too, but Darzek had stopped breathing through his nose the moment he entered the room.

"Some of you may have specialized knowledge," he said thoughtfully. "All of you should be able to give me useful information. I'm adjourning this meeting now. I'll visit each of you in your rooms to find out what you can tell me. Then I'll call you together again."

THREE grumbled, "You mean we have to wait here—"

"Not if you are concerned with other matters more urgent than the Dark," Darzek said sarcastically.

He watched with elation as the Councillors meekly left the room. He was firmly in control, and he might even learn something of value.

He hurried after EIGHT and asked him, "Do you have specialized knowledge?"

"The uncertified worlds," EIGHT said.

"What about the others?"

"ONE's is finance, but you already have unlimited solvency. TWO's is commerce. THREE's is the perimeter worlds. FOUR's—"

"I'll take them all in numerical order," Darzek said.

From ONE he received a surfeit of technical jargon and a quick awareness that the arena of interstellar finance held no charms for him. Neither could he think of any conceivable weapon that it might offer against the Dark. He extricated himself at the first moment that he could do so politely and moved on.

TWO was a surprise to Darzek. An old trader, a veteran of fantastic, far-flung business arrangements, his squeaky voice somehow rang with authority when he spoke of them.

At the first opening, Darzek came directly to the point. The lamented Biag-n had been a dealer in textiles and had thought to take Darzek into the business with him as a cover for his activities. Supreme would be asked to assign another of its agents to assist Darzek, but the new agent might not be so advantageously situated. Darzek liked the idea of an occupation that would give him an excuse to travel freely.

"I know nothing about this Biag-n," TWO said. "If he traveled freely, he must have been a mere peddler. What impression do you wish to make?"

"I don't know," Darzek said. "What do you suggest?"

"A peddler can go anywhere, but he is respected by no one. A factor commands very little respect, and a peddler none at all. A trader, on the other hand, whatever his volume of business, is respected according to his merit."

"I don't understand the difference."

"The trader works for himself. He buys, and then sells what he has bought. The peddler and the factor work for others. Both sell merchandise or products that others control."

"Can all of them move about freely?"

"The trader travels wherever business takes him, but he has a headquarters, a place of business. The factor has a headquarters, but he does not travel. His activities are restricted to one world, or even to part of a world. The peddler travels at will, but has no headquarters. Peddlers are wanderers. They remain on a world only until they achieve sufficient solvency to take them elsewhere. They normally specialize in cheap varieties of a single product, and they deal in small quantities—usually with native tradesmen. No one takes much notice of a peddler."

Darzek nodded politely. He could understand why an agent of Supreme would choose to be a peddler; but it was also obvious that someone had taken considerable notice of the peddler Biag-n. In the future any peddler would be suspect, and that was reason enough for not becoming one. And Darzek did not care to restrict his movements by becoming a factor.

"How does one get to be a trader?" he asked.

TWO's antennae twitched nervously. Or perhaps mischievously. "One trades."

"Trades what?" Darzek persisted. "What products would one start with? Remember that I know nothing. I don't know the value of anything, I don't know where or whom to buy from, or how to go about selling. Where would I begin?"

TWO gave his antennae a meditative flip. "Perhaps it would be better if you became a peddler. A peddler needs to know very little."

"I'll consider it. Right now I want to know how to be a trader."

"It would be very difficult. I'd suggest that you begin as an undertrader, learn a few specialities—"

"Trader," Darzek said firmly. "There isn't time for me to work my way up from the ranks. It doesn't matter whether I actually do any trading, as long as I *act* like a trader. How would I begin?"

"You would first have to choose a world for your headquarters."

"A world close to the Dark," Darzek suggested.

"You should consult THREE about that. The perimeter worlds are his concern."

"I'll pick the world later. First let's talk in general terms. Buying and selling, transferring solvency, that sort of thing. I should be taking notes. One moment, please. I have a notebook in my suitcase."

He hurried back to his own quarters, fumbled for his key, opened his suitcase. He stared for a moment. Then, notebook forgotten, he relocked the suitcase.

EIGHT appeared in the doorway as he turned away. "I heard you enter," he said. "Have you finished with the others?"

"Come in here, please," Darzek said. He waved EIGHT into the room and went to close the door. "You were wondering how the agents of the Dark could have learned I was coming. Would it surprise you if I said there was an agent of the Dark on the Council?"

It shocked him into speechlessness.

"Someone opened my suitcase and ransacked it," Darzek said. "Is there anyone here except the Councillors?"

"No."

"No service or maintenance people, or anyone like that?"

"No one is admitted except with a certified pass," EIGHT said. "You are the first outsider to be present at a Council meeting in my memory."

"Very well. Why would a Councillor want to search my suitcase?"

"None of them would," EIGHT said confidently. "It is unthinkable that *anyone* would molest the personal possessions of another."

"Then you'd better revise your thinking. Someone went through my suitcase. Nothing is missing, but that may be because nothing there was worth taking."

"Surely you are mistaken."

"When Jan Darzek packs a suitcase, he knows precisely what is in it, and where, and in what condition. When he finds the contents topsy-turvy and his one remaining pressed shirt wadded up, you can't convince him that no one was in his suitcase. Who among the Councillors would know how to pick a lock—a rather complicated lock."

"What is this *picking* a lock?" EIGHT asked.

Darzek explained and then demonstrated with his key. EIGHT pondered the lock silently. "I have never heard of such a thing," he announced.

"You must have locks. You have a word for them."

"But no locks like this one. Our locks do not have to be opened—cannot be opened. They open themselves, at the touch of the person they are attuned to. But they are rarely used because they are not needed."

"Personalized locks," Darzek said thoughtfully. "Are you certain that none of the Councillors would have experience of a lock that requires a key?"

"I do not see how any of them could. I did not know that there were such locks."

"I happen to know that even a person with considerable ex-

perience of such locks and their workings would have difficulty
with this one. And yet it was opened. I'm positive of that. I'd like
to have another talk with the Council."

"All of it? Now?"

"Yes."

With a last, frustrated glance at his suitcase, Darzek followed
EIGHT into the Council Room.

It had been done so *quickly*. Darzek had been with TWO no
more than twenty minutes, and with ONE much less than that.
And yet one of the Councillors had been able to enter Darzek's
rooms, open a lock of a kind he had never seen before and of a
quality that would have frustrated a trained locksmith for hours,
hurriedly examine the suitcase's contents, lock it again, and depart.

The thing *was* impossible, but it had been done.

So obsessed was he with the puzzle of how the suitcase had
been opened that it was some minutes before the realization
smote him that he'd made a momentous discovery. A traitor on
the Council of Supreme! The thought of it sent his pulse racing
feverishly. No wonder the Dark had seemed omnipotent, had
scored incredible victories with ease.

They entered one at a time through the arches opposite their
rooms. TWO lumbered in first. Darzek idly wondered if he
should apologize for not returning to him and decided that it
could wait.

TWO, he thought, was out of it. TWO would have had only
the brief ten minutes Darzek had spent with ONE, and that was
not enough time. EIGHT was out of it, or at least Darzek hoped
he was.

Of the others, ONE would have had twenty minutes, the rest
perhaps half an hour. As they took their places he looked at them
with a deepening sense of futility. If they had been humans he
might have had a ghost of a chance, but how could he read signs
of guilt in those grotesque features?

As soon as they were seated he got to his feet and backed away
slowly until he had all of them in his field of vision. He said
quietly, "You have brought me here to assist you in your struggle

with the Dark. Already I have made some progress. I have learned
one reason for the Dark's success." He paused to look at each of
them in turn and then snapped, "One of you is an agent of the
Dark!"

EIGHT stared at Darzek rigidly, as though refusing to comprehend the enormity of the charge. The others stirred, shifted
positions. Uneasily? Resentfully? He could not tell. He went on,
"One of you is in league with the Dark. He has betrayed the
secrets of this Council. I say to him now—will you confess your
error, or shall I, Jan Darzek, wrench your foul secret from your
wretched, perverted mind?"

He had never perpetrated a bluff with so little to back it
up—and with such a meager result. ONE had edged forward over
the table, his suckers gripping it, his multiple limbs trembling.
TWO's antennae waved wildly. THREE's faceless heads were
bent far back so that the row of eyes in his chest could stare at
Darzek. FOUR, a monstrous, shell-less snail in fur clothing, was
motionless, but his voice box emitted a crackling static. FIVE's
body was slowly deflating. SIX was plaiting his tentacles into two
pulsating braids. SEVEN—

Darzek looked again at SIX. The tentacles were long and
sinuous, tapering to fine threads. To strong, wiry threads. "What
a marvelous thing to pick a lock with," he thought. "A lock pick
with a sense of touch. Every well-equipped thief should have
one."

SEVEN was a blank blur behind his tinted hood. EIGHT was
still staring rigidly at Darzek. He turned again to ONE, but he
kept his eyes on SIX. The tentacles unbraided, fanned out, became longer and slenderer, braided again. The tips would have to
be extremely strong, to open a lock.

Darzek felt himself poised on a height, and about to make a
reckless, dizzying plunge.

He whirled abruptly. "You!" he shouted.

SIX jerked to his feet and reeled backward. The tentacles
lashed about, drooped, whipped forward. They held an Eye of
Death.

Darzek dove. The beam crackled above his head. He twisted and drew his automatic cleanly, but as he aimed EIGHT leaped in front of him. SIX pivoted as he fired again. The upper part of EIGHT's body splashed to the floor, spurting blood. His trunk teetered slowly and collapsed. Darzek emptied his automatic, deliberately searching for a vulnerable spot. Riddled with bullets, SIX staggered sideways and turned his weapon on FOUR, who had opened a panel and was touching out a message.

Keeping low, Darzek crept around the table. Screams of pain and terror rent the air as the Eye of Death crackled again and again. Ozone hung heavily in the room, and blended with it was an ominous smell of smoke. Glancing behind him, Darzek saw a wall in flames.

SEVEN leaped to grapple with SIX and died horribly. ONE scooted for an exit, and was sliced into segments as a section of wall burst into flame behind him.

Darzek's shots were slowly taking effect. SIX's tentacles jerked with violent tremors, and he had difficulty steadying his weapon as he attempted to bore through the table and kill Darzek. Darzek ducked down again, crawled, risked another glance. He saw THREE's two heads vanish in a snap of ozone and shouted a warning to TWO—too late. He heaved up a chair and sent it crashing across the table at SIX. Flames had reached the ceiling, and in a twinkling the upper part of the old building was a roaring inferno.

SIX stood motionless, tentacles quivering, his entire body seized with an uncontrollable spasm. Darzek edged around the table and rushed him, and he fell heavily. The Eye of Death rolled away. SIX's tentacles twitched once and went rigid.

Darzek snatched up his automatic and shouted, "Let's get out of here!"

FIVE had deflated completely, and was a motionless mound on his chair. The others were dead. Darzek seized FIVE, hauled him toward an exit. The leathery body was slippery, oozing fluid, and surprisingly heavy. Darzek lunged through a wall of flame, reached the transmitter alcove, pushed FIVE through. He dove after him, choking on the thick, pungent smoke.

FIVE lay on the floor of a red-lit tunnel, still deflated. Struggling with the slippery body, Darzek slowly made his way forward to the normal light of the corridor beyond.

Not until then did he realize that FIVE was dead, his body a sickly, grayish white.

He waited in the corridor for a long time, though he knew that no one remaining in that building could have lived. Finally he turned away, found EIGHT's transmitter, and stepped through.

Miss Schlupe was sleeping. She woke with a start when he bent over her. "You smell smoky," she said. Then she sat up abruptly. "What happened? Are you hurt?"

"I don't think so. Just my pride. I got seven innocent people killed and maybe lost the galaxy to the Dark—all in something under ten minutes."

"Nonsense!"

"It's true. The galaxy is now without a government. The Council of Supreme has been wiped out to the last Councillor, and because of the secrecy in which it worked, probably nobody will know that for years. Not even Supreme will know."

"Supreme—"

"Supreme is a machine. A computer. No one person could administer the millions of worlds of a galaxy. Not even an army of administrators could do it. A computer can, if it has reliable servants to supply the information it needs. My guess is that its most important source of information was the Council. Each member was a specialist in a critical area of knowledge. They kept Supreme informed, and maybe they made policy decisions. Now they're dead, and Supreme can't get along without them."

"Can't they elect a new Council?"

"Supreme chooses the Councillors. Only Supreme knows who they are, and they work in absolute secrecy. When one dies, the other Councillors notify Supreme, and Supreme chooses a successor. Supreme could choose a new Council, but it won't, because it doesn't know it needs one. The only person who could tell it is me, and I don't know how. Now the Dark has no opposition at all. It's a cancer eating away at the galaxy, and there's no one to prescribe medicine."

"What are you going to do?"

"I don't know."

"Should we try to go back—to Earth?"

"No."

Darzek backed into a chair and sat down gloomily. "I should have guessed that the traitor would be armed. If I could carry a weapon to a Council meeting, so could he. And I should have known how he would react. The fact that we polished off three of his invincibly armed agents probably had him thinking I was something supernatural. That was why he went through my suitcase. He was already scared to death and frantic to find out something about me. When I exposed him by apparently reading his mind, he went berserk. So now the whole Council is dead."

"EIGHT?"

"The whole Council. Don't you see what that means? Supreme has its agents, but the information they supply is useless unless someone can act on it, and Supreme can't act. It can't even recommend, unless someone asks it to." He got to his feet. "This affair has been blundered from the start. There wasn't any need to bring us here." He stared at her. "SIX! It must have been SIX's idea. The others, being nice monsters without a suspicious thought in their collective heads, or wherever they had thoughts, went along with him. He wanted to get rid of us before we got close enough to the Dark to do any damage. Pack up, Schluppy. I'm going to see if I can buy a new suitcase by transmitter. Then we'll get out of here."

"Where are we going?"

"To meet the Dark. That's the one good thing that's come out of all this. At least I have a general idea of where it is."

7

Gula Azfel was disporting with her mate when she heard her husband calling her. She gave his elongated snout a last, affectionate twitch, and he released her resignedly. "Big party tonight?"

"Full symposium," she said. "Azfel says it's good for business." She huffed disgustedly. "Why should anyone think about business at a symposium?"

"Traders always think about business. That's why they're traders."

Her husband called again, and she hurried away. She found him in full symp dress, squirming back and forth impatiently while his own mate looked on in rapt admiration.

"Someone has arrived!" he hissed.

"On time?" she gasped. She gazed at him in horror. "Who would have such filthy manners?"

"Why don't you go and find out? To think that I married you because I thought you'd make an excellent hostess! You don't even have your feathers preened, and there are guests waiting."

"It never happened before," she wailed. "It's your fault if you invite ill-mannered guests."

"Get yourself ready," he said disgustedly. "I'll go. I never thought I'd find myself playing hostess in my own home, but I'll go."

He returned a moment later muttering to himself. "It's all right," he said. "It's only Gul Darr."

"Ah! I hope you didn't speak harshly to him."

"Of course not. The poor chap has no manners at all, but he's such a charming person that it's impossible to feel resentful toward him. His arriving first at symposiums is almost becoming a tradition. I should have remembered. I'm sorry I hissed at you."

"I forgive you, dear. Did you apologize for my absence?"

"I told him you were preening. He said it was unthinkable that you should rush a task that produces such pleasing results."

"Tsk!" she murmured. "He *is* charming. Why didn't you ever invite him before?"

"I never had business with him before. By the way—he has an associate with him. A Gula Schlu. It might be a good idea for you to become acquainted with her."

"An associate? Is there a relationship?"

"They're of a kind, or at least nearly so, but I don't think she's his mate. He has no wife. There may be an opportunity for one of the daughters. He has prospered amazingly."

"Surely he wouldn't be attending a symposium with his mate! I mean—his manners couldn't be *that* bad. Would it be appropriate to introduce a few of the daughters to him?"

Gul Azfel arched himself meditatively. "Perhaps later. Take care to do it discreetly. Gula Dalg was disgustingly open about it at that little fete I attended last term. And Gul Darr asked—you'll never believe this—he asked if she were accepting bids on them. She collapsed on the spot—literally. I haven't heard such laughter in a leash of periods. Old E-Wusk practically exploded. It nearly broke up the party."

"I'll be discreet," she promised. "Perhaps I can arrange it so he *asks* for introductions. He sounds like a delightful person. I can't wait to meet him."

"I left him in the aquarium," Gul Azfel said. "He looked at the tank of pwisqs, and said, 'I see that some of the guests have already arrived.'"

Gula Azfel twittered shrilly and hurried off to finish preening. Gul Azfel curled up comfortably while his mate adjusted his tail ribbons.

"She'll manage discreetly," his mate said bitterly. "She'll manage discreetly for *her* daughters. Yours will be the last on Yorlq to find husbands."

"Now don't worry. Marriage is just a business proposition, and I'm a trader—and a good one. Don't you forget that. I'm capable of a little discretion myself."

* * *

Darzek leered at the pwisqs, who leered back at him. Miss Schlupe was contemplating a trio of equally repulsive creatures in the next tank. "Do they have interesting habits, or what?" she asked. "He certainly doesn't collect them for their beauty."

"He may. I've been trying to evolve a philosophy of non-beauty, strictly as a matter of self-preservation. I began by wondering if there was an ultimate degree of ugliness that would verge on the beautiful, but it didn't work out. Long before a thing becomes that ugly, it gets so repulsive that I can't stand it."

"I suppose that goes for the people, too."

"It does."

"I wish you'd left me home. I'm perfectly satisfied to run your office for you. I'd rather leave the socializing to you."

Darzek shook his head. "I need you, Schluppy. I can't cover even a small party as thoroughly as I should, and no matter how hard I try, I just can't seem to get next to people. I can't penetrate all this grotesqueness and find out what they're really like. Their society is appallingly superficial, if not downright frivolous, but I'm certain that the people aren't."

"Could the frivolity be a cover-up?"

Darzek shrugged. "I don't know. No one ever gets angry, or even excited. They act as if they're bored stiff without knowing it. I've made a character of myself by cracking a joke now and then, and from their reactions you'd think I'd invented the institution. The only other person who makes jokes is an old rascal named E-Wusk, and his humor is about as subtle as a charge of dynamite. If he ever discovers the pie-in-the-face and the fat-man-on-a-banana-peel routines, social life on Yorlq will be ruined."

"I'm just an emotional female," Miss Schlupe said sadly. "I

can't take some of these monsters—especially the snake-types. Either I'll laugh at the wrong time, or I'll be sick. I'm afraid I'll blight your business connections."

"You will not. You will observe in your own inimitable fashion, and we'll compare notes later."

"If you say so. Will they all speak *large-talk?*"

"Of course. But you would be wise to avoid the *efa*. They're a clan of *maf*-cousins, whatever that is. They have a nasty habit of vomiting from one of their stomachs to the other."

Gula Azfel hurried in breathlessly and sought to regale them with cheerful comment about those charming creatures, the pwisqs. It seemed that in mating season the male swallowed the female whole, and a term or so later, when he became aware of the fact that his offspring were escaping from his mouth, he regurgitated her.

"This would seem to impose a hardship upon the occasional female who is unfertile," Darzek observed politely.

Gula Azfel tittered and led them back to the reception room. The pwisqs, for all their robust peculiarities, offered a severely limited field for polite conversation, and when finally the next guests glided from the transmitter Gula Azfel met them with obvious relief.

The newcomers greeted Darzek with an unrestrained enthusiasm that on Earth would have been reserved for long-lost brothers. When finally he succeeded in detaching himself, he said quietly to Miss Schlupe, "For some reason not properly understood by anyone, it is considered bad manners to arrive first at a party. There is also a definite limit as to how late one can arrive without being unspeakably rude. It puts the guests in a magnificent dilemma. One of the reasons I'm so popular is that I always arrive precisely on time. I remain blithely innocent of offense, and the other guests don't have to risk the embarrassment of arriving late to avoid the embarrassment of arriving early. Watch the transmitter, and see how their faces light up when they see me."

"Those who have faces," Miss Schlupe said. "What's happened to the host?"

"He's not supposed to appear until all the guests have arrived." The reception room was kept at low illumination for the convenience of nocturnals, and as a result the other guests soon moved away in search of a brighter atmosphere. Darzek, having started Miss Schlupe on a whirl of formal introductions, began his own rounds.

In the shimmering aquaroom several guests were already dancing. They glided over the water with breathtaking grace and agility. Grotesquely fashioned bodies whirled in dazzling pirouettes, wove group patterns, performed magnificent, leaping solos. Darzek, who was willing to try anything once, had tried it—once. He lost his balance at the first stride, toppled into the water, and nearly drowned while trying to release himself from the gas-filled floats that enclosed his feet.

Whereupon he salvaged something from an acutely embarrassing situation by performing an *underwater* ballet that quickly reduced spectators and dancers to quivering hysterics. That marvelously amusing Gul Darr! He had to invent a rare water allergy that enabled him to decline, with regret, all requests for a repeat performance.

He skirted the pool, taking careful note of the dancers so that he could compliment them later. At the far side he joined a small group of spectators, several of them resting from dancing. They greeted him with a warmth tinged warily with apprehension; they never knew quite what to expect from the mysterious Gul Darr.

Frequently Darzek did not know what to expect from himself, but on this occasion he was not socializing. He produced a small phial and addressed himself to a veteran trader.

"By your leave, Gul Kaln, a minute favor. Would you sample this oil for me?"

Gul Kaln delivered the curious circular arm motion that served as a genuflection, extended sinuous fingers, took the phial, unstopped it. An arching filament stabbed through the opening and dangled limply, tasting. "What did you wish to know?"

Darzek prattled apologetically. He'd found two casks of the stuff in a warehouse he'd rented . . . no identifying marks, unfortunately . . . the oil had a distinctive cast to it that he didn't recognize . . . he thought he could find a market for it if it were available in quantity . . . he'd need a continuing supply, naturally, and he wouldn't know if one were available until he'd identified the oil.

"Distinctive," Gul Kaln agreed, withdrawing the filament. "There isn't anything distinguished about it, but it does have a certain individual quality."

"That's what I thought," Darzek said. "Do you recognize it?"

Gul Kaln inserted the filament again, tasted, withdrew it with a snap. "No. There's something vaguely familiar about it, but I don't quite . . . no . . ." The filament dipped a third time, dangled, agitated the fluid gently, slipped free. "No. My most humble apologies, but I cannot help you."

"But the apologies are mine to offer, for having troubled you," Darzek murmured. "It is a small matter. Probably it wouldn't have been of use to me anyway."

Gul Kaln genuflected; Darzek genuflected, included the group with a sweep of his arm, and moved away.

He had seen Gul Kaln perform that taste test a dozen times. Nine samples the trader had recognized; three he had not. But never did he dip the filament more than once.

Gul Kaln was lying.

Thoughtfully Darzek made his way through scattered groups of guests and entered the next room. Old E-Wusk sprawled in a far corner in a tangle of arms and legs, looking as pious as a cathedral and just about as immovable. Darzek had a genuine measure of affection for the old rascal. E-Wusk was the one creature he'd met on a dozen worlds whose laughter had a human quality, the ring of authentic jollity, of the sheer joy of merriment.

"Gul Darr!" E-Wusk chortled, waving at Darzek over an admiring circle of young undertraders. "Have you been—oh, ho ho— water dancing?"

"No," Darzek said gravely. "For that I wait until I have sufficient thirst."

"Oh, ho ho!" E-Wusk's enormous abdomen heaved and quivered.

Darzek waited politely and then extended the phial. "By your leave, Gul E-Wusk, a minute favor. Would you sample this?"

Darzek found Miss Schlupe seated at the entrance to the dark room, the special room maintained for nocturnal guests, deeply engrossed in conversation with a voice that emerged from its dim interior. It was a soft voice, and—a genuine rarity, this—musical.

"Gul Darr," Miss Schlupe said, "this is Gul Rhinzl."

"I have heard many complimentary things about Gul Darr," the voice murmured.

Darzek genuflected politely, keeping to himself the fact that the name Rhinzl held a special fascination for him. He had compiled a list of nine traders whose relationship with the Dark was, if not suspicious, at least singular, and Rhinzl was the only one on the list whom he had never met. In the depths of the dark room his appearance was shrouded in shadow, but still conveyed the impression of a truly exquisite ugliness.

At the first opportunity Darzek produced his phial.

"I have very little experience of oils," Rhinzl said, "but I am honored to share my feeble knowledge with Gul Darr."

An arm elongated out of the dimness; a circular hand unfolded to take the phial. Rhinzl removed the stopper, sniffed delicately, tasted. "This I do not recognize. I would gladly make inquiries for you."

"Thank you, no. I fear that it is much too rare an oil for my purpose."

Rhinzl politely changed the subject and began to talk of flowers. Unlike most traders, he had a hobby. He cultivated exotic plants and blooms, especially night specimens, and he delighted in displaying his collection to such cultured and perceptive friends as Gul Darr and Gula Schlu. He began to inventory his prize specimens, and Darzek felt mildly relieved when Gula Azfel came looking for him. He had some carefully composed questions for

Gul Rhinzl, but they would have to wait. They weren't the sort of questions that could be inserted into a conversation about flowers.

He was expecting Gula Azfel, for he had seen her quietly coaching her daughters. "I've been neglecting my hostess," he said with feigned remorse. He took his leave of Rhinzl and allowed Gula Azfel to lead him away.

He sensed a conflicting strategy in the Azfel family. Gula Azfel's daughters were in full display, feathers preened and ribboned, snouts polished. Gul Azfel's daughters were highly conspicuous by their absence, but their father had cornered Darzek earlier in the evening to suggest a joint enterprise that promised large profit for small risk.

Female-like, Gula Azfel was overtly emphasizing the feminine qualities of her daughters; her husband was subtly stressing the business connections of his. After a hard night's work Darzek thought he'd earned a laugh, and he was more than willing to go along with either of them.

Adroitly Gula Azfel shepherded him through the room where her daughters were waiting, tense with excitement. Darzek, spellbound with their beauty, begged to be introduced and spent the next half hour regaling the girls with compliments while Gula Azfel faded simperingly into the background.

Finally Miss Schlupe caught his eye from the doorway, and he excused himself.

"Can you drop the Casanova bit long enough to tell me when we eat?" she asked.

"We don't. No hostess would be idiotic enough to try to serve a banquet to a mixed crowd like this one. It would require almost as many different dishes as there are guests. If they're hungry they can go to the dining room and order food with a service transmitter, but very few guests bother. Parties are for scintillating conversation and group entertainments. Eating is something anyone can do in private, so why waste valuable party time on it?"

"I like high society less and less. Why the Romeo act with those, if you'll pardon the expression, chickens?"

"It's the solemn obligation of the unmarried male guest to pay court to the daughters of the host and hostess."

"Oh, joy! I've heard of mixed marriages, but that would be hilarious. How come all four daughters look like their mother?"

"Miss Schlupe!" Darzek said sternly. "I have been telling you to get out of the office now and then and find out what goes on in the galaxy. You are observing the inevitable result of the completely integrated interstellar society. Marriages between biologically incompatible species are bound to occur. Among the sophisticated classes they are the rule. One does not marry for such a trivial purpose as reproducing his kind. One marries for social, business, political, or economic reasons."

"Just like on Earth," Miss Schlupe observed.

"It's nothing like on Earth, and you know it. Stop interrupting. At the same time one strives to find a marriage partner who will be an intellectual companion and helpmeet. There are a surprising number of instances where people marry because they happen to like and admire each other—once the other requirements are satisfied, naturally.

"But there is no logical justification for forbidding a person to reproduce merely because he has married a wife from a species with which reproduction is impossible. Therefore we have two-dimensional marital arrangements. Every husband is entitled to a mate of his own species; and every wife is entitled to a mate of hers. These mates may be married to husbands and wives of other species, who will of course have mates of their own, and so it goes. In this society a household can become a rather complicated institution."

"It sounds scandalous to me."

"It is not. Scandal ensues only when a person is so unwise as to take both a marriage partner and a mate of his own species. A person stupid enough to do that is asking for trouble. Gula Azfel is a delightful hostess, and she and her husband have a successful marriage with many things in common, though not their children. With regard to marriage the society is scrupulously monogamous, but less so where mates are concerned. There are those

species that have more than two sexes, and for them the arrangements become vastly more complicated. The one colony here on
Yorlq keeps pretty much to itself, having perhaps all the social
problems that it can cope with at home. I am reliably informed
that the one-sex species have a rather easy time of it."

"You mean that they actually expect you—that you'd even
consider—"

"Making a nonbiological marriage? Of course. Every promising
young bachelor needs a wife to run his home and furnish intellectual companionship, not to mention providing him with all kinds
of important connections. I'm seriously considering it. Wouldn't
one of Gula Azfel's daughters make a charming hostess?"

"Ugh!"

"Have you seen the water dancing? Come along."

They lingered for a time in the aquaroom and then looked in
on the darkened arena, where in a central enclosure two luminous
dmo plants were locked in mortal combat. The spectators cheered
lustily; the glowing branches traced fantastic patterns in the darkness as they whipped about, grappled, struggled for a death hold.

"Eventually one will pull the other up by the roots and eat it,"
Darzek said. "Want to watch?"

"No, thank you. Isn't there an outside door anywhere? And a
terrace where one can enjoy the moonlight?"

Darzek shook his head. "Sometimes I wonder if these people
know that an outdoors exists. What do you think of them?"

"They're scared," she said.

"Rhinzl?"

She hesitated. "Maybe 'scared' isn't the right word. He's certainly uneasy."

"True. I wondered if you'd notice. Yorlq is poised on the brink
of the Dark like a house teetering on the edge of an abyss, and its
inhabitants pretend not to notice. The traders blithely carry on
with their trade, and their childish fun and games. The natives go
their native way and spice their mundane lives with the traditional cycle of folk festivals. When a common product is no longer
available because the Dark has taken the world of its origin, the

traders find a substitute without seeming to give a thought as to why a substitute is needed. It's as if all of them have made a pact not to mention the Dark, and they won't even think about it if they can help it. But they know it's there, and they're frightened."

"What was the angle with the oil?"

"It's a vegetable oil, and it comes from a world called Quarm. It was once in common use here, being readily available and cheap. Then the Dark took Quarm."

"Ah!"

"There were plenty of substitutes, so the passing of Quarmer oil didn't seriously inconvenience anyone. The point is that it was a well-known product. The native who found those two casks knew what it was. Anyone in this part of the galaxy having anything to do with oils would recognize it. The interesting thing is that no one did. I'm not sure about old E-Wusk—he deals mostly in luxury goods, which this Quarmer oil isn't. And as far as I know, your friend Rhinzl has never dealt in oils, so perhaps he was telling the truth. But all the others knew what it was and said they didn't. It's very interesting. You might even call it fascinating. Normally these traders are scrupulously honest, but tonight at least seven of them deliberately lied to me."

Darzek entered upon his career as a trader with a single objective—instantaneous status, which would place him wholly above suspicion before he did anything that might arouse suspicion. There was no time to start modestly and obtain a solid grounding in his new profession. He had to begin at the top and learn from his successes, with no leeway at all for failures.

He founded the Trans-Star Trading Company.

Miss Schlupe objected to the title. "It's bad enough to be running a trading company that has nothing to trade," she said. "Let's restrict our operations to one star until we have some operations."

"Think big, Schluppy," Darzek said cheerfully. "It won't hurt our chances if the local tycoons believe we have far-flung connections."

"Then you'd better get yourself some far-flung connections. They'll have ways of checking."

"You have a point," Darzek admitted.

He made a fast circuit of a dozen neighboring worlds and found a free-lancing factor on each who took no offense at Darzek's offer of modest compensation for displaying a notice that said he was the local representative of the Trans-Star Trading Company. Darzek also called on peripheral factors of vast trading concerns whose headquarters were located in the remote inner reaches of the galaxy and held forth the possibility of transactions that would not be detrimental to their reputations. They were receptive.

Darzek had his connections, but he still had nothing to trade. His one asset was his solvency credential. His unlimited solvency credential. Darzek was skeptical. *Large-talk* words had a disconcerting tendency to take on meanings not implicit in the translations he had been taught, or to mean different things in different circumstances.

"How unlimited is unlimited?" he demanded.

"Spend some of it and find out," Miss Schlupe suggested.

"I'll spend all of it," Darzek said. "Anything less than a colossal deal would be a waste of time."

He quickly found three natives who had talent for investigation—*that* kind of business he understood—and after several days of patient inquiry they reported to him that Gul Zarkun, a merchant who stood high in the local traders' pecking order, had a warehouse crammed with unmarketable *mosf* skins.

Darzek called on Gul Zarkun, who greeted him with polite reserve. "Trans-Star Trading Company? I don't recall—"

"We're just commencing operations in this sector," Darzek said glibly. "I understand that you have a surplus of *mosf* skins."

"I have," Gul Zarkun admitted, with truly confounding frankness. "A large surplus. I had a good market for them, but business conditions have changed."

Darzek nodded wisely. Gul Zarkun's market had been the world of Borut. He had astutely cornered the *mosf* supply, and then the Dark had swallowed Borut and the *mosf* market and left him with a surfeit of *mosf* skins that no one wanted.

"There are markets," Gul Zarkun went on, "but with transportation costs and the competition from local products I would have to take a heavy loss. I've been holding onto them in the hope that something will open up."

"I have a client who might be able to use them," Darzek said. "Quote me a price on the lot."

"The lot? All of them?"

"Of course. There's no solvency these days in handling small orders."

"No, indeed," Gul Zarkun breathed. "All of them, you say? Well—" The magnitude of the proposition made him wary. "What—ah—financial arrangement do you propose?"

"Full and immediate solvency. It's the only way I do business. I'll want a certified inventory, but if I'm unable to consummate the exchange I'll reimburse you for your trouble."

"That's fair enough. I'll have the inventory made and send it to you with a quotation."

For the next two days Darzek kept the transmitting relays sizzling with messages to his various connections, and when Gul Zarkun's quotation arrived he was ready.

He did not even consider haggling over the price. The money meant nothing to him as long as his solvency credential covered it. What he desperately needed was a reputation.

"A hundred thousand solvency units," he told Miss Schlupe. "Nice round figure, isn't it?"

"How much money is that?"

"No idea. A quarter of a million dollars, at least. Keep your fingers crossed."

With Miss Schlupe looking on nervously, he touched out the code that would transfer a hundred thousand solvency units from his account to Gul Zarkun's. After several interminable seconds the board clicked and cleared itself.

"Is that all there is to it?" Miss Schlupe demanded.

Darzek nodded.

"And—you've paid Gul Zarkun the hundred thousand?"

Darzek nodded again.

"Unlimited means—unlimited!"

"We still don't know that," Darzek said, "but there's no doubt that it means quite a lot."

He hurried off a memo to Gul Zarkun informing him that the quotation had been met and applied himself to the tedious task of shipping the *mosf* skins.

A full term went by before his factors disposed of the last of the skins and transferred payment to Darzek. Totaling up his expenses, he found that he'd recovered little more than a quarter of the purchase price. Transportation costs were high, factors' commissions took greedy bites out of the resale price, and he discovered to his consternation that galactic civilization was less beatified than he had supposed: there were taxes to pay, and assorted inspection and license fees.

A hurried calculation convinced him that he had lost, on this first business transaction, the equivalent of nearly two hundred thousand dollars.

He considered it a bargain. Gul Zarkun was overwhelmed. He came personally to pay his respects to Darzek, and he bragged to his friends—not about his own good fortune in disposing of a dead white elephant, but on Darzek's astuteness in finding a profitable market none of them thought existed.

"If I'm not careful, that astuteness will ruin me," Darzek told Miss Schlupe ruefully, but in truth he was elated. He paid for Gul Zarkun's *mosf* skins with Jan Darzek's solvency credential; when the skins were resold, payment was made to the Trans-Star Trading Company. He lost some seventy-five thousand solvency units he hadn't known he had, and Trans-Star gained a third of that amount in liquid solvency.

His company was in business, it had solid assets—and he had acquired the reputation he so desperately needed.

He quickly ran up a series of similar transactions, in each instance making payment with his personal solvency credential and returning the—considerably smaller—receipts to the Trans-Star Trading Company account. On each transaction he lost a fortune and his company became richer. He had the dizzying sensation of having discovered, quite inadvertently, a philosopher's stone of economics. In half a period he lost an enormous amount of solvency and became a millionaire.

Around Yorlq's trading community his status quickly became legendary. He no longer had to surreptitiously snoop out potential business deals. The other traders came to him with their surpluses, and, because he wanted to be known as a brilliant businessman rather than a magician, he had to exercise restraint and become severely selective in the offers he accepted. He could easily have lost four times as much solvency and become four times as rich.

He hired several promising young undertraders from the lower reaches of his competitors' organizations. His own radical ideas on how to run a trading company merely bewildered them, but left to their own devices they gradually developed a volume of business of a more prosaic sort, and Trans-Star began to show a modest profit.

He also expanded his staff of investigators, keeping that organization separate from his trading company and as anonymous as his ingenuity could make it. Its headquarters were a Trans-Star warehouse; certain alterations were effected before the trading company occupied the premises, and none of the trading personnel were aware that the building's internal dimensions were somewhat smaller than they had been originally. The rooms thus concealed were easily accessible by transmitter but in no other way; and by transmitter only to those who knew what transmitters to use, and how. With a secret headquarters, and with a staff of trained investigators, he felt that he was at last ready to learn a thing or two about the Dark.

But his trading company still required a disproportionate amount of time and energy that he would have preferred to expend on more vital matters. He had his reputation, but it would quickly wilt if he did not keep it nourished.

On the day following Gul Azfel's party, he sent for his first undertrader and flashed invoices on his ceiling screen until he found the one he wanted. "It says here," he remarked severely, "that you have just purchased two shiploads of *skruka*-gum."

"Yes, Sire," Gud Baxak admitted humbly. "It seemed like a very good price."

"Last evening I overheard Gul Meszk remarking that he had three full shiploads of *skruka*-gum on the way from Sesnav. His unit price, delivered here on Yorlq, will be a full fifteen per centum under what you paid. His ships will be unloading in four days."

Gud Baxak cringed with humiliation.

"I further find," Darzek went on, "that these two shipments, Gul Meszk's and ours, are the only supplies of *skruka*-gum likely to reach Yorlq in the next five terms. Does all of this suggest anything to you?"

"Yes, Sire. I shall divert my two shiploads to another world and salvage what I can from my stupidity."

"You will not," Darzek told him. "You will immediately post an anticipation of unlimited quantities of skruka-gum, availability within the half-term. You will invite bids, minimum price fourteen lurn-weights per solvency, which is at least ten per centum under what Gul Meszk could sell his for."

"But that would be twenty-five per centum under what I could sell mine for!" Gud Baxak protested.

"Gul Meszk will of course divert his three ships and attempt to dispose of the cargos before knowledge of an unlimited supply of low-priced skruka-gum on Yorlq becomes general. As soon as you learn that he has done so, you will cancel your anticipation and announce that you could obtain only the two shiploads at a higher price. You should be able to dispose of the lot at current rates, which will give you a tidy profit of twenty per centum."

Gud Baxak's bone-ringed face underwent contortions of incredulity. "But I can't post an anticipation unless we have an anticipation! And if we have one, there would be no need to cancel it!"

Darzek sighed and weighed the value of a small business coup against the possible suspicion that such sharp dealings might arouse. He doubted that it would be worth the risk. Gud Baxak was hard-working and no dunce, and would doubtless salvage a small profit. "No," he said regretfully. "You are quite right. Divert your two shiploads, and get the best price you can. And Gud Baxak—"

"Yes, Sire?"

"I want as few people as possible to find out about this little blunder of yours. Try to dispose of the two shiploads without posting availability or asking for bids."

"Yes, Sire."

Obviously relieved, Gud Baxak genuflected and hurried away.

Darzek sighed again, pondering the mysteries of interstellar business; more particularly, the mysteries of interstellar business-men.

They were incredibly, unnecessarily, even disgustingly honest. They worked hard, of course—fanatically hard. Their knowledge was encyclopedic, and they strove incessantly to keep it that way. And they were utterly devoid of shrewdness and imagination, and seemed incapable of the slightest machination.

"There isn't a one of them," Darzek mused, "who would make a tenth-rate poker player. God knows they all have the faces for it, but they're constitutionally incapable of the smallest bluff."

When he searched for the cleverness behind a brilliant business coup, it invariably turned out that the trader had scored his success merely because he knew more, and worked harder, than his competitors. The traders not only told the truth, but they believed everything they heard. Implicitly. On Earth, the wealthiest of them would have gone broke in a matter of months.

Darzek could have become a multibillionaire in record time, but money was the least of his needs. His only concern now was for his reputation, and it wouldn't do to have word get around that Gul Meszk had made an ass out of Trans-Star Trading Company's first undertrader.

Irritably he got to his feet and paced back and forth. "If they're so dratted honest," he growled, "why did they lie to me about the oil?"

Mentally he ticked off the names of the traders who interested him: E-Wusk, Azfel, Meszk, Kaln, Rhinzl, Isc, Ceyh, Halvr, Brokefa. All of them had been routed out of peaceful prosperity by the Dark—E-Wusk four times, the others at least once. Their property had been confiscated, their businesses ruined.

A trader thus burned should have feared the fire—should have taken himself with alacrity to a remote part of the galaxy, putting as many light years between himself and the Dark as the more than ample dimensions of space permitted.

Yet all had gathered here on Yorlq, on the very threshold of the Dark, and carried on as if nothing had happened. Brokefa had joined a group of *maf*-cousins already established here, but there was no explanation at all for the presence of the others. They were flourishing, but they could have flourished as easily on the other side of the galaxy.

"Except for E-Wusk, they're afraid of the Dark," Darzek mused. "They won't talk about it. If they're cornered, they'll lie to avoid even an indirect reference to it, and yet they remain directly under its shadow. When you consider that they won't lie about anything else, not even to make money—when their lives are dedicated to making money—it becomes highly significant, or at least meaningful. I wish I knew what it meant."

Miss Schlupe stepped out of the transmitter. She always did so with a look of surprise on her face, as though she never quite expected the blamed thing to work. "What did you do to poor Gud Baxak?" she asked.

"Shocked his moral fiber, I suppose."

"You shouldn't do that. The poor boy is half frantic."

"Really? What's he doing?"

"Working furiously. Checking references, getting messages off three a minute—"

"It'll do him good. What's that you have?"

She held out a long, narrow leaf. "What does it look like?"

"I haven't the vaguest idea."

"It's tobacco."

"No!" He stared. "It couldn't be!"

"I've been visiting Rhinzl," she said. "He's quite a horticultur- ist. He has lovely flowers, and all kinds of strange plants. And I found this."

"It couldn't be anything like tobacco."

"I'll dry some, and see."

"Fine. And then you can teach one of Gul Azfel's pwisqs to smoke, to see if the stuff is poison."

"Only yesterday you were threatening to buy a spaceship and send it to Earth for a load of tobacco. There's nothing to lose by trying, is there?"

"I suppose not," Darzek said absently. "Miss Schlupe, what

would you do if you wanted a trading empire with a truly impregnable monopoly?"

"I couldn't imagine wanting such a thing."

"That's because you're pure in heart. I've been thinking about these worlds that the Dark has taken. One moment they were receiving food, raw materials, and processed and fabricated items from all over the galaxy. The next moment they were receiving nothing. What did they do?"

"They did without."

"No, Miss Schlupe. They may have gone on trading with each other, but that's by no means certain, and even then I doubt that they could make themselves self-sufficient. The Dark has created a considerable void in interstellar trade. I find that idea fascinating. I'm wondering if I could fill it myself."

"You?"

"I'll put it another way. I'm wondering if, by making motions at filling that void, I may find that someone has already thought of it. Someone whose name is E-Wusk, Azfel, Meszk, Kaln, Rhinzl, Isc, Ceyh, Halvr, or Brokefa. One, or several, or all nine. It would account for their unnatural silence on the subject of the Dark. In short—"

"I like the way you talk for an hour, and then say, 'In short—' Why don't you start out with the short of it, so I can understand you."

"Item," Darzek said. "A revolution, a severance of relations, an eviction of foreigners, is unbelievable, staggering, incredible, inconceivable, and a number of other adjectives I can't think of at the moment. It can't happen. Since the worlds have complete autonomy, there's no need for it to happen. Suddenly it does, on a massive scale. It's so unimaginable that the only explanation anyone can think of postulates extra-galactic invaders armed with mind rays. It matters not that no one has ever seen one of these invaders, not even on the worlds that were revolting. When one rejects the possibility of their being invisible, which I do—"

"All right. Scratch the invaders. Where does that leave you?"

"With a question I should have asked myself months—excuse

me, terms—ago. Who benefits? Certainly not the revolting populations. If they merely wanted to rid themselves of foreigners, they could have done so legally and at negligible expense, and monopolized their own trade. They gained nothing by severing relations, and they ruined their economies. So who *does* benefit?

"I give up," Miss Schlupe said patiently. "Who?"

"Consider this: the one goal in life for a trader is trade. Business. Accumulating solvency. Supposing it occurred to a trader that he could have much more of all of these, with considerably less work and risk, if he devised a way to eliminate his grubbing competitors. A trader or group of traders who could invent a little device called the Dark, and use it to establish a trading monopoly over a large number of worlds, would have achieved a trader's idea of paradise. It wouldn't satisfy them, of course. Being traders, they'd want more and more worlds. The Dark would keep moving."

Miss Schlupe beamed at him. "That's it! You've wrapped it up beautifully. It explains everything, even why they won't talk about the Dark. Now all you have to do is figure out how they do it."

"It doesn't explain quite everything," Darzek said. "There's one small matter that it doesn't explain at all. What are they afraid of?"

9

At the edge of Yorlq's capital city stood the *Hesr*, the Hill of Traders, an unsightly knob of earth crowned with tangled vegetation and a haphazard crowding of enormous dwellings. Darzek, standing where the steep slope leveled off, gazed meditatively out over the city of Yorlez and pondered this inclination of foreign traders to settle upon a strategically located height.

He wondered if sometime in the distant past the belligerency of natives everywhere had forced traders into the habit of placing their enclaves where they could be easily converted to citadels. Perhaps the *Hesr* had once bristled with battlements and overlooked a lovely town of winding, flower-trimmed streets and quaint buildings. If so, time had obliterated the battlements to the last stone, and no one remembered when the cities and towns of Yorlq had been lovely.

Neither was anyone aware of the monstrous eyesores they had become. Time and indifference had worked together like an insidious blight to lay waste to cities that continued to flourish amidst their own ruins.

The orderly pattern of streets and spacious boulevards was still visible in the inner city of Yorlez, but the thoroughfares were choked with a raging tangle of blotchy brown vegetation that reached high to obscure the outlines of buildings whose colorful plastic facades had long since been bleached to sickly gray. Looking down from the *Hesr*, Darzek could trace the precise moment when the transmitter had influenced the city's growth. The buildings of the outer districts were arranged chaotically; the heaving sea of junglelike vegetation surrounded them and even lapped into narrow gaps where the buildings stood close together.

Studying the hideous thing that this city had become, Darzek felt a pang of apprehension for Earth. Yorlez had parks, circular oases of tamed greenery, but the few citizens who strolled there seemed not to notice the ugly, impinging jungle. The transmitter had turned their artistic vision inward. The external appearance of a building no longer mattered if no one saw it. No one could be concerned about the view from a nonexistent window. Would Earth, too, become a place where people lived out their lives in incubated comfort, surrounded by an unseen wasteland?

He whirled in alarm as the weeds behind him heaved ominously; but the ear-shrouded head that appeared belonged to Kxon, his chief investigator. Sheepishly Darzek holstered his automatic. He had faced the menace of the Dark coolly when he'd thought it was everywhere, but a menace that was nowhere was gradually unnerving him.

"I do not think it possible to locate any of the others," Kxon said.

Darzek turned to look at the nondescript exterior of the nearest dwelling. With no windows or exterior doors there seemed small chance of putting the information to use, but he'd thought it worth the effort to try to identify the dwellings of his nine traders.

They had found Rhinzl's, but only because of an addition Rhinzl had built to house his plant collection. It was not a greenhouse—the nocturnal preferred to grow his specimens in artificial light that could be turned off when he wanted to putter with them—but an extension to the original building, and the shimmering new walls stood out starkly. They had no luck at all with the other traders.

"They probably don't even know where they live themselves," Darzek said. "Ask them where their dwellings are located, and they'd show you a code on a transmitter's destination board. Strange. I don't suppose you've found any paths here."

"No, Sire."

"Or any paths leading up from the city? No? I don't know why there would be, but at least it would give us something to think about. We might as well go back, then, and think about something else."

Vegetation grew sparsely on the hill's steep slope, but as they approached the bottom it rose to meet them in a vicious tangle. The path they had broken on their way to the hill had disappeared without a trace. Blindly they hacked through the weeds, missed the park they were aiming for, and finally, perspiring, sticky with sap from dripping leaves, they stumbled upon another, slipped into it unobserved, and transmitted to Kxon's headquarters.

Darzek cleaned himself up and relaxed on a hassock to wait for Kxon. "How would you like to become a trader?" he asked him.

Kxon twitched his ears bewilderedly, which sent ripples of movement around his head. Nature had been unnecessarily lavish in its distribution of the tissue intended to reinforce a Yorlqer's aural sense. Kxon's ears encircled his head in a continuous band of taut flesh, forming a basket-like structure that added two feet to his height and inspired Miss Schlupe to label him a private eye with public ears. So accustomed had Darzek become to misshapen organs that he would not have thought twice about these had it not been for the paradoxical fact that Yorlqers were, all of them, extremely hard of hearing. The spectacle of an errant nature compensating for its goof in devising an inefficient hearing apparatus by enlarging upon its defects struck him as ludicrous.

"Trader," he said again. "Would you like to be one?"

"No, Sire. I would not care to leave Yorlq."

"All I had in mind was your obtaining employment with a trader. Gul Isc, for example. If you worked in his trading office, we might be able to learn the truth about such matters as why he recently sold two of his warehouses."

"I could try, Sire."

"We could also make a record of who visits him at his office, and perhaps of some of the people he visits. We can't get anywhere watching the outside of buildings that have no exits, and we've already learned that we can't follow people through transmitters. Let's see if we can plant investigators on all nine of the traders. Start with Gul Isc, and if he turns you down have one of the others try. Don't stop until someone has been hired, or until the whole staff has had a shot at every trader."

"Yes, Sire."

"But not all of them on the same day. And don't feel too badly if you aren't successful. None of the traders has a Yorlqer on his staff. I've been wondering why. If they turn you down, you might ask them. I'm going back to Trans-Star."

"Yes, Sire."

In his Trans-Star office Darzek activated the ceiling screen and arranged himself to study the Dark. An enlarged view of the galaxy's perimeter showed the black corridor looking like an immense, bottomless chasm. Darzek spent hours gazing at it when he could think of nothing better to do, and asking himself questions that only the Council of Supreme could have answered, and each time he was left feeling more frustrated.

He wasn't aware of Gud Baxak's presence until the undertrader said apologetically, "Sire?"

Darzek swore and darkened the screen. "What is it?" he asked wearily.

Gud Baxak stood before him unsteadily, face pink with fatigue, his strange, tripodic underpinnings arranged in exaggerated stance. He was obviously exhausted, but his great, faceted eyes were shining.

Darzek knew the symptoms. Gud Baxak had the endurance, determination, and infinite patience of a good trader, and several times a day his tireless search for bargains would strike pay dirt. Then he would rush to Darzek with the announcement that he was onto something big.

"I'm onto something big," he said, his voice squeaky with excitement. "Have you time to appraise the data?"

Darzek stirred resentfully. He'd had rather more than he wanted of inventories, product anticipations, solvency bids, and all the rest of it. He said dryly, "I'm onto something rather big myself. So big, in fact, that it's going to take all of my time from now on." He got to his feet. "Gud Baxak, I'm promoting you. Consider yourself a partner with Gula Schlu and myself. Handle your deals as you think best. I'll see that you have the privilege of solvency transfer. You have my full confidence."

"Yes, Sire," Gud Baxak said, beaming.

He departed, and Darzek sank back to contemplate the Dark. And his nine traders.

"If they're trading with the Dark," he mused, "they naturally want to keep their monopoly to themselves. If they aren't, or if some of them aren't, I should be able to play them off against each other. The question is how."

He had a faint glimmering of a plan, with E-Wusk as the central figure. E-Wusk, at least, was willing to discuss the Dark. Darzek paced the floor fretfully until he had shaped his idea into something he could act upon, and then he stepped to the transmitter and touched out the code for E-Wusk's office.

The old trader whooped when he saw him. "Gul Darr! Oh, ho ho! Have you come over for a little water dancing?"

"I was hoping you'd give me a lesson," Darzek said.

"Oh, ho ho!" E-Wusk quivered with merriment. "Me—water dancing! If they thought *you* were funny—oh, ho ho!"

"I have a business proposition for you," Darzek said.

"A business proposition from Gul Darr is a rare honor," E-Wusk said, instantly serious. "Rest yourself, and tell me about it."

"You have experienced the Dark—" Darzek began.

"Rather too frequently," E-Wusk agreed, "and it's about to happen again. You will soon experience the Dark yourself."

His train of thought completely derailed, Darzek could only gape in amazement. "How soon?" he demanded.

E-Wusk gestured absently with three arms. "Perhaps the word 'soon' was mischosen. But the Dark is coming—will come."

"I see. For the moment I am concerned with where the Dark has been. And I have had this thought: the remainder of the galaxy once carried on a vast trade with those worlds the Dark has consumed. What has happened to the needs that this trade once satisfied?"

E-Wusk shifted arms and legs uneasily but did not answer.

"What I propose is that we undertake to fulfill those needs."

"Trade—with the Dark?" E-Wusk whispered.

"What is the Dark?" Darzek demanded irritably. "Is it alive? Does it have a mind and a being of its own, or does it exist only in the minds of those who flee from it?"

"I do my thinking in terms of shiploads and solvency exchange," E-Wusk said slowly. "Such questions are not for me."

"You are perceptive. You have encountered the Dark four times. Have you ever seen it?"

"I have seen the fires and the raging mobs. I have heard them shout, 'Grilf, Grilf!' Do you know that word? No, and I should not have said it. Only the Dark pronounces it. My friend, I would not care to have dealings with the Dark."

"Nor would I," Darzek said. "As far as we know, the Dark has no needs that trade could satisfy, so I do not propose to trade with the Dark. My concern is for those worlds the Dark has cut off from trade. We know that they have needs."

E-Wusk had slowly shrunk into a tangle of limbs. "It is an attractive thought," he agreed awesomely. "Attractive—and terrifying. Who would dare?"

"I would. I intend to. I want your help."

"You, Gul Darr? But of course. You are a bold trader, you willingly accept risks, and because you have had no experience of the Dark you do not fear it."

"Do you fear the Dark, Gul E-Wusk?"

"Assuredly."

"I would not have thought so."

"I do not wear my fear," E-Wusk said simply. "I do not let it consume me. But I fear."

"Then why do you remain on Yorlq?"

"I am defying the Dark. It has routed me four times, and when it comes here I shall gladly flee with the others, but until it comes

I can defy it. I must defy it, to assuage in some small measure the humiliation I have suffered."

"Even when the defiance can only bring you more humiliation?"

E-Wusk heaved his enormous body with a sigh but did not answer.

"I think perhaps you *are* a philosopher," Darzek said with a smile. "But what about the other traders who have been routed by the Dark? Are they also defying it?"

"I do not know. The Dark is not a thing one talks about by preference."

"The others won't talk about it at all."

"I know. They wear their fear. This thought of yours is attractive, Gul Darr—to trade with so many worlds that have no trade. Alas, it would be impossible."

"How do you know that it isn't being done?"

E-Wusk's body jerked convulsively. "You mean . . . what *do* you mean?"

"My instinct tells me that those worlds cannot exist without trade. They have needs, and where there are needs there will always be a trader to fill them. Therefore someone must be trading with those worlds."

"Someone . . . must . . . be . . . trading . . ." E-Wusk repeated slowly. "I had not thought of such a thing. Proof will exist if this is true, though finding it would take much time and no small amount of solvency. Ship arrivals and departures would have to be tabulated. All the ships in half the galaxy would have to be traced. It would be a staggering chore."

"I believe you," Darzek said. "Even that would not suffice. Would arrival and departure records reveal that a ship rendezvoused in space with a ship from a Dark world and traded cargos with it?"

E-Wusk's body jerked again.

"I can think of a much simpler way," Darzek went on. "Some of the worlds of the Dark must have products that are unique. Are these products still in good supply? Are they being exchanged? If so, then someone must be trading with the worlds of the Dark."

"Yes. That would be much easier to check. One would need only to publish anticipated needs for such products and evaluate the response."

"Are you willing to make such publications? I should be happy to put my solvency at your disposal."

E-Wusk waved the offer aside. "The expense would be trifling. Mmm—it would not be necessary to investigate *all* unique products. Just a few that have considerable demand and a high value per volume unit, since the trader would want the most profitable use of his cargo space. Mmm—yes."

"It wouldn't do to list them all at once," Darzek said. "I'd suggest that you spread ten or twelve items over two terms."

"Of course."

"And the listings may bring you legitimate bids of small quantities which may still be available. You should think how to deal with these."

"I'll decline them. I never deal in less than shipload quantities. The handling costs are too high."

"What specific products do you have in mind?" Darzek asked.

E-Wusk mulled over the possible choices, and Darzek relaxed, and made mental notes, and attempted to quiet his conscience. He liked and admired the old rascal, and he wasn't proud of what he was about to do to him.

Darzek began avoiding the Trans-Star office, except to check the daily need anticipations for E-Wusk's listings. His presence was not needed; Miss Schlupe kept a wary eye on the company's solvency, the undertraders were performing competently, and profit per centums were improving each term.

After his investigators had tried unsuccessfully to obtain employment with the nine traders, Darzek could only keep them snooping futilely around the edges of the traders' apparently impeccable activities. There was so little for Darzek to do that he took the time to fashion a flimsy rocking chair for Miss Schlupe and carve a pipe for himself, and he tried out Miss Schlupe's alleged tobacco. It lacked even a fanciful resemblance to its namesake, but he smoked it anyway.

He spent most of his time in the apartment he shared with Miss Schlupe, pacing a fretful circuit of its compact dimensions, reception room to bedroom to bedroom to reception room, or stretched out in prone position racking his brain for ideas. He cursed himself for suggesting that E-Wusk spread his anticipations over so long a time interval, though he knew that haste could easily ruin this one positive action he had evolved since reaching Yorlq. There was nothing for him to do but wait. E-Wusk published his needs one at a time and advised Darzek that he'd had no response. Life on the world of Yorlq went its placid way; if the Dark was threatening, only E-Wusk seemed aware of it.

Darzek was engaged in a reverie in which he contemplated buying a fleet of spaceships, outfitting them as a private space navy, and invading the worlds of the Dark to find out what was going on there, when Miss Schlupe bluntly roused him.

"What is it now?" he asked resignedly.

"Prepare yourself for a shock," she said. "Your Trans-Star trading empire has gone smash."

"Schluppy, I'm in no mood for jokes, and even if I was I wouldn't appreciate that one."

"Do I sound as if I'm joking?"

"What's happened?"

"Gud Baxak has translated the irresistible force of Trans-Star's solvency into immovable objects."

Darzek got up reluctantly. "I'll go see him."

"It won't do you any good. He's delirious. I have three doctors looking after him, but what he really needs is some of my rhubarb beer."

"If he's delirious he needs a tranquilizer."

"That's what my beer is. A tranquilizer. Do you know anything about bark?"

"Bark? *Tree* bark? No."

"You will," Miss Schlupe said confidently. "You now own every scrap of one particular kind of tree bark in the galaxy."

Darzek sat down again. "How long has he been delirious? He wouldn't be buying bark without a darned good reason."

"He had a good reason—he thought. I got the gist of what happened before he became incoherent, and what I understand of it isn't good. Do you know what *tizc* is?"

Darzek reached out and tapped the wall. "Certainly. The common building plastic. It's produced everywhere from local materials, because it's cheaper to manufacture where needed than to transport through space. As E-Wusk would say, it has a low value per volume unit. Don't tell me Gud Baxak has been dabbling in that!"

"Indirectly, yes. He studies everything, you know, and he happened onto the alluring news of a revolutionary change in the manufacture of *tizc*. The new process requires a kind of unpronounceable crystal, which naturally Gud Baxak investigated, and he learned that it is derived from an unpronounceable fluid, which is obtained from the bark of an equally unpronounceable tree."

"Ah!"

"So he proceeded to corner the bark market." Miss Schlupe shook her head awesomely. "It was a brilliant operation. He didn't use a smidgeon of solvency, he bought nothing, and yet he tied up the entire available supply and also the anticipated output for more time than he now wants to contemplate. I never would have credited him with such imagination. He used a kind of promissory option, and just to show you how imaginative he got, I think he invented that, too. But it is binding. Oh, how it is binding!

"Then he learned that crystals obtained from bark fluid are too expensive for general commercial use. The new *tizc* process was made possible by the discovery of a cheaper source for them. Trans-Star now owns options on all that bark, and must eventually pay for it, and even the limited market the stuff had no longer exists."

"How did he manage to make such a mistake?"

"I don't know."

Darzek got to his feet again and paced the floor thoughtfully.

"Pay for it with your bottomless solvency credential, and burn the stuff," Miss Schlupe suggested.

"I can't. If my carefully contrived reputation goes up in a monumental smudge of bark I'll be a laughing stock, and the next trader I approach with a wild idea like trading with the Dark will spit in my face. I'll have to straighten this mess out quickly, or we might as well pack and go home."

It took him less than an hour to track down the basis for Gud Baxak's error. A description of the new *tizc* process had failed to mention the new source for the crystals. Darzek was not satisfied.

"It may have been bait," he said. "I'll have to look into that. Even if it wasn't, Gud Baxak managed his coup far too easily. I'm wondering if someone was leading him on—someone with a large stock of bark just rendered worthless by that new source for crystals."

The clues were few; the facts obscure and tenuous. The trail was crossed with the names of small, virtually unknown trading companies that on investigation proved to be owned by other equally unknown companies. After several days of driving both his undertraders and his investigators unmercifully and investing a small fortune in space transmissions, Darzek reached the top of the pyramid.

"Gul Rhinzl!" he breathed. "That's very interesting."

"It can't be," Miss Schlupe protested. "He wouldn't doctor a report."

"He didn't. At least, I don't see how he could have, or why he would have wanted to. Every trading firm in this part of the galaxy received that identical incomplete announcement. The others—those who were interested—investigated it properly and ignored it, as Gud Baxak should have done. If a firm is intent on squandering solvency, there isn't anything unethical about cooperating with it. Rhinzl cooperated like the master that he is. Any other trader would have done the same, or tried to."

"What are you going to do?"

"I haven't any choice. I've got to show Rhinzl that my bark is worse than my bite."

Gud Baxak, wan from his bout with high fever and hallucinations, came timorously to Darzek with the latest industrial bulletin. "I suppose I should give up reading these, Sire," he said humbly, "but I did happen to notice this, and I couldn't help wondering—"

Darzek glanced at it. A textile firm on the world of Terlbs had developed a new fiber from a vegetable sheathing. Cloth woven from this fiber could be worn by animates with the most ultrasensitive epidermises. The market was vast and virtually untouched, and production in commercial quantities was expected in the near future.

"I can't keep you from wondering," Darzek said, "but before you buy any more bark I'd suggest that you make inquiries."

"Yes, Sire."

"*Careful* inquiries."

Gud Baxak went away and made careful inquiries. Before he had quite completed them a pharmaceutical notice came to his attention. A certain bark that had been successfully made into a textile fiber that did not affect sensitive skins was being tested for its medicinal qualities. The firm making the tests was guardedly optimistic. Gud Baxak made inquiries about that, too.

"It seems to be true, Sire," he exulted. "It's the same bark. The textile firm informs me that it has enough on hand for experimental purposes, but will be buying stock for production very soon."

"In that case your bark venture may prove highly profitable."

"But—what shall I do?"

"Nothing," Darzek told him. "We have title to the bark. When they're ready for it, they'll call us."

At Gul Halvr's symposium that evening Darzek did some exulting of his own. "Never saw anything like it," he remarked. "Certainly the lad has a touch of genius. We control the entire supply, and yet we don't have a sliver of solvency tied up in it. Until the market develops, our sources are obligingly storing the bark under optimum commercial conditions and at no cost to us. Eventually there'll be an unlimited market, over which we'll have absolute price discretion."

"Amazing," Gul Azfel murmured, and offered his congratulations. The other traders, being envious, were less enthusiastic. Gul Azfel's enthusiasm may have been genuine; he was still cultivating Darzek as a potential son-in-law.

The conversation took place within earshot of the dark room, and Darzek was mildly disappointed to learn later that Rhinzl had not been present. It did not really matter; he would know everything Darzek had said before the next midday, and in a way his absence was quite as gratifying as his presence would have been. It meant that he had something on his mind other than symposiums.

Bark, perhaps?

"Schluppy," Darzek said when they were alone, "did you by any chance bring a genuine silk handkerchief with you?"

"I think I have a couple of them. Why?"

"My phony textile firm has had a request for a sample of its new miracle-type bark cloth."

"Rhinzl?"

"Not directly, but we both know where the sample will ultimately end up. My study of textiles has been rather hurried, but I did notice that there are no listings of any made from anything approximating insect fibers. Earth's fiber-producing insects may be unique in the galaxy. Even if they aren't, Rhinzl's experts will have had very little experience of silkworms. I'll cut a circular sample from one of your handkerchiefs, and we'll save the trimmings to present to Rhinzl at a later date."

"Tsk. Let's not be vindictive about it."

"Of course not. Rhinzl is simply playing the game, and because I haven't time to start building my reputation all over again I'm cheating a little to beat him at it. He won't lose anything except solvency, of which he has plenty. What I'm wondering is how long it will take him to realize that even in this enlightened civilization possession is nine points of the law, a bird in hand is worth two in the bush, and so on. We have title to the bark, but he's *got* it. He should be doing some very serious thinking about that."

Darzek waited with increasing uneasiness and finally risked a cautious message to one of the smaller trading companies, advising it that he would soon complete his purchase of the optioned bark. Gud Baxak brought the reply, trembling with anger.

"They say they sold it—by mistake!"

"Indeed," Darzek said. "Do they apologize?"

"They offer a per centum settlement in compensation. A per centum!"

"That doesn't sound particularly generous. Ask them for twenty, and settle for ten."

"But it's a trap, Sire! If we settle for ten on this option, all of our other options can be settled for ten. It's the *doctrine of equal preference.*"

"It's a trap," Darzek agreed with a grin. "Act as tough as you like, threaten whatever iniquities you can legally threaten them with, and hold out for fifteen if you think you can get it—but not too long. I'll be perfectly satisfied with ten."

"But, Sire—"

"Unless you have a special craving to eat bark, do as I say!"

Gud Baxak returned the next day and said bewilderedly, "I settled for fifteen per centum. I asked for twenty, and they *offered* fifteen!"

"Good. Now listen carefully. When you receive the next cancellation, I want you to refuse a settlement and demand the merchandise. Tell 'em they'll have to buy the bark back and deliver it according to contract. Let *them* bring up this doctrine of whatchamacallit, and fight that a little, too. It's a trap, but until we're out of the bark business I'd rather friend Rhinzl didn't know who trapped whom."

An undertrader brought the message and delivered it with a

politeness so studied that it seemed rehearsed. Gul Rhinzl earnestly sought an interview with Gul Darr, at the latter's convenience.

"Make him come and see you," Miss Schlupe suggested.

"Let's not be vindictive," Darzek answered. "He's an interesting person, he's charming company, and he has a lovely herb and flower collection. He also has all of his bark back, plus what he bought to unload on Gud Baxak, and now he's learned that my dummy textile and pharmaceutical firms encountered unexpected problems in their bark processing and are no longer in business. Probably he's sitting there in his dark room crying all of his eyes out. He rarely goes anywhere, and we wouldn't be equipped to entertain him if he did."

"Is it safe to go there?"

Darzek laughed. "You aren't seeing this in the proper perspective. A transaction large enough to wipe out Trans-Star is piddling stuff to traders who control sizable hunks of trade with hundreds of worlds. Rhinzl wouldn't willingly lose that much solvency—he wouldn't willingly lose any—but he'll still show a profit for the term."

Darzek sent back word that he would call on Gul Rhinzl when convenient, and treated himself to a pipeful of Miss Schlupe's tobacco before he left so as not to appear too eager.

As he stepped from the transmitter, Rhinzl's lilting voice called from the remote corner of his unlighted office. "Gul Darr! I had that room illuminated for you, thinking that you would be more comfortable there."

"I don't really mind an absence of light," Darzek said, and moved on into the office until he stumbled upon a chair.

"There you have the advantage of we nocturnals."

"How is that?"

"The darkness is only an inconvenience to you, but the light is an intensely painful experience to many of us." An arm telescoped out of the gloom to wave something at Darzek. "What can you tell me about this, Gul Darr?"

Darzek peered at it unsuccessfully, and had to step forward and touch before he recognized it.

A circle of silk.

"Very little," he said.

"Where does it come from?"

"Would you be offended if I refused to tell you?"

"Not *offended* . . . no . . . every trader is entitled to his secrets."

"Thank you. I can tell you this much. The sample you are now holding represents almost the entire available supply, and there is no possibility of obtaining more."

"That is information enough," Rhinzl said. "I am sorry to hear it—very sorry. It is an interesting fabric. It would find a good market if you could supply it in commercial quantities."

"I'm sure it would. Unfortunately, I can't."

"In fact," Rhinzl's soft voice went on, "it might be the very fabric to satisfy the needs of animates with sensitive skins." Suddenly he laughed. It was a gurgling, giggling sort of laugh, and in the darkness Darzek could only imagine telescoping arms waving and a grotesque body jerking with merriment. "Gul Darr! We are even. You are more than even—you, at least, have made a profit. Shall we call it quits?"

"It suits me," Darzek said.

Rhinzl laughed again. "Gul Darr! You are a terror!"

"It takes one to know one," Darzek murmured.

10

So absorbed had Darzek become in his contest with Rhinzl that he completely forgot E-Wusk and the need postings. Worse, he forgot the Dark.

He made his rounds, to Azfel, Meszk, Kaln, Rhinzl, Isc, Ceyh, Halvr, and Brokefa, and the following day all of them met in Gul Rhinzl's office. There was a subtle point of courtesy involved, Gul Rhinzl being the only nocturnal among them. Nocturnals were not numerous on Yorlq, and few of the traders maintained dark rooms in their offices. All well-furnished homes had them, but one could not hold a business meeting in a home. One could *talk* business there, but one could not meet there to talk business.

Rhinzl occupied his usual remote corner, and the others were grouped together in half-light near the open doorway. Darzek regretted that he could not see them well enough to observe their facial expressions and gestures. He confidently expected to shock them, and he would have given much to be able to see their reactions clearly.

There was incredulity enough in Rhinzl's voice when Darzek made his opening statement. "You assert that E-Wusk is—*trading with the Dark?*"

"I do," Darzek said firmly.

Clothing rustled, feet scraped uneasily on the spongy floor, arms, tentacles, heads swayed. All of them were stirring uneasily.

"But how—" Rhinzl's normally smooth voice broke momentarily. "It is not possible!" he protested.

"Not possible!" Gul Isc echoed.

"I asked Gul Rhinzl to have available the anticipation manifests of the past two terms," Darzek said. "The interstellar lists. If you don't mind, Gul Rhinzl—"

The ceiling screen flickered on, and a moment later the anticipation manifests began to flow across it—dim patterns in a dim room, but they were legible.

"There!" Darzek exclaimed. "*Hsof* crystals; E-Wusk, Yorlq." The manifests flowed on. "There. Kiln-dried *fren* leaves, pressure packed; E-Wusk, Yorlq. E-Wusk had twelve such entries, scattered over two terms."

The incredulity quickly changed to bewilderment. "What could E-Wusk's anticipated needs possibly have to do with his trading with the Dark?" Gul Azfel demanded.

"Think!" Darzek said. "*Hsof* crystals, *fren* leaves—there's another, *wkelm* shells, cut and polished. *Every one of those listings concerns a product that is unique to a world the Dark has taken.* Is that not correct?"

"As far as I know," Gul Azfel admitted hesitantly.

"It is correct. You may take my word for it—I spent several days investigating the matter."

A long silence followed. The manifests ran on to the end, but no one was looking at them. Finally Gul Meszk spoke. "You must pardon my obtuseness, Gul Darr, but I should think that the manifests prove exactly the opposite—that E-Wusk is *not* trading with the Dark. If he were, why would he publish anticipated needs in these products and ask for bids? He could obtain all he wanted. Rather than publishing them as needs, he would be asking for bids of purchase."

"Any trader who is familiar with the worlds of the Dark might experience a need for one of their products from time to time," Darzek said condescendingly, "but E-Wusk has never before published an anticipation for even one. Why would he suddenly need twelve? Even as a coincidence it would be extraordinary."

"Extraordinary," Gul Isc echoed. "But I still have difficulty in seeing it as proof that E-Wusk is trading with the Dark."

"I have a suggestion," Darzek said. "Suppose one of us were to go to E-Wusk and say to him, 'I know where a quantity of *hsof* crystals can be obtained. What are you willing to pay?' Would you do that, Gul Isc?"

"*I?* I have no such knowledge."

"I have," Darzek said. "Perhaps as much as half a shipload. Would it not be interesting to know how badly E-Wusk wishes to obtain these products for which he has posted needs?"

"Why don't you ask him?" Gul Isc demanded. Darzek smiled and turned to the others.

"I'll ask him," Gul Azfel said. He slithered from the room, and the click of the transmitter sounded a moment later. He returned almost immediately, seated himself, and announced, "E-Wusk has no interest in bids of less than shipload quantity."

"Surely if E-Wusk had a genuine need, half a shipload would interest him," Darzek said. "Are you convinced?"

"Gul Darr," Rhinzl said, "it is difficult to concede that you have proved your point when we are not certain what your point is. Would you mind explaining?"

"*Someone* is trading with the Dark," Darzek said. "Can you refute that?"

"Can you prove it?" Gul Meszk asked politely.

"Only by logic. The worlds of the Dark have needs. The Dark, whatever else it offers to them, cannot supply them with products that are available only on worlds the Dark has not touched. They must trade for those products, or starve, and they can trade only if someone trades with them. So I say that someone must be trading with them. Can you refute it?"

Again they stirred uneasily, but none of them said anything.

"Supposing that a trader such as E-Wusk made contact with the Dark and arranged to trade. The most urgent needs of those worlds would be made known to him, and he would be asked what he wanted in return. He would compile a list of the products he thought he could handle most profitably. They would be products unique to the worlds of the Dark—why suffer the difficulty and risk of such trade to obtain things that are more easily available elsewhere? They would be products with an established market and a high value per volume unit, since the trade must be conducted on a small scale and he would want to realize a maximum profit per shipment. All of the products E-Wusk lists satisfy these requirements. Finally, to gain the highest immediate profit he must select products of which all available stocks have been exhausted. He can do this most quickly by publishing his full list as anticipated needs, and asking for bids. If he receives any he will find a pretext for declining them, and he will trade only for those products on which no bids are received. And therefore I conclude that E-Wusk is trading with the Dark, or is about to do so."

He looked from one to the other, damning the dim light. All seemed to be laboriously unraveling his arguments and attempting to weave the threads into patterns more to their liking.

"What has this to do with us?" Gul Ceyh asked suddenly. "E-Wusk's trade is no concern of ours."

"My humble apologies. I thought you were a trader."

Silence.

"Why should E-Wusk have all of the Dark's trade for himself?" Darzek demanded.

Silence.

"All of you have some experience of the Dark. How would one go about trading with it?"

Silence.

"You know native merchants on those worlds. You know their needs. My idea is that we form a partnership and seek a just share of this trade. What would be the best way to proceed?"

"There is no way," Gul Brokefa said flatly.

That was as much as he could get from any of them. There was no way. The thing was impossible. There must be some other explanation for E-Wusk's listings.

The meeting broke up, and Darzek ceremoniously took his leave of them. He had gotten as much as he dared to hope for: no information or action, but at least he had them discussing the Dark.

Individually, they would think long about this supposed coup of E-Wusk.

They were traders.

Miss Schlupe had left a note for him at the Trans-Star office. "E-Wusk wants to see you." Darzek did not want to see E-Wusk, but he went immediately to E-Wusk's office and was greeted with the familiar roar of laughter.

"That fool Azfel was here," E-Wusk said. "Told me he thought he could furnish half a shipload of *hsof* crystals. I said I wasn't interested in such piddling quantities. Oh, ho ho!"

"I wouldn't attach much significance to half a shipload of *hsof* crystals," Darzek said.

"Of course not. I wouldn't suspect Azfel anyway. He's never impressed me as being an adventurous type."

"No, but he's a good trader. He might become adventurous, if there was enough profit in it."

"Mmm—he might, at that." E-Wusk chuckled softly. "Any of them might. I might myself."

"By the way—I've just come from a meeting at Gul Rhinzl's."

E-Wusk leaned forward attentively.

"Some of the traders are indecently curious about those anticipated needs of yours. They're wondering what you're up to."

"Oh, ho ho! They're wondering how to get their fat digits onto some of the profits. I know them."

"You certainly do. It was they who sent Gul Azfel to you."

"They did? Oh, ho ho!" He squared his huge figure around and faced Darzek. "If anyone *is* trading with the Dark, he's not disposed to trade with me. Except for Azfel's crystals, I haven't received a single bid."

"He might be trading only for markets he has already developed," Darzek said thoughtfully.

"I think that's likely."

"Perhaps we need a different approach. I'll try to think of something."

He gave E-Wusk a brief and wholly fictitious account of the

traders' meeting, left him laughing uproariously, and stepped through to his apartment. There he froze in consternation with one foot on the alarm rug, oblivious to the rasping buzzer.

Miss Schlupe's rocking chair lay on the floor in the center of the reception room, smashed flat. Darzek stared at it in horror.

"Schluppy!" he called.

He dashed from room to room. The apartment was empty.

He returned to the chair and examined it carefully. It had been much too flimsy for Miss Schlupe's usual violent rocking—the wood was soft and porous and Darzek's workmanship erratic—but she had been able to rock gently, and she loved it. Something heavy had knocked the chair over and crashed down upon it. Other than that blunt evidence of violence, the mute pile of splintered sticks offered no clue.

Darzek needed none. While he had been contriving elaborate stratagems to uncover the Dark, the Dark had found him.

His first thought was to look for her at the Trans-Star offices and at Kxon's headquarters. He took a step toward the transmitter, and then turned away helplessly. If she had smashed the chair herself she would have given the remains a decent burial, not left them strewn about the reception room. Her departure had not been voluntary.

His investigators could follow her trail no further than the transmitter. The planet's proctors, if he informed them that his associate had disappeared leaving her chair wrecked, would suggest that he wait for her return and ask her what had happened. The traders, if he asked for their help, would be simply bewildered. Abduction was unheard of—inconceivable, even—on the peaceful world of Yorlq. People did not vanish on Yorlq.

Miss Schlupe had vanished.

Someone had devised a way to get through a personalized transmitter. He would have to look into that later. For the moment—

"Think, man!" he told himself sternly. "There's no sign of blood, so they didn't gun her down on sight. She had a chance to struggle and she did, hence the smashed chair. They wanted her alive. They wanted—"

He regarded the transmitter warily. "They wanted both of us, and they found Schluppy as much as they could handle. Otherwise, some of them would have been waiting for me. Which means that they'll be back for me later, as soon as they patch themselves up and get their broken bones set."

He went to his bedroom and stretched out there, face close to the wall. A gun slot looked out onto the transmitter. He drew his automatic and waited.

They came. Darzek blinked as the first bounded out of the transmitter, hurtling over the alarm rug. It was the same tall, stalklike type of nocturnal he'd encountered on Primores, and which he now knew (he'd taken the trouble to investigate) came from the lost world of Quarm.

He hadn't known there were Quarmers on Yorlq.

A second bounded into the room, and then a third and a fourth, each taking a soaring leap to avoid the alarm rug. "I hope it scared the acorns off them the first time they came," Darzek muttered. "Five, six—have they called out their army?"

He counted and recounted incredulously. There were ten of them, several wearing bandages. Not even Miss Schlupe could have put up a struggle against so many. More likely she had given the original abductors such a bad time that they brought in reinforcements to deal with Darzek.

"If I can frighten them enough," Darzek mused, "scare the twigs off them so they'll want to get back to where they came from but fast, and then as soon as one of them touches out the destination on the transmitter—"

He edged away and opened a secret wall panel where part of his arsenal was cached. Thoughtfully he studied it; thoughtfully he selected a tear gas grenade. He opened the bedroom door silently. They were huddled together in the reception room, talking inaudibly. He eased himself to the floor and slid the grenade toward their feet.

He darted back to the gun slot. "Lie down on the floor!" he ordered in a booming voice.

Echoing from the bedroom, the command must have sounded like a message from a remote dimension. The Quarmers whirled in one movement and looked about wildly. Then the grenade went off with a pop and a hiss, and instantly they were a choking, panicky mob.

One leaped to the transmitter, touched out a destination, and turned to escape. Darzek coolly placed a shot in his abdomen, and he collapsed.

"Stay away from the transmitter!" Darzek roared, and fired again. The second Quarmer fell on the alarm rug, and the buzzer added its clamor to the confusion. The others backed away slowly, their bodies shaken with convulsive coughing. One by one they folded into heaps of segments, shuddered violently, and subsided.

Darzek approached them cautiously. The ventilation system cleared out the gas almost at once, but enough traces remained to make his eyes smart uncomfortably. He bent over the nearest Quarmer. Dead. All of them were dead.

He paused only to reload his automatic and memorize the transmitter setting. Then he stepped over the bodies by the transmitter and leaped through.

A single Quarmer faced him. He was immobilized on a chair, limbs swathed in bandages, and he regarded Darzek with helpless horror. "I don't want *you* to die of fright," Darzek muttered. He skirted him widely, assured himself that the Quarmer was incapable of movement, and moved on into the next room.

There he found a figure wrapped mummylike from shoulders to feet. Miss Schlupe. She smiled at him.

"Just like a Class D movie," she said brightly, "except that the heroine should be young and beautiful, and the hero probably wouldn't be shedding tears of joy."

"I'm not shedding tears," Darzek growled, stripping away her bindings. "I mean, I am shedding tears, but it's from tear gas."

"Now you've hurt my feelings. Did you find one of those overgrown weeds dead on the floor? He grabbed me from behind, and I flipped him, and he smashed my rocking chair. I hope it killed him."

"Maybe he's the one in the next room. He looked as if he'd fallen on something—or vice versa. Can you walk?"

"They cut off the circulation in my legs, drat them!"

She stretched and manipulated her legs, and when she could stand he helped her into the next room. The Quarmer had fainted, but was still breathing.

Darzek examined him anxiously. "They seem to die upon very slight provocation. Remember the one you frightened to death on Primores? I just frightened ten of them to death. Either that, or they're allergic to tear gas."

"*Ten?* The apartment must look like a brush pile."

"A very apt description. I'm sorry they died. I really am. I was looking forward to a long talk with them. Let's handle this one carefully."

"Maybe the tear gas is also a weed killer."

"Maybe it is, at that." He handed his automatic to her. "Now you're starting to cry. My clothing is contaminated, so I'd better stay away from him. Hold the fort, and I'll be back in about twenty seconds with help."

Kxon and another of Darzek's investigators carried the Quarmer through the transmitter to their secret headquarters, handling him like the priceless, fragile item that he was. Darzek rounded up his entire staff and sent investigators scurrying in all directions —four to search the Quarmers' apartment and ambush anyone arriving there, one to find a trustworthy individual who spoke Quarmer, three to inquire into the presence of Quarmers on Yorlq, six to his own apartment, to clean up the place and figure out a way to dispose of ten bodies, three to inquire into the matter of uninvited strangers passing through a personalized transmitter.

"The first thing you and I are going to do is move out of that apartment," Darzek told Miss Schlupe grimly. "We're taking a dwelling large enough to house a garrison for around the clock duty. The next time anyone drops in on me unannounced, I want to know about it. What is it?"

"The Quarmer is dead, Sire," Kxon said.

Darzek shrugged resignedly. "All right. That makes eleven to dispose of. See that it's done, and then find out if there are any dwellings available on the *Hesr*."

He seated himself wearily. Miss Schlupe remained standing, tapping her foot with a thoughtful frown on her face. "This is a funny kind of funny business," she announced.

Darzek nodded. "The approach is entirely different from what we encountered on Primores. No Eyes of Death. They wanted us alive. It'd be interesting to know why. Tell me what happened."

"I don't know what happened. I walked through the transmitter, and one of them jumped me from behind. I flipped him, but there were at least five more. They wrapped me up and carted me away."

"You impressed them," Darzek said with a grin. "That's why they sent ten after me."

"I snapped a few branches and peeled off some bark, but those dratted things are *strong*. And *heavy*."

"Still, they wanted us alive. I've been wondering if maybe they aren't certain, and they didn't want to stir up a fuss over our disappearance until they'd found out."

"Found out what?"

"That we're us. We couldn't have covered our tracks on Primores any better if we'd done it deliberately. SIX was running things in that neighborhood, and he died before he could get off a report. The Dark probably knew that an agent of Supreme was coming there. Suddenly its most important spy ring was wiped out, and it was getting nothing from Primores but a loud silence. The Dark would naturally credit this to Supreme's agent, and it's been nursing its ulcers all this time while wondering what the agent will do next, and where, and what manner of creature he might be. So we were wanted alive. The Dark wants to know if we're it."

"Why the sudden interest in us? Have we done something?"

"I have. It can't be a coincidence that this happened right after I made noises about trading with the Dark."

"You shouldn't have done that."

"I should have done it a long time ago. Only the nine traders know about this idea of mine. I suspected that one of them might be an agent of the Dark, and now I'm sure of it. All I have to do is figure out which one it is."

"What if it's all nine?" Miss Schlupe asked.

11

The fabulous and mysterious Gul Darr was hosting his first symposium. "Gul Darr can't let his public down," Darzek proclaimed oracularly. "They'll expect something different from him, and they'll get it."

The rooms were bedecked with custom-made ornaments. Nets of colorful imitation crepe paper hung from the ceilings, balloons floated with the air currents, molded figurines of Gul Darr himself dangled from strings and performed graceful genuflections when the feet were squeezed, cleverly arranged lights bathed the rooms in soft, ever-changing colors. Three of Darzek's investigators stood in plain view near the transmitter to guard against gate-crashers and incidentally to ensure that no guest would suffer even a momentary apprehension that he was the first to arrive. Another lurked nearby to shower the arrivals with confetti.

Darzek's undertraders, decked out in pert uniforms, circulated among the guests with trays of refreshments. Their real mission was to listen in on what Darzek hoped would be choice tidbits of conversation. He had wanted to give this assignment to the investigators, but Kxon and his Yorlqers were too hard-of-hearing for effective eavesdropping.

Darzek passed out noisemakers and conducted guided tours of his new dwelling, which was as fine as any on the *Hesr*. There were certain modifications that the guests thought peculiar—an outside door opening onto an outside garden overlooked by windows, for example—and other modifications that would have seemed much more peculiar had the guests known what they were.

Gula Azfel, daughters in tow, inspected the building ecstatically. A dwelling of this size could only mean that Gul Darr was at last contemplating marriage, and she monopolized him for an hour, waiting alertly for an unguarded remark that might be construed as a proposal. He finally made his escape, still safely single, and hurried off to look after his other guests.

They were as delighted as children at their first party. The aquaroom enthralled them because the foot floats gave off dyes that had already converted the surface of the pool into a shimmering swirl of color. The arena, however, where instead of the customary pair of battling *dmo* plants Gud Baxak was operating a bingo game, was all but deserted. Darzek had imported a choice assortment of prizes, but the game's few players were finding it puzzling. The guests preferred to wander about squeezing the feet of the Gul Darr figurines and throwing confetti at each other, or to watch Gul Meszk, who was delighting bystanders by leaping into the air and popping balloons with his horns.

The refreshments had taxed Miss Schlupe's .investigative and culinary ingenuity to the utmost, but she seemed to have provided an acceptable morsel for everyone, from Gul Kaln's pickled insects to the prickly pastries that Gul Isc was fond of munching.

"An overwhelming success," Darzek announced when he finally located her. "Congratulations."

She shrugged. "It was nothing. Any parent who's ever given his child a birthday party has had to cope with the same problem—how to entertain a houseful of monsters."

"There does seem to be something childlike about them," Darzek agreed. "Everything is going nicely, though." He winced as an undertrader floated a tray of food past his nose. "That's the strangest looking salad I've ever seen. I hope you didn't put one of the guests into it."

"Tsk. Have you made the rounds lately?"

"No. I've been looking for you."

"The guests seem to be disappearing. Haven't you noticed how quiet it's become? I haven't heard anyone blowing a horn for at least twenty minutes. They wouldn't go home without the formal leave-taking, would they?"

"I don't think so. I'll have a look."

The guests had thinned out alarmingly. Darzek went quickly from room to room, finally glanced into the aquaroom and saw to his amazement that even the water dancers were gone.

On the far side of the aquaroom a crowd had formed around the entrance to the arena. Somewhere inside Gud Baxak could be heard chirping numbers in a high-pitched tremolo. Darzek pushed his way through the crowd. At the first table inside the door Gul Ceyh, who had eleven arms, each equipped with an eye, was playing twenty-two bingo cards with ease, and others were doing almost as well. Every place was taken at the tables; players filled the open spaces on the floor and ramps. Spectators had crowded in among them, watching avidly and waiting for an opening to play.

Darzek managed a half-circuit of the room, wedging his way through the spectators and gingerly stepping over the players on the floor. A few glanced up as he passed, but all were concentrating too fiercely to be bothered with paying respects to their host. Outside the opposite entrance he found a group of his undertraders watching idly. They were finding few customers for their trays of food and fewer conversations to eavesdrop on. Even such versatile animates as Darzek's guests had no free hands for eating and neither the time nor the mental agility for serious talk when playing a sheaf of bingo cards.

Darzek resignedly sent word to Miss Schlupe that bingo had caught on with a vengeance and more cards were needed.

The exodus to the arena had left old E-Wusk without his usual following of young undertraders. He did not seem to mind. He sat huddled in a corner of the aquaroom, gazing morosely at the patterned water.

Darzek stopped to talk with him. "Aren't you feeling well?" he asked. "I haven't heard you laugh all evening."

E-Wusk's body heaved with an enormous sigh. "I see little

cause for laughter, Gul Darr. I can only think that this excellent society is soon to pass forever."

"If this is true I share your sorrow."

"It is true," E-Wusk said, and sighed again. "Had I known you contemplated acquiring a dwelling, I should have given you mine. I shall leave Yorlq before the end of the term."

"I'm sorry to hear that," Darzek said, and meant it. "But why this sudden decision? Have you given up defying the Dark?"

"I have seen it come four times. I have been caught by it four times. Suddenly I find that I am not eager for it to happen again."

"Where are you going?"

"There is no place to go," E-Wusk said gloomily. He heaved himself to his feet. "If you care to come to my office, Gul Darr, I should like to show you something."

Darzek hesitated, uncertain of the propriety of the host running out on a symposium. "You will be back before anyone has missed you," E-Wusk assured him. "They are all obsessed with this Gobing."

Darzek summoned an undertrader, and while E-Wusk methodically absorbed the contents of his tray, showing an amazing catholicity of taste, Darzek whispered a message for Miss Schlupe.

"Splendid idea," E-Wusk enthused, drawing the broad ribbon of an arm across his mouth. "I'm truly sorry that I must leave. Social life on Yorlq should be much more interesting with you giving symposiums. But there is so little time left—"

"How much time?" Darzek asked, as they moved toward the transmitter.

"So little that I do not dare remain to the end of the term. Only the Dark knows precisely how much."

They stepped through to E-Wusk's office. Darzek seated himself, and E-Wusk bent over his desk and activated the ceiling screen. "This is what the Dark has taken," he announced.

Darzek nodded. He could have drawn that sinister black corridor from memory.

"And this is what it will take."

The blackness leaped forward. It thickened hardly at all, but sent its awesome emptiness far into the galaxy. Darzek said incredulously, "So much?"

"I, E-Wusk, predict it. I guarantee it."

"How do you know?"

"I have my factors," E-Wusk said simply. "I have told them what to look for, and they have told me when they found it."

"I, too, have factors," Darzek protested. "They have told me nothing."

"They do not comprehend what they see. Your factors are like everyone else, saying, 'The winds blow as always, the factories produce, the people eat, the traders trade. All is well.' But all is not well. The Dark is already here. One only need know where to look to see the marks of its presence, just as one sees the passing of the wind in the eddies it creates."

"The Dark is already here," Darzek mused. "*Here*—on Yorlq?"

"True."

"And yet I have seen no mark of its presence, not so much as a single eddy."

"I, E-Wusk, say it is here. I have seen the marks."

"I heard that you foretold when the Dark came to Quarm."

"Then hear well when I make this new foretelling."

"The Dark seems to take in area in a regularly accelerating progression," Darzek said. "In your predicted move the width hardly changes, which is why it moves so far. Did you work it out mathematically?"

"Not I. I merely recorded the reports that I received. Of course I do not have information from all of these worlds—that would be impossible—but I have enough, and I made a special effort to predict the new boundaries. And with those new boundaries the Dark will be poised—you did not say it, but I know you thought it—the Dark will be poised only one move from Primores, and from Supreme itself. Do you not see what that means? *Supreme!* When the Dark takes Supreme it will capture all the secrets of the galaxy and destroy every vestige of galactic organization. The galaxy as we know it cannot exist without Supreme and its Council. The galaxy is doomed!"

Darzek wrested his gaze away from the ceiling, started to speak, and thought better of it. "Where will you go?" he asked finally.

"I do not know. I hope to find myself a peaceful world on the remote perimeter, a world where there is little that the Dark could want. Perhaps I will be able to pass the remainder of my life there unmolested. And you—what will you do?"

"I'll fight," Darzek said with a smile.

"It would be well to prepare for every eventuality. I hear that the *efa* have purchased a ship. This is something you should consider. While I was waiting on Quarm for those clods to release me, I spent much time in wishing that I'd had a ship in point connection when they came for me."

"Thank you for the suggestion. By the way—are there any Quarmers here on Yorlq?"

"I don't know of any. Please convey my apologies to Gula Schlu. Delightful as it was, I'd rather not return to your symposium."

"I hope to see you again before you leave."

"Come any time," E-Wusk said. "But come soon!"

The symposium had degenerated into a crowd of fiercely concentrating bingo players. Darzek turned his back on them and went looking for Miss Schlupe, whom he found in the dark room talking with Rhinzl.

"What was on E-Wusk's mind?" she asked.

"The Dark," Darzek said bluntly. "He thinks the Dark is coming soon. He's making plans to leave Yorlq before it gets here."

"That would seem to refute your previous conclusions about E-Wusk," Rhinzl said politely.

"What conclusions?"

"That he has been trading with the Dark. If that were so, why would he want to run away from it?"

"A trader might do business with the Dark, and still not want to live with it," Darzek said dryly. "There is also the question of why he is so certain that the Dark is coming. Have *you* seen any portents that point to its imminent arrival?"

"No," Rhinzl said after a brief silence. "What sort of portents would one look for?"

"E-Wusk knows, or thinks he does."

"E-Wusk is an astute trader, and a student of the customs of many worlds. I would not disparage his conclusions. And yet—I have seen no portents."

"You have experienced the Dark," Darzek said, peering narrowly at Rhinzl's dim hulk. "Its coming here should be no surprise to you."

"No. But I was not expecting it soon. It rested much longer between its last moves. I must discuss this with E-Wusk."

"You'd better see him tomorrow, then. I have the impression that day after tomorrow may be too late. Have you ever heard of a world called Quarm?"

"That was my last headquarters. Why do you ask?"

"I have acquired something that is purported to be Quarmer art. I wondered if there were any Quarmers here on Yorlq who could authenticate it."

"I don't recall having seen any."

Darzek excused himself and moved off to play host. All of the bingo prizes had been distributed; many of the guests found the game fascinating enough to play without prizes, but the others drifted away to other diversions. The water dancing had started up again, and Darzek sat down to watch it. A short time later Kxon came to deliver a negative report. The undertraders had overheard nothing of interest.

When Miss Schlupe joined him she added her own succinct appraisal of the evening. "It's a total flop."

"Not quite," Darzek said. "E-Wusk told me something that I find extremely interesting. Fascinating, in fact. But the party is a flop. We can't work spies into their offices, and when we corner them away from their offices they keep their mouths shut. It's downright discouraging."

"If only that Quarmer hadn't caught the blight," Miss Schlupe said sadly. "We should have sprayed him."

"There's Gul Halvr. Excuse me—I want to see what he thinks of E-Wusk's prognosticating."

Gul Halvr thought very little of it and said so. He also knew nothing about Quarmers on Yorlq. Darzek moved on to talk to Gul Kaln, who dismissed E-Wusk's prediction with a shrug.

"Sitting around worrying about the Dark won't keep it away. If it's going to come here it will come. I think all of us have learned, by now, to record our solvency in safe places and keep our inventories low."

Solvency . . . inventories . . . trade. Darzek listened politely to Gul Kaln's latest exploit with *rucb* hemp, expressed his regrets that he could not relieve him of an unfortunate surplus in *dlk* sugar, and escaped on the pretext of looking after his other guests. They were enjoying themselves, which meant that they would stay late.

Quietly he slipped away to his garden. Yorlq's three small moons hung one above the other like saucers in a juggling act. The night was strangely silent—insectlike life on Yorlq was either mute or vocalized beyond the range of human hearing—and laced with pungent odors from plants Miss Schlupe had obtained from Rhinzl on the remote chance that some of them might have Earth-like characteristics.

The garden was restful, and the dwellings that loomed nearby had no windows from which curious or malicious stares could be directed; but Darzek quickly found that he could think no more easily there than he could surrounded by the hubbub of his symposium. Not that thought would be of any use to him; every turning he had taken had been wrong, every opening he had discovered led only into a blind alley. He knew little more about the Dark than he had learned in the one thorough briefing from EIGHT.

"But it seems that the Dark itself is about to advance my education," he told himself. "All I have to do is wait."

The door ripped open. Kxon cried shrilly, "Is that you, Gul Darr? Come quickly!"

Darzek sprinted. In the reception room he came upon several guests, Gul Ceyh among them, writhing on the floor and vomiting.

"Get a doctor!" he snapped.

"Gud Baxak has gone for them," Kxon said.

"*Them?*" Darzek whirled and ran toward the aquaroom, fearing the worst.

He found it. His guests had been felled as if by sorcery, and they lay twisting in agony, retching, moaning. Miss Schlupe fluttered about helplessly, wringing her hands, and when Darzek spoke to her she answered with inarticulate babble.

Then Gud Baxak's corps of doctors marched in, and the crisis passed as mysteriously as it had arrived. As each guest voided whatever had offended his stomach he got unsteadily to his feet, wounded in dignity, shaken, sometimes disgustingly soiled, but— to Darzek's amazement—apologetic rather than angry, as though the fault were entirely his own.

The symposium ended abruptly. As soon as a guest could shakily negotiate the distance to the transmitter he went home. The doctors made puzzled rounds, shrugged, and departed, apparently convinced that the sick were in nature's competent hands. Darzek started up a robot cleaner and sent Kxon to bring others from the Trans-Star office and the investigation headquarters. Obviously there was more cleaning to be done than one could handle in a night.

Miss Schlupe, calm at last, faced Darzek like a small child expecting a whipping.

"What happened to the food?" he demanded.

"It wasn't the food," she confessed timorously.

"Then what was it?"

"Well, none of them would talk, so I thought I'd try something to loosen them up a bit. So I had each of them served—"

"Served what?"

"A shot of my rhubarb beer."

"You couldn't!" Darzek protested. "We drank the last of it when we left Smith!"

"I just made some more."

"Where'd you get the rhubarb?"

"From Rhinzl."

"You couldn't!"

"Well, it *looked* like rhubarb. And it tasted like rhubarb—a little. And the beer is *good*."

"Is there any left? Let me try the stuff."

She produced a flask. Darzek tasted, spat hurriedly. "Schluppy! That stuff is at least fifty proof!"

"I thought it had a rather nice kick to it."

"It loosened them up, all right. We'll be airing out the house for a week, and we may never live it down."

"I'm sorry. All I wanted to do was make them talk."

"They will. They'll talk about it for periods, but I'll be surprised if they ever speak to us again."

"I thought they were very nice about it. They all apologized. They didn't seem in the least offended. Gula Azfel even thanked me for a pleasant evening."

"She's probably delighted. This fiasco is proof positive that I need a wife to look after my entertaining. Well, it served one good purpose. It got them out of here. I was afraid they'd stay all night."

The last guest had teetered homeward; the cleaners were humming busily. Darzek started for his room, and was flagged down by Gud Baxak. "Gul Rhinzl wishes to speak with you, Sire."

"Rhinzl? Still here?"

"In the dark room."

"Great Scott! The doctors wouldn't think to look there. He may be dying!"

But Rhinzl was still seated in his dim corner, apparently in good health. "Are you all right?" Darzek demanded.

"Quite all right."

"You see, everyone else got sick, and I was afraid—"

Rhinzl laughed softly. "It was rude of me, of course, but I didn't drink. I only pretended. I offer my apologies."

"Please don't. I'm immensely relieved that you didn't drink the stuff."

"I waited because I wanted to ask your advice. My dwelling is of ample size. You are familiar with my business reputation. I have lived alone for many periods, and it makes it difficult for me to maintain my social position. I wondered if you would have any objection to my marrying."

"Why should I object?" Darzek exclaimed in amazement.

"I thought it best to obtain your approval. You see, it is Gula Schlu that I wish to marry."

"Gula Schlu!"

"She is a charming person. I have long admired her—ever since we first met. She will make an excellent hostess, and she shares my interest in plants and flowers. I am uncertain as to the customs of your kind, so I need your advice. How should I proceed with a proposal of marriage?"

"I am sure that Gula Schlu would feel honored—"

"Thank you. In that case I'll make the necessary legal arrangements immediately."

"But she could not possibly accept," Darzek added quickly. "As my kind ages, she is beyond the age for marriage."

Rhinzl pondered this and pronounced it exceedingly strange. "I have heard of minimum ages for marriage," he mused, "but never a maximum age. Both in appearance and in actions Gula Schlu seems commendably, even invigoratingly, young."

"That will please her very much. I have no right to give you an answer for her. My kind considers marriage a personal matter that one must decide for oneself. I'll gladly tell her of your proposal and send you her answer tomorrow. I feel certain, though, that she will not accept. As I said, she is beyond the age for marriage."

"This would not matter to me if she did not find it an obstacle. But I'm sure that you understand your kind better than I."

Darzek dimmed the reception room and bowed Rhinzl to the transmitter, murmuring regrets and condolences.

"My first proposal of marriage," Miss Schlupe said tearfully, a few minutes later. "He's such a nice person, too. You could have at least let me decline it myself!"

12

The vault of stars above the Yorlq transfer station palled beside Darzek's recollection of the awe-inspiring view he had seen at Primores. The Primores stations had looked out upon the glowing majesty of the heaviest concentration of stars in the galaxy, but Darzek dourly wondered if the apparent difference might not also be due to his sense of awe becoming jaded.

He said, "They're loading nothing but *lwip* nuts? You're certain of that?"

"Yes, Sire."

"What are *lwip* nuts?"

"I don't know, Sire," Kxon said apologetically.

Darzek abandoned the stars to regard Kxon with amazement. "A native product, and you don't know what it is?"

Kxon blushed white to the remote ridge of his ears and sputtered confusedly.

"Never mind. Send someone to ask Gud Baxak. Let's concentrate on finding a way to get aboard."

A short time later Gud Baxak delivered his reply personally. He was mystified and anxious to forestall a business *gaffe*. "There is no market for *lwip* nuts," he said.

"Of course there's a market," Darzek told him. "Someone has sold a shipload. The trader who bought them is no fool and wouldn't be shipping a load of nuts as ballast. That wasn't my question. What *are* the damned things?"

"There has never been any trade in them," Gud Baxak protested. "There was a market, a very good market, but the *efa* had

a monopoly of it. Then the Dark took it. The nuts continue to
grow, so there are probably mountainous surpluses and no bids."

"Where was the market for *lwip* nuts?"

"A world called Quarm."

Darzek nodded sagely. Quarm seemed to be running through
his personal saga like a thread—a dark thread.

"Listen carefully," he told Gud Baxak. "I want you to go back
to Yorlq and make some motions toward buying *lwip* nuts. Mind
you, I don't want to buy any. I don't even want a free sample. I
just want to know if *lwip* nuts can be bought."

Gud Baxak said slowly, "But if you don't want to buy any—"

"Never mind. You've told me what I wanted to know."

He dismissed him and signaled to Kxon.

Enormous tubes fanned out from the base of the transfer station, and arriving ships were netted and carefully guided into
berths that lay at right angles beneath them. Darzek and Kxon
rode a conveyor down a tube to the *efa* ship and stood looking
down into its cavernous interior. Even though an unbroken pro-
cession of passenger and freight compartments traveled this same
route to be packed into the ships, there were far more workers
about than Darzek had expected. He concluded that the handling
of the huge compartments under zero gravity required finesse and
judgment that machines could not be trusted to exercise without
constant supervision.

No one challenged their presence there. The workers seemed
never to have heard of stowaways. Kxon boldly took a step
forward and floated down into the ship, and Darzek followed
him.

"What's that?" Darzek asked, pointing.

"They've installed a special transmitter," Kxon said. "A transmitter with a viewing screen."

"What do they use it for?"

"I don't know."

Kxon rippled open a door and dropped to the deck in midstride
as he moved into the light gravity of the ship's service and control

section. It was primarily a cargo ship, and the lounge was tiny. Darzek quickly investigated a row of storage compartments, rippling open doors, closing them.

"What's this stuff?" he asked.

"Vacuum suits. For emergencies."

Darzek backed into the compartment. "This is for me. It won't be too uncomfortable, and they shouldn't be looking in here before they get under way. If there is an emergency I'll have first crack at a suit. Run along, before someone sees you and gets suspicious."

"You'll have a long wait," Kxon said. "The ship is only half-loaded."

"A long wait will be good for me. I have several things to think about."

"You won't let me come?"

"I need you here on Yorlq. You know what to do. Off with you, now."

He rippled the door shut and sank back upon the billowing softness.

The *efa* were trading with the Dark. There wasn't a *lwip* nut to be had on Yorlq, which meant that the *efa* still exercised its monopoly and thought it could make a greater profit by handling the entire crop itself. Probably it had a number of ships trading with Dark worlds. It had gotten overconfident and handled the purchase of this one so clumsily that E-Wusk had detected it.

"The *efa* may be agents of the Dark," Darzek mused, "or they may be astute traders who know an opportunity when they see one. In either case I'll be getting my first look at a Dark world. It's up to me to see that it isn't the last."

He had given Kxon a verbal message for Miss Schlupe, a written message to be handed to her if he was gone more than three days, and another written message to be held against the possibility that he might not return at all.

He had only one real worry about her. He hoped she wouldn't do something foolish, such as elope.

He dozed off, found the lounge still deserted when he awoke, and went back to sleep. He was awakened by a muffled babble of talk. The low, rumbling tones were familiar; at least two of the *efa* were present, but he had never been able to distinguish their voices. Carefully holding the door to keep it from collapsing, he opened it a crack and peeked out.

An argument was in progress. Brokefa, the most remote from Darzek, was sullenly silent. Three of his *maf*-cousins were discussing something with much heated waving of tendrils. An animate of a type Darzek did not recognize, probably the ship's captain, stood at the far side of the room and studiously pretended to ignore the argument, if indeed he understood it. The language was a strange one, perhaps a private *maf* dialect. Darzek listened for a time, attempting to pick out the words, and then he disgustedly edged the door shut.

Much later he detected the subtle, almost imperceptible vibration that preceded the ship's first transmission. He released the door for another peek at the lounge. Only Brokefa was there, sitting dejectedly in the same position. Darzek closed the door again. Whatever the *efa* were up to, Brokefa didn't care for it.

Darzek's position, close to the hull of the ship, received vibrations and sounds he had not experienced in a passenger compartment. Time stretched out tediously in the darkness as he tabulated the transmitting leaps, the long waits between them, and finally the interminable, humming approach by rocket.

The rockets cut off. They should have been jockeying into a berth at a transfer station, and Darzek strained his ears for sounds of a net scraping across the ship's hull and tensed himself for its telltale jerk. He heard nothing, felt nothing.

He opened the door a crack and took a deep breath of fresh air. The time had come, he thought, to make his presence known. He allowed the door to collapse soundlessly and stepped out.

The lounge was empty. Beyond a distant, open door were the fantastic complexities of the control room, which was also deserted. Darzek turned the other way and stepped into the cargo section.

A narrow alley led between the stacked cargo compartments to an open space by the newly installed transmitter. The *efa* and all of the crew were gathered around it, watching its screen intently. A curved sliver of light hung there, motionless against a backdrop of deep black. It swooped toward them and gave Darzek a dizzying sensation of rushing headlong on a collision course. Surface details appeared: a range of snowcapped, cragged mountains marching in stately formation off into the night shadow; the green oval of an inland sea; a dark patch of forest.

Quarm.

As it moved closer Darzek realized that their approach was illusory, a process of the screen's magnification. They were in a remote orbit, and the lighted crescent widened as they circled toward daylight.

Quarm. A primitive world. Darzek saw a network of roads, which no fully transmitterized planet would need. The viewer finally centered upon a village, and as the magnification brought it closer Darzek thought nostalgically that he was receiving a distorted glimpse of Earth. The dome-shaped buildings were capped with odd-looking cupolas, and the one principal street coiled out from a central, ovular park, with smaller ovals and their surrounding clusters of buildings threaded onto it like symmetrical ornaments.

The viewer focused on the central oval and brought it closer.

"Put down the transmitter," the captain ordered.

A crew member thrust a frame with a weighted base into the ship's transmitter; the others watched the screen in tense silence.

Suddenly Darzek understood what they were doing: they were attempting a difficult "point" transmission, the transmitting of an object to a precise point without the benefit of a receiver. If their calculations were even slightly off, the frame might materialize a hundred feet in the air and fall to its destruction.

But were there no transmitters operating on Quarm? He watched incredulously.

"It's down," the captain said, as though he could not quite believe it himself. "It's operating."

The *efa* turned in one motion to Brokefa, who gloomily said something in the *maf* language, stepped into the transmitter, vanished.

Darzek pushed past the crew members, excusing himself politely. The other three *efa*, suddenly aware of his presence, regarded him with mingled amazement and blank consternation. Before anyone could move to intercept him Darzek flung himself at the transmitter.

The sudden emergence in full gravity staggered him. His momentum sent him stumbling forward. He slipped to one knee, scrambled to his feet, and hurried after Brokefa. "Wait for me!" he called.

Brokefa turned. "Gul Darr!" he exclaimed. His amazed features assumed an expression remarkably akin to relief. He said simply, "I'm very glad to see you."

They crossed the oval, wading through knee-high, yellowish grass that crackled protestingly with every step. What Darzek could see of the village had the lazy, unhurried aspect of a rural town on a quiet Sunday afternoon. Only the automobiles were lacking. There was no traffic.

There were no people. As they came closer, Darzek revised his first impression and thought of the place as a ghost town. The yellowish grass grew in cracks in the pavement. The gardens around the dwellings were choked with riotous growths of tall, yellowish weeds.

Brokefa panted an explanation as they walked. He was obviously frightened, and he kept glancing about apprehensively. "Naturally the dirty work falls on me," he grumbled. "I once had headquarters on Quarm, so I know the language. I obtained gems from this region, and I had two agents in this village. So I have the job of making contact with them. The others—" He gestured disgustedly. "They remain in the safety of the ship and share in the profits. It's all your fault, really. You and your talk of trading with the Dark."

"Then—this is your first attempt?"

"Of course. We had the monopoly of *lwip* nuts. They won't

grow anywhere except Yorlq, and only the Quarmers have found uses for them. They extract their oil and use the pressed kernels as a confectionary. They even make a flour out of the ground kernels. It's a favorite Quarmer food."

"I didn't know anyone had a favorite food."

"Primitive peoples often have strange tastes. Anyway, the Dark took Quarm, and we were left with our commitment for the entire *lwip* nut production on Yorlq, with no market for it. So when you produced your proof that someone was trading with the Dark, my *maf*-cousins determined that they could do the same, and dispose of our stock. And the dirty work falls on me."

"Then that's why there were no nuts available on Yorlq," Darzek said. "When you decided to trade with the Dark, you took them off the open market. Isn't anyone home?"

They had stepped from the central oval onto the coiling street, but there was still no sign of life. "They're nocturnals," Brokefa explained. "When the sun is highest, they sleep the slumber of midnight."

Hesitantly Brokefa led the way along the cracked pavement to the first cluster of dwellings. He approached one of them and stepped onto a flat stone before the door.

"Something is wrong," he said a moment later. "The call slab doesn't operate."

"What's it supposed to do?"

"It makes a light flash. You can see it through the air vents." He stomped heavily on the slab. Puzzled, he turned to look about him. "Something is wrong. I've never seen the ovals so overgrown. The gardens, too. The Quarmers are fond of night flowers, and they cultivate them with care." He moved toward the nearest garden. "Look—there's nothing left but weeds."

"The place certainly looks deserted," Darzek agreed. He turned back to the dwelling, heaved against the heavy sliding door—another mark of a primitive society—and opened it.

At first he could make out nothing in the dark interior. A damp, fetid odor smote him. Gagging, he took a step backward as a clicking sound approached the door. A Quarmer appeared in the opening and stood staring out at him. He wore no light shield, and the sunlight instantly made his large eyes drip copiously. Suddenly he lunged at Darzek, bleating a word, and Darzek backed away warily.

Brokefa called something in a strange language. The Quarmer ignored him and continued to mouth the same word until the sound became a blurred moan.

"What is he saying?" Darzek asked.

"Food," Brokefa said.

"Is that what the word means? *Food?*"

"Yes."

The Quarmer stretched out multiple, segmented arms in a pathetic, pleading gesture. Others stumbled from the open doorway, cupping strange, handless fingers to protect their dripping eyes. Darzek looked about uneasily. Quarmers were staring down at them from the tinted cupolas of neighboring houses, or excitedly pouring into the street with light shields flapping.

Abruptly Darzek and Brokefa were surrounded by a crowd of bleating natives.

Brokefa said indifferently, "They ask for food. They say they are starving."

"How can they be starving? Doesn't this world produce food?"

"Ample food. Its principal exports were food. It imported only *lwip* nuts."

Quarmers filled the street and began to press closer, bleating their piteous cries and importuning with knobby, clicking arms. Their odd bodies did not look emaciated. The only evidence of malnutrition that Darzek could detect was the jerky unsteadiness of their movements.

"There is no trade here," Brokefa said. "Let's go."

"They need food. They'll certainly trade for your nuts."

"They have nothing to trade. Let's go."

"We can't leave them to starve."

"Why not?" Brokefa demanded bitterly. "They ran us out, burned our warehouses, took our property. Now they bleat for food. Well—let them bleat!"

"Ask them why they have no food."

Brokefa shouted the question, but the Quarmers could only sob brokenly for food. Darzek and Brokefa began to back away slowly. Darzek had his own bitter memories of the strength in those bristling arms, and though he very much wanted to feed these Quarmers, he vastly preferred to do it from the safety of the spaceship.

Surrounded by Quarmers, they moved along the street toward the central oval. No attempt was made to stop them, but the stumbling crowd matched their pace and mouthed its pleas with mounting frenzy. "Food! Food!"

Then the Quarmers saw the transmitter frame. They fell silent for a moment as they pondered the significance of this strange object. "Tell them we'll send them food through the transmitter," Darzek suggested.

He was too late. Brokefa could produce only an inarticulate sputtering as the Quarmers surged toward the transmitter with full-throated howls of rage. They deduced that these aliens were about to step into it and vanish forever, and all hope of food with them, and they sought to prevent that the only way they could. They tore the transmitter apart. The first Quarmer to reach it stumbled through and vanished. Others seized the frame and furiously bent and twisted it until its members parted.

"They may have something similar in mind for us," Darzek observed. He turned the horrified Brokefa around and briskly walked him away.

The Quarmers abandoned the dismembered transmitter to chase after them, but they broke into a run and easily outdistanced their stumbling pursuers. They followed the curving street for a short distance and then veered off through a weed-choked garden. Brokefa, despite his quaking fright, could still mutter angrily as he ran. His indignation was directed mainly against his maf-cousins, Gudefa, Tizefa, and Linhefa by name. He had known what would happen. He had told them what would happen. He'd had his fill of running away from Quarmers, but they, who had never been away from their smug Yorlqer safety—

they had to trade with Quarm, and here he was: running away from Quarmers.

They crossed the spiraling street, circled a cluster of dwellings, crossed the street again. The Quarmers, tottering blindly in the bright afternoon sunlight, were left far behind, but from the dwellings they passed came a new horde, to string after them bleating, "Food! Food!"

"Will your cousins be able to see what is happening?" Darzek asked.

"I think so. Yes."

"I hope they have another transmitter."

"They have several. We didn't expect to put one down safely on the first attempt."

"May they be as successful on the second attempt. Let's open up more distance, so they can try."

They skirted another cluster of dwellings, and saw, around the buildings ahead of them, a group of Quarmers milling about uncertainly. Their pursuers were still huffing and staggering in their wake, and the cries grew louder.

"Is there a shortcut out of town?" Darzek demanded.

Brokefa, who was huffing himself, did not answer.

"We're surrounded," Darzek said bluntly. "If we don't get clear soon, the ship won't have time to connect with us before dark."

"Dark!" Brokefa sobbed. "They're nocturnals! They can see in the dark! We could never get away from them at night."

"Come on."

They turned back toward the dwellings they had just passed, picked their way through an overgrown garden, circled around to the front of a house. The door stood open; the oval was deserted, its inhabitants probably having drifted off to join one of the mobs. Darzek grabbed Brokefa's shoulder and firmly steered him into the house.

"We'll be trapped here," Brokefa sobbed.

"They can't all get through the door at once. I'd rather face a few at a time here than take on the whole village out in the open."

Darzek pushed the door shut and they faced each other in a dim shaft of light from an air vent. A peculiar, sweetish, musky odor filled the room. From somewhere in the darkness came a steady drip, drip of water. Quarmers began to stream past the house with a noisy clicking of segments, still gasping feebly for food. Darzek nudged a chair into position and climbed up to peer through an air vent. Quarmers were converging on the oval from three directions.

"Is there a back door to this place?" he whispered.

"*Back* door? No—"

"Then we're stuck here until they get tired and go home."

"They won't get tired," Brokefa said gloomily. "They're nocturnals."

"Even nocturnals have to get tired sometime, and these are starving."

"You weren't here when the Dark came. Once they're roused, they stay active until the next morning. I *know*."

"We'd better see if there are any in the house."

From the back of the room a curving ramp led up to the level above. Darzek started up; Brokefa, after a moment of hesitation, scrambled after him.

The odor became stronger as they climbed, and long before they reached the top its fetid pungency had sickened them. Darzek clenched his teeth to keep from gagging and peered into the dim light. Abruptly he turned, pushing Brokefa back toward the ramp.

"What is it?" Brokefa whispered.

"Dead Quarmers."

They returned to the lower level. Darzek said soberly, "The Quarmers told the truth. They're starving. The entire planet must be in the same fix. Why would the Dark take a world only to let its people starve?"

"We're marooned here," Brokefa whimpered. "We'll starve, too."

"Nonsense. Your cousins won't go off and leave us."

"Marooned," Brokefa whined. "I'm hungry already."

"Oh, be quiet! I want to think."

He paced back and forth, occasionally going to the air vent for a look at the milling Quarmers. The dripping water irritated him. He went to investigate and found a queer type of water clock. Obviously there was no shortage of water; but even on a primitive planet the utilities, if properly automated, would continue to function long after there were people to use them.

It was the economic system that had collapsed. The socialism that assured life's necessities to everyone had ceased to function as soon as its odd veneer of capitalism had been removed. "The Dark is a more horrible menace than anyone seems to have imagined," Darzek announced thoughtfully. "I thought it was enslaving the populations of the worlds it has taken. Instead, it's exterminating them. How could the Dark or anyone else possibly benefit from killing off every intelligent life form in the galaxy?"

He had no fear for their immediate safety; the house's taint of death probably offered a better defense than any that he could devise. When daylight routed the nocturnals, the ship would put down another transmitter.

But the night, in a house reeking of death, would be a long one.

Most of the Quarmers went home at dawn. Those who did not lay dead in the tall, brittle grass. With the sun high in the sky Darzek and Brokefa walked quickly toward the central oval. A transmitter materialized as they approached, fell twenty feet to the ground, and smashed. Another was waiting when they reached the center of the oval, and they stepped through.

The first person Darzek saw was the Quarmer who had inadvertently stumbled through the transmitter the day before. He sat beside a pile of shells, happily munching on *lwip* nuts.

"There is no trade," Brokefa said bitterly, in answer to the *efa*'s first question. "They have nothing to trade. Let's go home."

"They have nothing to trade," Darzek said quietly, "but they have a tremendous need. They are starving."

"That is no affair of ours," Brokefa snapped. "Let them starve."

"It's an affair of mine. Has the Quarmer given you any trouble?"

"Only at first, when we did not realize he was asking for food," Linhefa said.

"Talk to him," Darzek told Brokefa. "Find out what's been happening on Quarm."

Brokefa put the question, listened to the answer, and said disgustedly, "Nothing has been happening on Quarm."

"Has he seen anything at all of anyone representing the Dark?"

"He says not. He says we're the first strangers—foreigners—he has seen since the foreigners left."

"Ask him if there is hunger in the other villages, and in the cities."

The Quarmer jabbered excitedly, and Brokefa interpreted, "There is hunger everywhere, except that it is worse in the cities. The food ran out sooner in the cities. The villagers smashed their transmitter so people from the cities would not come to take their food."

"Ask him why an agricultural planet ran out of food."

"He does not know. Suddenly the food supplies were gone, and there were no crops to harvest."

"We should congratulate Gul Darr for his brilliant deduction," Gudefa said sarcastically. "The Dark worlds do need trade. Unfortunately, no one will trade with them if they have nothing to offer in payment." He whipped his tendrils in a gesture of disgust. "We'll return the Quarmer to his village and retrieve the transmitter."

"I want to know why they have nothing to trade," Darzek said.

"They have seen nothing," Brokefa said scornfully. "They have done nothing. They know nothing. They have not operated their mines, nor planted their farms. Now they wait for the foreigners to return and feed them. When last I saw them they shouted *Grilf! Grilf!* meaning what they could not tell me themselves.

Now they shout only *Food! Food!* Let us leave them to the fate they have chosen."

"Their emotional orgy must have continued long after the foreigners left," Darzek mused. "But that was—Great Scott!—a couple of periods ago, at least. I've had some personal experience of how emotional Quarmers are, but I hardly expected that. Do you suppose they went right on rioting until their food gave out?"

"It would seem so," Brokefa said. "Then it was too late to produce more, and they starved. Whatever happened, it does not concern us."

"Ask him why the Quarmers ejected the foreigners."

Brokefa interpreted disgustedly. "He doesn't know. He says he doesn't remember."

"If we could find out what got them worked up to such a peak of excitement, we'd be well on our way to understanding the Dark." He moved on into the lounge and slumped wearily onto a chair. The suspenseful night had taken its toll; he felt utterly exhausted. "We can't return to Yorlq with a shipload of food when all of Quarm is starving," he said.

"How can we trade with them when they have nothing to trade?" Tizefa demanded.

"How can you think about trade when they're starving? Give them the food!"

"One shipload of nuts won't feed a planet. It won't even feed a city."

"It'll keep some people alive until we can get back here with more food."

"We?" The *efa* gazed at him dumbfounded.

"Look," Darzek said. "I'll buy your ship. I'll buy your load of nuts."

"What do you offer?" Linhefa asked politely.

"For your ship, what you paid for it plus the cost of this voyage. For the nuts, whatever the price used to be on Yorlq."

The *efa* exchanged glances. "Agreed," Linhefa said.

Darzek turned to the captain. "You're working for me now.

Start breaking out the cargo. We'll return this Quarmer to his village with a ration of nuts, and then we'll put nuts down at every populated place as long as the supply lasts."

"You mean as long as the transmitters last," the captain said. "We have only four left, including the one that is down now."

"Then put them down carefully. A lot of lives depend on it."

The *efa*, though they made no effort to conceal their puzzlement, obediently opened shipping compartments and began counting bags of nuts. Brokefa rationed them out, drawing upon his amazingly detailed recollections of towns and cities and their pre-Dark populations. Darzek didn't want the nuts dumped into the overgrown ovals where they might not be found, so the captain meticulously placed the transmitter in the street near the center of each town.

It required only seconds to unload a ration of nuts, but putting down the transmitter and retrieving it took tedious calculations and tense, nerve-wracking minutes. They followed the line of day around the planet, and when finally they finished, tossing out all of the ship's emergency rations at the last stop, the captain had made several hundred of the difficult point transmissions and lost only one more transmitter. He gleefully called himself the galaxy's foremost expert.

"I'll pay you a bonus," Darzek promised him. "Now take us home."

But captain and crew were too exhausted even to perform the routine functions of the return to Yorlq. All of them sprawled about the small lounge and went to sleep. Darzek dozed off thinking wryly that few men had ever begun a journey as a stowaway and ended it owning the ship. Equally amazing was the fact that none of the *efa* had asked him what he was doing there. Perhaps each of them assumed that one of the others had invited him.

When he awoke the ship was safely under way, so he went back to sleep. He awoke a second time to find the lounge deserted. *Efa*, captain, and crew were all crowded into the small control room.

"What's the matter?" Darzek called.

"We can't catch a beam from the Yorlq transfer station," the captain said.

Darzek blinked sleepily and covered a yawn. "Something wrong with our equipment?"

"No," the captain said emphatically.

"Something's wrong with their equipment, then. What about the other stations?"

"There aren't any beams, and none of them answer our signal."

"There's nothing to do but keep trying," Darzek said cheerfully.

"And you had to give away all of our rations," Brokefa complained.

"I'll buy you any food you want at the transfer station," Darzek promised. He said quietly to the captain, "Can you go in without a beam?"

"No. It would be too risky, both for the ship and the station. Difficult, too. Anyway, it's forbidden, and—just a moment."

"Got something?"

"Yes."

The captain jerked out the message strip and glanced at it wonderingly. "It says—'Go away, Grilf!' "

Grilf. They stared at each other.

During their brief absence the Dark had taken Yorlq.

13

They avoided the orbital plane of the transfer stations and slipped unnoticed into an orbit around Yorlq. Yorlez and the *Hesr* lay under the night shadow, where the captain, for all of his recently acquired experience, found point transmitting to be an entirely different matter. While they watched the screen tensely he smashed two of their three remaining transmitters, and then scored a perfect bull's-eye on Darzek's garden.

Darzek leaped through into the feeble light of Yorlq's diminutive moons. Without breaking stride he dashed to the house and pounded on the outside door. The *efa* positioned themselves to guard the transmitter and waited anxiously.

Darzek pounded again, bellowing "Schluppy!" and finally poised himself to kick in the door.

It opened soundlessly. Miss Schlupe faced him, belligerently brandishing a revolver. "You scared me to death," she announced resentfully.

"Is everything all right?"

"Nothing is all right."

"Don't tell me you're here alone."

"Are you kidding? I have the whole Trans-Star staff, and all of their families. Their hungry families, I might add. The service transmitters haven't worked since yesterday, and there's no food in the house. I don't suppose you happen to have a ham sandwich in your pocket."

Darzek signaled to the *efa*, who carefully carried the transmitter frame into the house. "Where's Kxon?" he asked.

"I haven't seen him since he brought your message."

"Message? Didn't he bring two?"

She shook her head.

"That's odd. He was to hand you a note if I wasn't back in three days. Are the regular transmitters still working?"

"They were a moment ago. I just came back from Rhinzl's."

The *efa* were stirring impatiently. "You want to know how things are at home," Darzek told them. "Go ahead. But I want you back here at once with the rest of the traders. All of them. Tell them their presence is urgently required at a meeting, and if they won't come bring them anyway."

"Meeting?" Brokefa exclaimed. "What is there to meet about? We need only to obtain the necessary supplies, and leave."

"Suit yourself. But this particular ship belongs to me, and it isn't going anywhere until I'm ready. And," he added darkly, "it isn't accepting any passengers who refuse to come to my meetings." He waved them away and turned to greet Gud Baxak, who hurried in slobbering joyfully.

"This transmitter connects with a spaceship," Darzek told him, patting the portable frame. "Put some of the undertraders here, and tell them to guard it with their lives. The ship is short of supplies. It has no food at all, and not enough water and air for the number of passengers it may have to carry. We'll make better arrangements later, but for the present everything will have to be brought here and passed through this transmitter. Do you know what to do?"

"Yes, Sire," Gud Baxak said, beaming.

"Then do it." He said to Miss Schlupe, "Tell me what's been happening."

"I really don't know. The natives whoop it up all day, but so far they've just wandered about in mobs and made a lot of noise. Except for cutting off the service transmitters, they've left us alone. Do you need me at your meeting?"

"No. Go to bed. You look worn out, and this is only the beginning. Get some sleep while you can."

"Where are you going?"

"To find Kxon. I can't make any plans until I've talked with him."

He stepped through to Kxon's headquarters. The place was a shambles. The carefully compiled files were strewn from room to room; furnishings had been tossed about and smashed. Stunned, Darzek righted a chair and seated himself wearily.

He'd lost the battle for Yorlq before it began. At the moment he most urgently needed his investigators—the moment he'd trained them for—they'd gone mad along with the other natives.

"That's why the traders hired only foreigners," he thought. "Their experience with the Dark taught them not to trust natives." He told himself defensively that he'd had to trust natives, that no foreigner could have moved about Yorlq unnoticed the way Kxon did. But he should have been prepared for this.

Minutes slipped by, and still he sat huddled in bleak despondency, unwilling to move, reluctant even to think or plan. He had called the traders together, intending to rally them to a battle that was already lost. Now he could only ask their help in collecting supplies and organizing an evacuation. They'd help eagerly, of course. The same mental weapon with which the Dark maddened the natives probably paralyzed the traders' will to resist.

He started. Was it possible that the Dark's mental weapon was working on *him?* Angrily he got to his feet and strode to the transmitter.

At dawn Miss Schlupe found him sitting meditatively in the garden. She handed him a dish of her synthetic rhubarb beer, and he sipped it appreciatively, saying, "This is the right time for it."

"Did you get any sleep at all?"

He shook his head.

"Are the traders going to cooperate?"

"They have no choice if they want to leave here on my ship. It took me hours to get that point across, but it finally registered."

"I wondered if you'd found an obstructionist among them."

Darzek smiled. "Which is a polite way of saying, 'agent of the

Dark.' No, but I'm watching all of them very carefully—watching them and having them watched. Each of them now has one of my undertraders as an assistant, supposedly for liaison duties. It'd be difficult to say which were deliberately obstructive and which were merely scared stiff, but all of them are cooperating, albeit reluctantly.

"Gul Meszk owns an interest in a factory that produces compartments for spaceships, or did before the Dark put a damper on the spaceship business in this sector. He thinks there are enough finished passenger units on hand to fill my ship. Gul Kaln is what would be called an electronics nut back on Earth, and he has enough equipment available to put together any number of outsized transmitters. The two of them are working at getting the passenger compartments up to the ship. As for the others, Rhinzl is willing to do whatever I want, but only at night when he knows there'll be very little that I want done. He's going to muster the few available nocturnals and organize a night watch. I have the rest out collecting supplies, but I'm afraid I'll have to prod them constantly."

"I hope you have something for me to do. I've never felt so useless in my life."

"You can take charge of the evacuation. The natives may turn off the broadcast power at any moment, so I'm having outside doors cut in all of the dwellings. As the compartments are made ready you can bring the women and children over here, one household at a time, and pass them through to the ship."

"Are you really going to fight the natives?"

"The hill is a perfect defensive position. Any native who climbs it won't feel much like fighting when he reaches the top."

"You didn't answer my question."

"I'm going to make a show of fighting," Darzek said. "There's something I want to find out—something I *must* find out—and this is the only way it can be done."

"Can it be done before we starve?"

"We're culling all of the warehouses for anything that might be of use to us. Gul Kaln has some self-powered transmitters ready so we can keep moving supplies after the power is cut off. As fast as the noncombatants move out we'll convert the dwellings into supply depots."

"Water?"

Darzek laughed. "We'll stock that, too. And if we need more, every dwelling has a lovely aquaroom with a reserve of I don't know how many thousands of gallons."

"All right. We'll be prepared for a siege. Will it take that long to find out what you want to know?"

"I don't know," Darzek said soberly. "No one has ever resisted the Dark before, so I have no idea what will happen. The more I learn about the Dark, the more confused I get. Why would any rational entity go tearing through the galaxy on an orgy of conquest, and then leave the conquered worlds to starve? The Dark doesn't merely induce insanity—it *is* insanity. I can't make any sense out of it."

"Those howling natives certainly didn't make sense to me."

"If we could hold on here until they regain a measure of sanity, it would be a tremendous morale booster to the whole galaxy. A victory here could be the turning point. On the other hand, there aren't enough of us to defend this place if the natives attack in force, even if their only weapons are their bare hands, and I hate to think what will happen if there are a few Eyes of Death among them. So I'm going to make a show of fighting. Perhaps I'll learn . . . something . . ."

"Have you learned a substitute for breakfast? No one on the *Hesr* has eaten since the day before yesterday. Your army will fight better on a full stomach."

"I'll take it up with Gul Ceyh," Darzek promised. "He's appointed himself quartermaster general."

A few minutes later he sought out Miss Schlupe again and said remorsefully, "Schluppy, you just changed jobs. Behold the harvest of total automation. There isn't a person in the entire trading community who knows how to cook!"

Already exhausted, Darzek spent a frustrating, exhausting day dashing frantically from place to place, never quite finishing one task before he was urgently needed elsewhere. He inspected warehouses, browbeat balky traders into making plans and doing something about carrying them out, saw that the hilltop's thick vegetation was cut and stacked in barricades, and organized the undertraders and youths into squads and platoons. Along the way he dealt with an unending succession of messengers who dashed up breathlessly for decisions on problems of truly Gordian perplexity.

In one of the warehouses he found a stack of stout poles of unidentifiable wood, intended for an undiscernible purpose, and he armed a company of shock troops with them. No officer had ever commanded a more motley group, but they responded eagerly and learned quickly. Their attitude pleased Darzek, even though he could not watch their slithering, ambling, gamboling, shuffling, gliding, and skating charge without laughing.

Gul Kaln's unlimited resourcefulness provided Miss Schlupe with a makeshift kitchen, and she supervised an endless preparation of food with helpers drawn from every type of animate on the *Hesr*, who also served as tasters for their own kinds. Darzek inspected the place—once—and found its variegated outpourings astonishing and largely nauseous.

When the turmoil had taken on a semblance of organization, Darzek slipped away to a warehouse at the center of Yorlez, cut a slit in an outside wall, and watched the natives. Their coarse shouts, their ferocious cries of "Grilf! Grilf!" carried only faintly and fitfully to the *Hesr*, but in the narrow defiles between buildings the clamor became terrifying. As they threshed and tore their way through the thick vegetation, Darzek watched with increasing perplexity. Ruefully he weighed his two critical mistakes: the first in trusting the natives, and the second in knowing so few of them. He should have lived and worked with them, instead of cutting a dazzling figure in trader society.

But that could have been a worse mistake. Had he done so, would he now be sharing their hate-twisted frenzy and raising his own cries of *Grilf?*

"What is the Dark?" he muttered.

A panting messenger arrived to stammer out a more immediate problem, and he had to turn away.

At the end of the day Darzek again sat in his garden, watching one of the last remaining groups of women and children waddle through the dusk to the nearest transmitter link with the spaceship. His supply problem was under control. His defense was organized and ready. Most important, his lines of retreat were secure. With their families in safety on the ship, and with transmitters spotted about the *Hesr* for instant use in case it became necessary to evacuate, the traders seemed much less frightened. Two or three of them even showed flashes of boldness.

Miss Schlupe materialized out of the gathering night. "The power's been cut off," she announced.

"We can do without it."

"When did you sleep last?"

"On the spaceship," Darzek admitted. "Last night, or yesterday, or maybe the night before. That must be what's wrong with me. I've been trying to blame it on the Dark."

"If it isn't what's wrong with you, it soon will be."

"I'll get to bed as soon as I've made the rounds," he promised.

The city below had receded into silent darkness. All seemed peaceful there. The night had stoppered up the natives' frenzy, but it would go on fermenting, and perhaps, when the dawn released it, the explosion would follow.

Darzek moved from post to post, exchanging banter with the sentries. Abruptly light flashed in a doorless opening, and a shadow loomed monstrously beside him. He whirled in alarm, but it was only Rhinzl, who chuckled softly.

"Did I frighten you, Gul Darr?"

"You startled me," Darzek admitted. "If I'm flinching at shadows, I need sleep worse than I realized. Are there any natives about?"

"None within the range of my vision. I do not expect them to come by night unless they bring lights, and then they themselves will give us warning. Have your sleep, and fear nothing. My nocturnals are placed so that no one can approach without their seeing."

"What is your opinion of what's happened so far?"

"Things have begun almost exactly as they did on Quarm, except that the Quarmers were active at night. This worked a hardship on most of the traders. The darkness has a property of magnifying the terrors of those who prefer the day."

"True," Darzek agreed.

"Have your sleep. I will send for you at once if you are needed."

"Thank you," Darzek said.

He found his bedroom crammed with crates of foul-smelling foodstuffs. There wasn't sufficient space for lowering a hassock into a reclining position, so he made one into a chair and slept sitting up.

It was late morning when he awakened. He strolled out into the sunshine and found Gul Azfel, who had charge of the morning watch, calmly scanning the horizon.

"Greetings, Gul Darr," Azfel said cheerfully. "Gula Schlu would not permit that I awaken you, so I could not report the beginning of my service as ordered."

"Is anything happening?"

"They are burning a warehouse," Azfel said, gesturing at a thin column of smoke. "I have been trying to identify it. I think it is E-Wusk's."

Darzek started. "I'd forgotten E-Wusk. Did he leave as he had planned?"

"He is gone," Azfel said. "He did not confide his plans to me. His warehouse is empty, or there would be more smoke."

"I thought these buildings were fireproof."

"It requires special combustibles to ignite them, but when sufficient heat is applied they burn fiercely. And dangerously," Azfel added, savoring the thought. "There will be many deaths among the natives."

Miss Schlupe sent over a basket of fresh fruit, and Darzek

picked out a vantage point where he could look down at the city and seated himself to eat his breakfast. Occasionally he could see the mindless surges of the mobs, as they threshed through the vegetation or charged blindly along paths that had already been beaten clear. Their cries billowed up louder when they were hot on the scent of something—a foreigner's home, a warehouse, perhaps his person. Darzek had made his invitation general, but so awed by the *Hesr* were the lesser traders and factors and peddlers that few had responded.

He turned to Azfel, who waited respectfully at his elbow. "Did anything happen during the night?"

"Gul Rhinzl said not."

"Is this the way it went on Quarm?"

"Not at all. There the natives had easy access to our dwellings. They filled the ovals the first night, and from that time we had no food and were isolated from each other when the natives were about."

"And an empty stomach, like the night, magnifies terrors," Darzek murmured. "Is everyone getting enough to eat?"

"Perhaps some are not getting as much as they would like, but no one is hungry."

"When will the natives come here?"

"Today," Azfel said confidently. "Their anger is feeding on the warehouses now. It grows as it feeds, and the more it grows the more food it demands. I expect them today."

"Then I'd better make certain that we're ready for them."

He moved off, carrying his breakfast with him, and Azfel slithered along at his side.

By late afternoon a pall of smoke hung over the city, and separate mobs, drifting about aimlessly, merged, meandered closer to the *Hesr*, merged with other mobs. They converged from a dozen directions to stand at the edge of the city looking up at the hilltop.

"A thousand of them, at least," Darzek muttered.

The cries of "Grilf!" crescendoed to a peak of frenzy, and the natives charged.

For a hundred yards they moved at top speed. Then, as the slope became steeper, they gradually slowed to a panting walk, and their cries faded to piping gasps. They doggedly continued to stagger upward, but only a small vanguard approached the top; the rest were scattered over the face of the hill.

Darzek moved his shock troops forward and held them poised at the barricade. They waited quietly with leveled poles, and a thin line of natives, enormous ears drooping with exhaustion, gathered twenty yards below and stood looking up at them.

"Charge!" Darzek ordered.

The shock troops swept down the hill, and the natives fled.

A cheer went up. Darzek had difficulty in recalling his troops, who would have chased the natives down into the city. Scenting a trap, he reorganized them quickly and rushed them to the other side of the hill in anticipation of a coordinated attack. There was none.

Thoughtfully he returned to his headquarters. There he found Gul Halvr and Gul Isc cavorting about with unrestrained jubilation. The shock troops dropped their poles and joined in, the watch deserted its positions, and in a twinkling Darzek's army was milling about with the casual enthusiasm of a community picnic.

Angrily he shouted it back to order and shrugged off the outpouring of excited congratulations. The Dark was performing so ineptly as to make him highly suspicious, and he immediately ordered a practice evacuation maneuver.

Soon after dark Rhinzl sent for him. The night was deeply overcast and Darzek could see nothing at all, but Rhinzl pointed into the gloom at several small groups of natives who had climbed partway up the hill. "I am uncertain of what they are trying to do," Rhinzl said.

"If any of them get to the top, grab them and ask them. Do you still think they won't attack at night?"

"They *shouldn't* attack at night. Of course there is no way to *know* what their madness may move them to do. But I think they will come by day—every day, as long as we are here. And each time there will be more of them."

Darzek went back to bed. He learned in the morning that the natives had not approached the top of the hill and had left long before dawn. Thoughtfully he ordered another practice evacuation.

"Everyone is wondering why you're getting ready to run away when we're winning," Miss Schlupe told him.

Darzek made no answer. The previous day's victory, instead of buoying up his hopes, had deepened his pessimism. He wondered again if the Dark's weapon could be working on him.

At dawn the rampaging mobs were already converging at the foot of the hill. There they waited, sending an incessant cacophony of insult toward the hilltop. Their numbers grew steadily. When Darzek made his midday rounds the hill was surrounded.

"There seem to be such a lot of them," Gul Azfel observed plaintively.

Darzek nodded and grimly contemplated his thin line of defense. His defensive perimeter was a long one, and there was no way that he could shorten it. He had to defend the entire hilltop. His only hope was that the natives would reach the top in driblets. Then he could defeat them in detail with his shock troops.

He invoked phase one of the evacuation plan and ordered to the ship all of the nocturnals and kitchen helpers. Then he made another circuit of the hilltop to bolster his commanders. Some of the traders were performing magnificently. Gul Halvr had positioned himself in front of the barricade, where he stood peering boldly down at the natives like an Indian scout. Gul Ceyh paced back and forth, exuding confidence and chanting in a strange language something that might have been a hymn to battle. Gul Isc was also pacing back and forth, but he blurted nervously, "I don't know what to *do!*" Darzek told him what to do.

The *efa* posed his major command problem. They had refused to serve under another trader, but they led their sector of the defense like an embattled board of directors. Darzek located them in a nearby dwelling, furiously engaged in argument, and he did not bother to interrupt them. He promoted an undertrader to take their place and moved on.

Gul Kaln had the bored aplomb of a tourist out sight-seeing. Gul Meszk seemed mainly concerned that the work of the kitchen force had been interrupted and he might miss a meal. Darzek told him he could spend the rest of his life eating, but that the fun of winning a war might never come again, and left him.

The natives began to move up the hill.

It was not the wild charge of the day before, but a deliberate advance. Watching, Darzek told himself gloomily that this time they could not be frightened away. They were so solidly massed that they would fill the hill from top to bottom. Pressure from the rear would force the front ranks forward.

He summoned Gud Baxak, who was carrying his arsenal, chose a position with care, and, as the screaming natives neared the top, lofted a tear-gas grenade down the slope. The chorus of hate changed to one of terror, and the natives charged. Darzek threw' one more grenade, and then desisted; the gas was simply driving the front ranks forward. They reached the top and began to grapple with the defenders.

As Darzek turned to signal his shock troops into the melee, he heard a cry of alarm behind him. Whirling, he saw a group of natives moving between the dwellings.

His first horrified thought was that the line had broken on the far side of the perimeter. He faced the shock troops around, but even as they moved forward a new threat developed on his right. This time he could see natives pouring out of a dwelling.

They were coming in through the transmitters.

Off on his left the same thing was happening. Darzek did not hesitate. He raised both hands above his head, signaling the evacuation.

His troops disengaged and drew back. The natives followed them closely, shouting, "Grilf! Grilf!" and smoke was already curling from the central dwellings; but there was no panic. Darzek breathed fervent thanks for the practice evacuations and watched with a flush of pride as his shock troops formed up to protect the transmitters while the others filed through them in orderly fashion.

Darzek circled the hilltop, making certain that no one had been cut off. The natives trailed after him, screaming derisively, but they made no attempt to interfere. Flames were leaping high from a dozen dwellings when Darzek finally convinced himself that the evacuation was complete. He signaled Gud Baxak into a transmitter and turned to follow him. His last visual impression was of Kxon and three of his ex-investigators pouring oil to fire another dwelling.

The ship's captain had been watching everything on the transmitter screen, and he looked shaken. Silently he approached Darzek for orders. Darzek asked for a complete roll call.

Miss Schlupe touched his elbow and said anxiously, "What'd you do to Rhinzl?"

"Nothing. Why?"

"This is the first time I've ever known him to be angry."

"Where is he?" Darzek asked.

He found the trader in a darkened compartment with the other nocturnals. "You sent us away before the fight started," Rhinzl said bitterly.

"I had the impression that you didn't care for daylight action," Darzek said. "Anyway, there was no fight. It would have been silly to fight. We were outnumbered a hundred to one in all directions."

"Indeed?" Rhinzl said coldly. "But I suppose you are to be congratulated on running away so efficiently."

Puzzled, Darzek returned to the ship's lounge. In one corner the *efa* were entangled in one of their loud arguments, Brokefa shouting, "How can we know, when we didn't even try to fight? I'm telling you, Gul Darr—"

His voice dropped. Darzek walked toward Gul Halvr, who slowly and deliberately turned his back. Darzek moved on, and was suddenly conscious that traders and undertraders were drawing away from him.

Again he found Miss Schlupe at his elbow. He said bewilderedly, "Can it be that they actually think—"

"I'm afraid so. It was those practice evacuations that started it. They wondered why you wanted to rehearse running away when you were winning. And then you did run away without a fight, after you won so easily yesterday. A lot of them think they could have won again."

"That's nonsense. Once the natives got inside the perimeter the situation was hopeless. The practice evacuations were what saved us."

"I know. But some of them are saying that you surrendered to the Dark. Did you get what you were after?"

Darzek shook his head. "I wanted to find out whether the natives really were an unreasoning mob, or whether they had intelligent direction that was able to adapt to unexpected circumstances. I still don't know. Turning the power back on and using the transmitters was the work of a crafty mind, but the natives could have thought of it themselves. So I don't know. I muffed it, and now I won't be able to find out until the next time."

"Next time? The next time the Dark moves?"

Darzek nodded. "When it tries to take Primores. And by then I may be too late."

14

They had been on Primores for nearly a term when Gul Isc convoked a meeting. The summons came as a surprise to Darzek; he had been too furiously occupied with his own affairs to keep in close touch with the traders, and he had mistakenly assumed that they were already engaged in rebuilding their businesses.

The heavy influx of refugees from the Dark so taxed the housing accommodations that they had to meet in the diminutive reception room of a small apartment. The place was obviously unsuited for the hosting of nocturnals, and Rhinzl had not been invited. There were not even enough chairs for those present.

Gul Isc stammered through a long-winded explanation for the meeting, and it gave Darzek no small measure of satisfaction to answer bluntly, "No."

They gazed at him in consternation. "You refuse to join us?" Gul Azfel demanded wonderingly.

"I am very tired," Darzek said. "Like E-Wusk, I have seen too much of the Dark. I hope to find a world beneath its notice and live in peace."

"E-Wusk did not find such a world," Gul Halvr said. "Or perhaps he did not look. He, too, is here on Primores."

It was Darzek's turn to stare. "E-Wusk? *Here?*"

"I saw him only yesterday."

"You will not reconsider, Gul Darr?" Meszk asked politely. "We had counted on your help. We need it desperately."

Darzek said dryly, "When we left Yorlq several of you gave me the impression that your opinions of my abilities were less flattering."

"We were hasty," Meszk admitted. "In our distress over the outcome, we did not properly evaluate your accomplishment. You showed us that the Dark can be resisted. With greater numbers, and with more time to prepare, we might have won. And if the Dark can be defeated on Yorlq, it can be defeated anywhere."

"Primores is not 'anywhere,'" Gul Ceyh said. "It is the home of Supreme. The Dark must not take Primores."

"We have ample time to work and plan before the Dark moves again," Meszk said. "Will you not supervise that planning, Gul Darr?"

"Regretfully—no. As soon as I can liquidate the affairs of the Trans-Star Trading Company, Gula Schlu and I are going home— or to some remote world that we can call home. I did what I could on Yorlq, and I failed. Others may do better. I hope so. I wish them well, and I think them more likely to succeed without my counsel."

"If you are firm in that belief, then of course there is nothing more to be said," Meszk said resignedly. "If your thinking changes, we will welcome your assistance. Do you plan to leave soon?"

"Not immediately. There is still much work to be done." He turned to Brokefa. "Would the *efa* care to purchase a spaceship?"

Brokefa wheezed in amusement. "No. The *efa* have no need for one."

"Nor does anyone else," Darzek said gloomily. "The Dark's last move has so restricted trade that there is a surplus of spaceships. I haven't received a single bid for mine."

He took his formal leave of them.

"Come and see me before you go," Gul Ceyh called.

"Of course," Darzek said. "I hope to see all of you. And if I find my refuge, all of you will be welcome there."

He joined Miss Schlupe in a public park, where she stood looking through the transparent dome at the looming profile of the city.

"I hate parks without benches," she announced.

"The parks are walking places. People can sit down at home."

"I also miss the birds. A park without benches and birds is like beer without alcohol. Are you sure you aren't making a mistake? They have substantial resources, and they'll probably have help from other wealthy traders. If they had someone to tell them what to do, they might even accomplish something."

Darzek shook his head. "I had a private talk with Gul Isc before the others arrived. He thinks I performed brilliantly on Yorlq, and he gave me the inside story of this little meeting. Gul Meszk bought a plantation on Primores II and converted it into a military training base. He sought help from every trader he could contact, recruited a force of some five hundred, and started training it. Rhinzl was his second in command, and of course the others meddled in whenever they saw fit. In this short time they've gotten their troops into such a muddle that they may never be able to straighten them out. They're bewildered, because it all looked so easy when I was doing it on Yorlq."

"Then what they really want you to do is straighten out the mess."

Darzek nodded. "Train an army for them, get it ready to fight—and then turn it over to them, or use it under their orders."

"You still might be able to make use of them."

"It's the wrong approach. The riots are only symptoms. The problem isn't to resist them, but to find out what causes them. We can only do that by studying the natives. On Yorlq we didn't even bother to learn their language. I don't intend to make that mistake twice."

"I don't see what you expect to accomplish by going native. You can't alter the fact that you're a foreigner."

"I can't *be* a native," Darzek said slowly, "but perhaps I can learn to think like one."

"The traders will find out that you haven't retired. You can't trade with thousands of worlds without anyone knowing about it."

"I think I can."

"All of them helped on Yorlq. Don't you trust any of them?"

"No, but they can still be useful to me. They helped me today. Gul Halvr told me that E-Wusk is here, and that's the most intriguing thing that's happened since Smith unloaded the million dollars on us."

The old trader seemed to have shriveled since Darzek saw him last. He had lost weight, and his leathery flesh was puckered with deep wrinkles. He greeted Darzek congenially enough, but the note of exuberance was gone from his laughter.

"Gul Halvr told me about your fight with the Dark," he said.

"It wasn't much of a fight."

"Any fight with the Dark has but one ending."

"So it would seem. I was surprised to learn that you were here."

"I thought to ask Supreme to suggest a place of refuge, but there are so many who wish to consult Supreme—so many who have fled the Dark." E-Wusk sighed. "One must wait one's turn, and I fear to wait much longer. Would it surprise you if I said the Dark came here before me?"

"The Dark? Here on Primores? I don't believe it!"

"I, E-Wusk, have seen its work."

"I, Darr, have not," Darzek said boldly. "Therefore I cannot accept what you say."

E-Wusk's enormous face assumed an expression of hurt astonishment. "You cannot accept what E-Wusk tells you? Come. You shall see for yourself."

Darzek followed him to one of the city's many beautiful parks. They walked through it slowly, and paused for E-Wusk to stare searchingly at each native they met. "Not here," he announced finally. They moved on to another park. And another.

He found what he was looking for. "There!" he whispered.

A small group of Primorians had gathered at an intersection of paths. One, speaking stridently and with jerky gesticulations, seemed to be lecturing to the others, who stood grouped together a short distance away from him and did not seem to be listening.

"There!" E-Wusk whispered again.

They stopped to watch. The audience, if it was one, soon began to edge away, and the speaker broke off and stood looking after it disgustedly. He marched to the other side of the park and began to address another group of natives, which broke up almost immediately.

Puzzled, Darzek demanded, "This is the Dark at work?"

"It is," E-Wusk said.

Darzek scratched his head fretfully. "What did he say?"

"I can not tell you precisely, for I do not understand the language. I know the sort of things he is saying. 'The foreign traders are greedily drinking the lifeblood of our solvency. They take their huge profits and live in their lavish homes and drain the wealth from our world while leaving us only enough to subsist. Let's rid ourselves of foreigners, and keep the wealth that rightfully belongs to us for ourselves.' He, and many like him, are saying this all over Primores. This and much more. They say vile things. The natives don't want to listen, but soon they will listen in spite of themselves, and then they will become angry. Finally the madness will come. The Dark's madness."

"This happened on the other worlds?"

"On all of them. When the speeches begin, the Dark is never far behind."

"I see. Are there other signs?"

"Many. As the Dark approaches, the world's pattern of trade changes. The people eat more and consume fewer luxuries. Soon they stop buying clothing and ornaments. Those with occupations neglect them. They are afflicted with strange sicknesses. Some remain in their homes and brood, but more gather in the parks where always there is a speaker to talk against the foreigners. By watching places of public assembly, and by studying trade records, medical reports, patronage of the transportation systems, and many such things it is possible to predict within a quarter-term when the Dark will strike."

"Are you making such a study of Primores?"

"I? I have no intention of remaining here that long."

"Could you teach me how to do it?"

"There is no time. Surely I will be able to consult Supreme very soon, and then I shall leave. Immediately."

They separated at the transmitting exchange, Darzek to look for a young native he had hired, named ᴜʀsDwad. He took him on a tour of the parks, and when they found another speaker haranguing a small group of natives, Darzek ordered, "Translate!"

ᴜʀsDwad listened with signs of incredulity. "He says the foreign traders devour the wealth of our world and leave us the dregs. He says we should force them to leave and destroy the symbols of their greed."

"Ask him what foreigner has paid him tainted solvency to make such statements," Darzek suggested.

ᴜʀsDwad did so; the haranguer glared in speechless fury and then flounced away.

"Touché!" Darzek murmured. "A shot in the dark—at the Dark."

He should have discovered this on Yorlq. He should have investigated E-Wusk's prognostications there, though by the time he found out about them it was already too late.

Perhaps it was too late on Primores.

He told Miss Schlupe about it, and she exclaimed, "Great! It's a dratted Communist conspiracy."

"Nonsense. An out-and-out Communist couldn't get to first base around here. No one is underprivileged, and anyone can become a capitalist who wants to work at it. All this means is that someone has discovered how effective rabble-rousing can be, and the custom of leaving one's home planet to go into business makes all the traders foreigners and an obvious target."

"What are you going to do about it?"

"Just as fast as possible I'm going to train a staff of private detectives. I want to find out where these characters go when they climb down off their soapboxes, and whom they talk to. Especially whom they are taking orders from. There must be a tremendous organization behind this, to bring off riots on so many worlds almost simultaneously, and the thing is self-perpetuating. Foreign agents work through susceptible natives to arouse the populace against foreigners. Then they're evicted along with the innocent foreigners to start over again on a world the Dark hasn't touched. Schluppy, this comes as a terrible letdown. The Dark's mysterious mental weapon is the rabble-rouser!"

"The people can't be that stupid. Maybe the rabble-rouser uses a mental weapon to make them believe him."

Darzek winced.

"You're going to train a staff—of *natives?*"

"They'll have to be natives."

"They'll turn against you in the end, just as they did on Yorlq."

"The idea is to see that there won't be any end. I'm putting you in charge of this. What with my trading operations, and keeping tabs on the traders, and trying to figure out E-Wusk's statistical analysis, I won't have time for it."

"Won't E-Wusk help you?"

"No. He's leaving as soon as he can. He's changed so much that you'd hardly know him. They've all changed. Now E-Wusk is wearing his fear, and the others aren't. I wish I had time to investigate that." He gestured absently. "E-Wusk reminded me of something else I should have done the moment I arrived here, only I didn't know it was possible. So today I registered a request to consult Supreme."

Darzek had established ten of his undertraders on the outer planets. Ensconced in obscure, unmarked offices, these novices in interstellar trade had as much solvency at their disposal as the largest trading companies. Already they were operating fleets of spaceships and providing essential supplies for worlds the Dark had isolated. Starving worlds, such as Quarm, were fed and encouraged to dispose of their dead and get to work supporting themselves. Most worlds had recovered their sanity before their food stocks were exhausted, but all had critical shortages, usually of metals and fuels. These Darzek's trading team obtained for them, whenever possible from other Dark worlds.

Gud Baxak moved energetically from office to office and journeyed far into the realm of the Dark, supervising, coordinating, displaying a high genius for trading organization. He had an ecstatic vision of an absolute trading monopoly of thousands of worlds, and he was extracting a pledge from every world he supplied to ensure that no ships except Darzek's could handle a fractured solvency of its trade. Darzek approved of such Machiavellian tactics. He could always open the territory to other traders later; his immediate concern was to prevent the return of agents of the Dark.

Darzek made the rounds of the traders, seeing one or two a day in an apparent gesture of good fellowship. Gul Meszk had evolved the grandiose scheme of uniting all the traders in the galaxy against the Dark, but several of the traders were less than wholly enthused with the idea.

"There are too many traders in this part of the galaxy now," Brokefa grumbled.

"Then you should be pleased that E-Wusk and I are leaving," Darzek said lightly.

"Bosh. I wasn't thinking of you. When are you leaving?"

"Like E-Wusk, I shall consult Supreme. There is, alas, a long waiting list."

"Of course. There always has been."

"At present it's longer than usual. Everyone fleeing the Dark seems to proceed by way of Primores."

"I'd be happier about this plan of Gul Meszk's if you would join us," Brokefa said. "Gul Meszk is no leader, and he knows it. He wanted to give the job to Gul Rhinzl, but Gul Rhinzl said a commander who could fight only at night would be worthless."

"On Yorlq we fought only during the day, at the convenience of the natives. If we'd had enough nocturnals to harass them at night, we might have won."

"I never thought of that," Brokefa said, wide-eyed.

"I found Gul Rhinzl to be a valuable assistant. Whatever position he holds, he certainly won't be worthless."

He departed, leaving Brokefa in a thoughtful mood. If what Darzek had said got back to Rhinzl—and he was certain that it would—there was a good chance that when next Darzek called on him the nocturnal would be more generous with his confidences than he had been the last time.

Miss Schlupe had a squad of her detectives out for training. She was lurking unobtrusively behind some shrubbery and casting scathing glances in the direction of an agitator who was haranguing a small group of natives.

"How many of them are yours?" Darzek asked.

"Are you kidding? Mine have strict orders not to go near one of those jolly gatherings. If they hang around listening to that bilge they may start believing it. I've got them studying the agitators, and they've made a lovely collection of three-dimensional photographs, and they're to tail them whenever they can, as far as they can, but if I ever catch one listening I'll fire him."

"Good idea."

"When I think of the time we wasted on Yorlq with Kxon and his group I feel sick. By the way—has it occurred to you that our education has been neglected?"

"Several times. What did you have in mind?"

"I wanted ursDwad to go over and call that snake a liar, and I don't know the word for it. Do you?"

Darzek thought for a moment. "No."

"We should sue Smith for dereliction of duty."

Darzek chuckled. "He was indoctrinating us for a meeting with the Council of Supreme. Even if he'd known there would be liars present, he wouldn't have wanted us to say so."

"How would we go about getting ahold of Smith? There must be a Primorian headquarters for his certification groups."

"We wouldn't know whom to ask for. He didn't tell us his official name or status. We don't even know how they refer to Earth."

"Drat him!"

"If I could get ahold of him I'd use him for more critical things than vocabulary building," Darzek said, watching the agitator. "Is it my imagination, or are these characters drawing more people?"

"Their crowds get larger every day. If we don't find out who's behind this, and soon, Primores is going the way of Yorlq."

"Carry on. I'm going to see E-Wusk."

E-Wusk was out. Darzek went instead to call on Gul Halvr and found him grumbling about Meszk's latest idea. "He's called a meeting of five hundred traders," he said. "He wants to organize them against the Dark."

"Will they come?"

"Why not? Any trader would be interested in defeating the Dark. Gul Meszk wants each of the five hundred to organize more traders, and so on. If he brings all the traders in the galaxy to Primores, who will there be left to do business with? Do you think this idea has a chance?"

"What's the native population of Primores?"

"Perhaps as many as a million million."

"If Gul Meszk raised a force of a million, which would be a staggering task, he'd still be outnumbered a million to one. Of course a large part of the million million is made up of nonfighters, and the rest would have very little organization. Gul Meszk might have a chance if he could get his force organized in time and deployed in the right place. Unfortunately, he has very little time and no one knows the right place."

"Now you sound like E-Wusk," Gul Halvr said disgustedly.

E-Wusk was waiting at Darzek's apartment, his huge, wrinkled form tense with excitement. "I have consulted Supreme!" he blurted.

"Splendid! With what result?"

"I asked Supreme to suggest a world where I would be safe from the Dark. And Supreme answered—" E-Wusk paused for breath. "Supreme answered, '*Primores*'!"

15

Officially it was Primores O, the only planet in the galaxy thus designated, called nothing to distinguish it from its sister planets Primores I through IV—and because it was everything.

It was the innermost planet of its solar system, the first world of the central sun of the galaxy, and it was a beautiful world, as perfect in each of its parts as a masterfully fashioned miniature.

The numbered cities were typical sprawling, streetless conglomerations of windowless buildings; yet startlingly untypical because their profiles revealed plan and symmetry, the spaces between buildings were lush, carefully kept gardens of grass and flowers, and the numerous parks were incongruously enclosed in tinted domes—incongruously because the climate of Primores O was everywhere a sublimity of balmy perfection.

Darzek shook the ugliness of Yorlq from his memory and felt reassured. The transmitter-orientated city did not have to be a monstrous blight.

Beyond the cities, white-crowned hills thatched with the orange plumage of a lofty forest loomed on every horizon, the cultivated fields of automated farms radiated in wedges from a central building like a meticulously carved pie, small rivers flowed endlessly and unbelievably in circles, geometrically shaped patches of vividly hued vegetation were splashed about the landscape like colors on an artist's palette, and distant, ovular lakes shimmeringly mirrored a rainbow sky, where an enormous sun swam from horizon to horizon like an egg in a bowl of intermixed Easter egg tints.

Darzek found the sun as much of a mystery as the varicolored sky: he could look at it steadily with naked eye.

Obviously Primores O was an old, old world. The harshness of nature had long since been controlled and softened, and someone with an eye for beauty had rearranged and remolded the landscape, at the same time that those seeking comfort had rescheduled and revised the weather.

Darzek's one regret was that there was no air travel. The only broad glimpse of Primores that he could obtain came from the observatories, the white crowns on the hilltops where the Primorians went to eat a quiet meal and look out at their lovely world.

But Darzek had little time for sight-seeing. He visited the observatories, not to enjoy the view, but to observe the natives.

They were another of the disconcertingly humanlike species. Darzek had long since learned that he was much more at ease with the utterly inhuman than with those types that possessed superficial human resemblances. With the latter he experienced the normal reaction of one of his kind encountering the maimed or the deformed: a temptation to stare, and a feeling of acute embarrassment. For this reason he was more relaxed in the presence of a Rhinzl, for example, or an E-Wusk, than with such distortedly human types as a Kxon or a Meszk.

He was extremely uncomfortable in the presence of the Primorians.

Their heads protruded from their chests, and their bodies loomed above and behind in bulging humps. Their faces were small, the large eyes wide-set with an enfolded nostril slightly above and a mouth invisible under a blunt chin. They swathed themselves in thick wrappings that completely obscured the contours of their bodies, a custom of which Darzek heartily approved. He preferred not to know what their bodies looked like.

Their slow movements, their quiet, meditative manner, their soft, hesitant speech gave no indication of blazing powers of intellect, and yet Darzek had the uncomfortable suspicion that their misshapen heads housed enormous brains. The crude, lying propaganda of the Dark should have received from them the derision it so richly deserved, but it did not. They were listening to it in ever-increasing numbers—listening phlegmatically, but for all Darzek knew they were capable of unimaginable heights of frenzy.

These were the people to whom Supreme was entrusted. They filled the ranks of civil servants, custodians, even guardians, if such existed. The entire galaxy would be plunged into anarchy if they revolted.

They must not revolt.

The traders saw this as clearly as Darzek. Rhinzl invited Darzek to come and see him, and there he met Gul Meszk and Gul Isc. Meszk asked him bluntly, "What do you know about Supreme?"

"Very little," Darzek said. "I've requested a consultation, but half the galaxy seems to be waiting for consultations."

"Some of the traders I invited to Primores have already arrived," Meszk said. "We must perfect our plans, and quickly." He paused. "Gul Darr—where *is* Supreme?"

"I haven't the vaguest idea."

"Nor has anyone else. A world is too large a place on which to seek even such a large object as Supreme must be. The governmental departments and offices are connected with Supreme in some fashion, but they are staffed entirely by natives, who pretend to know nothing."

"Have you asked them?"

"I've done nothing else since we arrived here."

"I'm afraid I can't help you."

"We are agreed on two points," Meszk said. "For one, the absolutely essential task we must undertake is to protect Supreme. For another, if anyone knows where Supreme is located it will be certain natives responsible for its maintenance, which means that when the Dark comes all natives will know. The Dark will know."

"I agree."

"Gul Darr, how can we protect Supreme from the natives when they know where it is and we don't?"

"Has anyone thought of asking Supreme where it is?"

Meszk blinked his eyes in rapid succession. "No. No one has thought of that."

"When I receive my consultation I'll ask."

Meszk brightened. "Thank you, Gul Darr. You always seem to know what to do."

"Yes," Darzek agreed. "It rarely works out, but at least I know what to do."

He stopped off at one of the parks before returning home. There were two agitators at work there. Darzek was not yet fluent enough in Primorian to understand everything they said, but he grasped enough of it to leave him feeling both angry and depressed. He counted the natives: nineteen in one group, twenty-seven in the other, all listening impassively without looking at the speakers. Vainly he searched their faces for the clue that seemed to be there for the taking but somehow eluded him.

At the park transmitting station he found another group gathered at one end of the small building. He edged his way to the front, and saw a word smeared onto the smooth wall. The natives were contemplating it silently.

Darzek had made no attempt to master the written language. He had to return with ursDwad and ask him to translate. The puzzled native announced that the word had no meaning. Not until Darzek thought to suggest that ursDwad pronounce it was he able to understand.

It said, in the Primorian alphabet, "Grilf."

They called it the Hall of Consultations.

It was an enormous, circular room, its wall lined with doors leading into the small consultation chambers. The consultants trudged patiently around the circle waiting for a chamber to become vacant just ahead of them, or positioned themselves strategically between two doors. When a door rippled open there was a politely restrained scramble to be next.

Darzek watched for a moment, and then took his place with those circling the room. He found, somewhat to his surprise, that he was in no hurry to consult Supreme. He felt very much like a bridegroom getting cold feet a moment before the wedding ceremony began. Belatedly he was realizing that the action he was about to take was irrevocable.

Supreme might have embarrassing questions as to why he had been squandering solvency like a spendthrift who unexpectedly comes into possession of a sheaf of credit cards. There was also the possibility that Supreme, once it learned Darzek's whereabouts, would address a stream of communications to him marked ORDERS. He was prepared to welcome Supreme's assistance, but the decisions Jan Darzek carried out had to be his own. He was not about to become a lackey to a computer, even when the computer was called Supreme.

He drifted with the others, making no attempt to enter a consultation chamber himself. They were as variegated a crowd as he had ever seen. "The dregs of the galaxy," he found himself thinking, but of course they weren't. They only looked like dregs. Traders, administrators, industrialists, scientists, scholars, perhaps even artists, all were exercising their traditional right to consult Supreme.

It was, Darzek thought, a glowing picture of democracy in action, and one made possible only by the fact that the head of the galactic government was a computer. No mere intelligent being could possibly cope with the demands of such a democracy.

A door rippled open just ahead of him. He took a deep breath and waited for another to snatch the opportunity, but so close was he that the others acknowledged his priority and moved around him.

He stepped through the open door, and it clicked shut behind him. He took in the room at a glance: a desk, a native clerk, a transmitter, a chair.

"State your problem, please," the clerk said.

"I request a private interview with Supreme."

"A . . . *private* . . . interview . . ."

"Private," Darzek said firmly. He was determined that no

native would listen in on his conversation—not with the Dark's agitators ranting in the parks. "Just Supreme and myself. Please arrange it as quickly as possible. It's urgent."

The native's chest heaved, tilting his head toward the ceiling. "I'll inquire," he announced finally. He stepped through the transmitter.

Darzek perched tensely on the edge of a chair and waited. The native returned, said politely, "Come with me, ·please."

They emerged in another office, where a second native stood waiting for them. "You wish a—a *private* consultation?" he demanded.

"Private," Darzek agreed.

"What did you wish to consult Supreme about?"

"That, too, is confidential."

"I don't know . . . I gravely fear . . ."

"Ask Supreme," Darzek suggested.

"I could not, without some justification for your request."

Darzek extended his right hand. "My solvency credential. Show that to Supreme, and tell Supreme that its owner requests a private consultation."

"Come with me, please."

He turned Darzek over to a committee of three, one of whom silently placed his hand on a solvency scanner and indited a message. The inditer clicked off a reply.

"Granted!" the native exclaimed awesomely.

Darzek modestly remained silent.

The native motioned Darzek into a transmitter, and he found himself at the end of a dimly red-lit corridor. He stepped forward confidently. This time he knew what to expect: the sensation of icy needles probing him, the dizziness, the tremendous weight, the growing feeling of numbness. He reached the opposite end of the corridor in a bath of blinding perspiration, and the weight lifted. A door stood open before him. He mopped his face and flexed his numb limbs before he moved into the room beyond.

Triumphantly he approached its desk, and then he froze in

consternation. The inditer was a strange model, and he had no idea how to work it.

"So much for my private consultation," he said bitterly. He seated himself and waited for someone to come for him.

Abruptly the room spoke. It said, "Why have you not reported?" Its precise tones were utterly devoid of emphasis or expression. The question was a flat statement.

Darzek controlled his amazement and said plaintively, "I didn't know how. I still don't know how."

"Why have you not reported—" A pause. "—through the Council?"

"There is no Council," Darzek answered.

"Why have you not reported through the Council?"

Darzek hesitated, apprehensive that he and Supreme might be embarking for a ride on a conversational merry-go-round. Obviously he would have to phrase his statements carefully. "You have had no report from any member of the Council for a long time," he said.

"Affirmative."

"You have had no report from any member of the Council since the day I was admitted to a meeting of the Council."

The pause, if there was one, was a mere flicker. "Affirmative."

"All members of the Council of Supreme are dead," Darzek said.

This time the pause was noticeable. "More data requested," Supreme said.

"SIX was an agent of the Dark. When I exposed him, he tried to kill me. I escaped, but he killed the other members of the Council before I killed him. His Eye of Death burned down the meeting place. There is no Council. All of the members are dead."

"You killed the members of the Council," Supreme said.

Darzek hoped that it was a question. "Negative!" he snapped. "I killed SIX, who was an agent of the Dark. SIX killed the other members of the Council and set the building on fire."

It sounded unbelievable even to him. Suddenly he could envision himself telling that story in court with no witnesses to support him. *How did it happen that you survived, Defendant Darzek, when everyone else died? How did it happen that this disaster overtook the Council at the precise moment of your one and only visit?*

But he would defend himself when the need arose. The immediate problem was to make Supreme understand what had happened. He said, "Check your circuits, if that's the word for it, and you'll find that nothing is operating in the building where the Council met."

The pause was a long one. "Affirmative," Supreme said finally.

"Nothing is operating because the building no longer exists. You'll also find, if it's possible to check, that no member of the Council has used his official residence since that day."

"Affirmative."

"I didn't know how to report to you that the members of the Council were dead, and I didn't know what other agents of the Dark might be active on Primores. I left as quickly as possible, and my assistant and I went to Yorlq to learn what we could about the Dark. Do you want a report on what I did there?"

"Affirmative," the flat voice said.

In concise sentences Darzek described what had happened on Yorlq, and on Primores since his return. At the end he asked lamely, "Did you understand all of that?"

"Affirmative."

"Do you want me to go over any of it again?"

"Negative."

"Have you any instructions?"

"Negative."

"None at all?" Darzek exclaimed unbelievingly. "The Dark will soon move again. Primores is in danger. *You* are in danger!"

"Negative."

Darzek took a deep breath. "Am I to continue supplying the Dark worlds?"

"Affirmative."

"I'd like to be placed in charge of this world's proctors."

"More data requested."

"If we can squelch the agitators, it may not be too late to save Primores."

"Primores is not in danger," the voice said laconically.

"If you're wrong, and I happen to think you are, I want to be able to protect you when the Dark comes. Where on Primores is your main location?"

"Everywhere."

Darzek hesitated, and then asked again, "Where are you?"

"Everywhere."

"Should the traders be encouraged to organize a resistance?"

"Negative."

Suddenly Darzek realized that he was not alone. A native stood near the door, waiting respectfully.

"What do you want?" Darzek demanded.

"I am URSGwalus. Supreme has appointed me to assist you. You are to report to Supreme through me."

Darzek regarded him coldly. "Why?"

"Supreme prefers indited reports."

"I see. Would you kindly inform Supreme that I prefer a non-native as an assistant?"

"Non-native?" URSGwalus repeated bewilderedly.

"Someone from another solar system."

"There is no such person available."

"Not even one?"

"Not among the servants of Supreme."

"The situation is worse than I thought."

"I beg your pardon?"

"Kindly inform Supreme that in the absence of precise instructions I shall carry on along the same lines, as I see fit."

URSGwalus tapped out the message and read the reply. "Affirmative."

"May I have a private consultation with Supreme whenever I deem it necessary?" Darzek asked.

"If Supreme consents."

"Then I have nothing more to say. Kindly show me the way out of this place."

"I don't like it," Miss Schlupe announced.

"Neither do I. Supreme insists that Primores is not in danger. Supreme must exist in a dream world. How many agents do you have?"

"Twenty-eight."

"I wish it was ten times that many. The traders would help, but what I have in mind requires natives."

"What do you have in mind?"

"Action. For once I'm going to act *before* the Dark does."

16

The crowd was the largest that Darzek had seen. At least fifty natives had gathered at a convergence of park paths, and as the first arrivals drifted away others took their places. They came, they listened impassively, they moved on.

urSDwad hung back at the rear of the crowd, waiting for a signal. Darzek gave it to him and watched what followed as tensely as a playwright enjoying an opening night performance.

urSDwad edged forward, waited until the agitator paused for breath, and then brushed past him. Darzek was too far away to hear what was said, but he had rehearsed the lines a hundred times, and he mouthed them himself as urSDwad spoke. *Something important has happened. I must talk with you at once.*

urSDwad walked away quickly without a backward glance. The agitator delivered a final, screaming rant, and hurried after him.

urSDwad spoke over his shoulder. *We're being watched. Go on ahead, and wait for me at the end of the park.* They separated, and met again at the park transmitting station. urSDwad touched out a destination. *You first. Hurry!* The agitator stepped through, to a wholly unexpected reception. urSDwad turned away with something remarkably akin to a smirk of triumph on his ugly face.

"Will you come into my parlor said the spider to the fly," Darzek murmured. "It's a smash hit. Let's take it on the road."

"urSDwad should have followed him," Miss Schlupe said. "And he'd better stage his next performance in some other park."

"I agree. Speak to him about it. He also should try to do something about that smirk. But it works. Now I want to see if our ex-agitator has anything constructive to say."

But the agitator, when he got over being incoherently bewildered, would say nothing at all. By then ᴜʀsDwad had brought in three more agitators, and the remainder of Miss Schlupe's detective squad was moving into action. In three days Darzek had a thousand prisoners on his hands, none of whom would speak except to recite, parrotlike, the all-too-familiar cant against foreigners.

Concentration camp facilities were difficult to come by on Primores. Just as the operation seemed about to break down because there was no accommodation for more prisoners, and no one to guard them if accommodation should be found, Gud Baxak arrived. He had purchased a hundred more spaceships, and Darzek ordered one of these fitted for passengers, and shipped the agitators off to a Dark world whose populace was properly grateful for Darzek's ministrations and in no mood to tolerate any nonsense from those who had been spreading the gospel of the Dark.

Gud Baxak brought a distressing report on the activities of agitators on surrounding worlds. Even if Primores were defended successfully, it seemed likely that it would become an island completely surrounded by the Dark.

"But there's nothing I can do about that," Darzek told himself. "One world at a time is as much as I can handle."

They were five days in accumulating another thousand prisoners, and the third thousand required ten days of intense work. Every abduction came off smoothly, but there had been a sharp falling off in the number of agitators available. Darzek shipped out the last thousand and went with Miss Schlupe on a tour of the parks.

"I'd like it better if some of them would talk," Miss Schlupe said.

"I doubt if any of them know anything. The first agitators had to be recruited by foreigners, but after that the natives would do their own recruiting. Probably none of our three thousand has had any contact with the persons behind this."

"Then your smash hit is a flop. All they have to do is recruit more agitators."

"Not at all. At the very least we've upset their time schedule, and they can't recruit them anything like as fast as we can pick them up. From now on I want your detectives to work in teams—one to do the abducting, and the others to watch carefully for a foreigner who seems unduly interested in the proceedings. He might even try to interfere. He's the one we want."

"Right. It's high time they started getting curious about what's happening to their agitators. These foreigners won't come willingly, so there'll have to be enough muscle to stuff them into the transmitters. I'll set up four teams of seven."

"That should do it."

Darzek patiently made his rounds. He went first to E-Wusk, who had submerged himself in statistics relating to the Dark's next move. E-Wusk said bewilderedly, "Everything is proceeding according to pattern except here on Primores. The parks should be full of agitators; instead, they've almost disappeared."

"Fancy that," Darzek murmured.

He found Gul Meszk in the throes of despondency. Having recruited an army, he didn't know what to do with it. Worse, the housing shortage had forced him to scatter his recruits through all of the worlds of the Primores system, and he had no better than a vague idea of where his army was.

"Isn't anyone in charge?" Darzek asked.

Meszk gestured despairingly. He had been too busy recruiting to look after the recruits he already had. Gul Ceyh had heroically accepted the task, but he had accomplished nothing. Gul Kaln was acting as his assistant, but he was kept busy trying to persuade the recruits not to give up and go home. Gul Isc had accepted the task of locating Supreme. He had not done so. Gul Halvr was trading again, doing a brisk business importing food to Primores. (Darzek winced, remembering E-Wusk's prediction of an increased consumption of food when the Dark threatened.) Gul

Rhinzl also was trading again, but was helping as much as he could whenever anyone could think of anything for him to do. The *efa*, despite their ignominious Yorlq behavior, were posturing as military commanders and seeking to oust Gul Ceyh—who was perfectly willing to be ousted. Gul Azfel had become disgusted with the whole business. Dark or no Dark, he wasn't forgetting that he had daughters to marry off, and he was planning a symposium.

Meszk said pleadingly, "Come with me to see Gul Rhinzl."

Darzek went without protest, and from the murky depths of an impromptu dark room Rhinzl greeted him enthusiastically. "Gul Isc just left," he said. "He has two hundred people making inquiries, and for all they've been able to find out, Supreme might be located at the end of the galaxy. Either end." He paused. "Gul Darr, the fate of an individual becomes unimportant when the fate of an entire galaxy is at stake. I sympathize with your desire to find a refuge from the Dark, but if the Dark takes Supreme there will be no refuge anywhere. I ask you in the name of all of the traders: Help us."

"What do you want me to do?"

"Join us. Take command of the defense. You seem to understand such things. The rest of us don't, but we do understand the need for action. We are willing to do anything, to make any sacrifice, if only someone in whom we have confidence will tell us what must be done."

"If I could be certain that all of the traders agreed with you—"

"They do," Meszk said quickly. "I've asked them."

"I see. I know the time is short, but I must think about this before I decide."

Alone in the small room he called an office, he attempted to sort out his jumbled impressions. He had never completely abandoned his notion that one of the traders was an agent of the Dark; but the Dark's area of conquest was so vast, its conquered worlds so numerous, that no one trader could be contributing more than local assistance. He rejected emphatically the notion that the Dark was a conspiracy on the part of many traders. No group of traders would participate in a plot that was ruinous to trade.

"The more I learn," Darzek muttered, "the less I know."

The Dark's weapon, for example. The idea of a force that twisted minds was absurd, and yet—surely the natives of so many worlds should not have succumbed to the agitators' crude lies. There had to be *something* that aroused them to frenzies of hatred.

Darzek opened the door and summoned URSGwalus into the room. The servant of Supreme had taken his appointment as Darzek's assistant as a license to haunt him. He camped out in Darzek's apartment, waiting expectantly for the reports to Supreme that Darzek had no intention of entrusting to him.

"Have you ever heard the word, 'Grilf'?" Darzek asked him.

"Grilf, grilf, grilf," URSGwalus ruminated. "No, I do not think so."

"Ask Supreme about it. I'd like a report on its etymology."

URSGwalus departed happily, and Darzek resumed his pacing.

Later that day URSQwor, one of Miss Schlupe's younger detectives, came with a strange tale to tell. "I was resting at home during the *tompl*—" he began.

Darzek nodded. Among the natives, the *tompl* was the time of day's end relaxation and casual visiting.

"A stranger called and invited me to attend a *sef*."

"What's a *sef*?" Darzek asked.

"I don't know. That is, I didn't know then, and I'm not sure that I know now. He was very friendly about it. He assured me that I'd find it interesting and enjoyable, so I went with him. He led me to an apartment. There were thirty-seven people present when we arrived."

Darzek whistled, and URSQwor added apologetically, "I counted them."

"Good for you."

"Seventeen more arrived shortly."

Darzek whistled again. "Where did they put them?"

"In all of the rooms. Then we were spoken to—the way the agitators speak in the parks. When it was over I reported to ursDwad, my team leader, and he went with the others of my team and took possession of the place and the three who were in charge of it. They were already starting another *sef*."

"Is this the first you've heard of these *sefs?*"

"It's the first that any of us have heard of them."

"I see. You've done a good job of work. Congratulations."

ursQwor demurely murmured his thanks.

"Have you told Gula Schlu about this?"

"She was out, and ursDwad thought the matter sufficiently important for your attention."

"Quite right. Tell ursDwad to call everyone in. There'll have to be a general briefing on this."

Miss Schlupe returned, took one glance at Darzek's face, and asked, "What's the matter now?"

"We have a crisis on our hands. The Dark has gone underground on us. While we were concentrating on the parks, it subjected the entire population of Primores to an indoor lecture course."

Miss Schlupe chased her detectives into action, and when finally they reported back they'd been unable to find a single citizen of Primores who hadn't attended several *sefs*. Some had attended a dozen or more.

"So why haven't we heard about them?" Darzek demanded.

"I've been working my detectives too hard. Today was the first time in ages that any of them have been free when these *sefs* were going on."

Darzek regarded her stonily. "The Dark isn't very inventive, but it certainly is ingenious about adapting its techniques to local conditions."

"If only these Primorians weren't so confoundedly polite," she wailed. "When they're invited somewhere, etiquette demands that they accept. What can we do? We can't police every private dwelling and apartment on the planet."

"Raid the *sefs* just as fast as you can locate them."

She threw up her hands despairingly.

"We're too late to stop it anyway," Darzek said. "The entire native population has already been exposed. But we have to try, and there's always a chance that we might stumble onto a really important agent."

"We should have thought of something like this. Maybe the Dark's mental weapon *is* working on us."

"I'd like to blame the Dark, but I'd have to admit that it would be a strange kind of weapon that could induce stupidity. But carry on. The only thing left for me to do is take charge of the traders' army and try to protect Supreme."

The traders' purportedly vast army had dwindled to a mere ten thousand potentially active traders and undertraders. Gul Meszk was humiliated, but Darzek said grimly, "We haven't the time to train half that many. Let's get on with it."

He chose ten competent leaders, told each of them to select a hundred of the youngest, sturdiest and most agile types available, and moved the whole contingent to Meszk's Primores II plantation. He ordered Gud Baxak to keep a ship standing by, just in case—as he expected—he needed emergency transportation back to Primores O.

Rhinzl located a stock of light but sturdy metal piping, and Darzek had this cut into suitable lengths for weapons and trained his troops as he had the shock troops on Yorlq. The promise of action worked wonders for their morale, and they drilled tirelessly.

Darzek added another thousand troops as quickly as Gul Kaln could obtain housing for them, and then a third thousand. He drove them mercilessly during the day, held a night school for his officers, and tried to convince himself that at last he was doing the right thing. Rhinzl put together two companies of nocturnals and trained them himself, and several dozen times each night disturbed everyone's sleep with his screeching order, "Charge!"

They had been at it for ten days when Miss Schlupe came to look on. She watched two battalions stage a sham battle, and announced cheerfully, "They look *good!*"

"Better than on Yorlq," Darzek agreed. "We had a better selection of troops, and we've had more time to train them."

"Then why are you so gloomy?"

"I still don't know what to do with them. If there was one vital area to defend, I think I could do it. But Supreme is everywhere. It said so itself."

"If you can't find a vital area to defend, maybe the natives won't be able to find one to attack."

"No." Darzek shook his head emphatically. "That won't do. Who charges Supreme's batteries and polishes its transistors? There have to be natives who know all about Supreme—thousands, probably, but if even one knows, Supreme is doomed."

"Tsk. Any moment, now, you'll have me believing in that mental weapon. Cheer up. Things are going well, or at least no worse than they were. I have a packet of news for you."

"Let's have it."

"Your ursGwalus is still haunting the place, waiting for you to report to Supreme. He says Supreme knows nothing about the word 'Grilf' except that it appears in reports on the Dark."

"Supreme knows only what it's told, and no one has been able to tell it much about the Dark."

"The Chief of Proctors is haunting me," Miss Schlupe went on. "Someone tipped him off that I'm responsible for the *sef* raids, and he's against them."

"Did you tell him the *sefs* were threatening the public safety?"

"Not in those words, but I tried to get the idea across. He wouldn't believe me. It seems that I'm violating a whole list of unwritten regulations. He ordered me to turn everyone loose and not do it any more."

"Refer him to me."

"I did. I told him I was following your orders, and you were working directly for Supreme. He retired to think it over. Probably he'll ask Supreme about it."

Darzek shrugged. "What about the *sefs?*"

"We're raiding them as fast as we can locate them. Gud

Baxak's shipped off another thousand agitators. He's complaining again about our tying up his ships."

"Tell him to buy more ships."

"I did. E-Wusk wants to see you. He keeps sending messages."

"I'll go back with you, and see him and have another heart-to-heart talk with Supreme. What else?"

"Did you know that the Dark was running a courier service? It is. One of Gud Baxak's captains intercepted it. The person in charge—this will slay you—claimed he was working for Supreme."

"That's very interesting. They're bringing him back, of course."

"Gud Baxak was indignant when I suggested it. Worlds are starving, he's building a trading empire, and how can he get any work done if he has to reroute a spaceship because of one lousy agent of the Dark? This is what comes of not letting your left hand know what your right hand is doing. No, it's all right. I convinced him, but I'm afraid he'll take his own time about it."

"Schluppy, what would I do without you?"

"Work harder, probably. You certainly wouldn't have any time for playing soldier."

URSGwalus escorted Darzek to a different consultation room, one that did not require him to run the gamut of Supreme's identification system, and Darzek thanked him sincerely. As soon as he was alone he began to describe the *sefs*. "The situation is hopelessly out of control," he said. "Every native on Primores has been exposed to the Dark's propaganda. We have to assume that the planet will be lost whenever the Dark decides to move."

Supreme's flat voice announced, "Primores is not in danger."

Darzek counted to ten—slowly—and went on, "I am training a small force drawn from the staffs of traders. I can't defend Primores with it, but I think I could effectively protect Supreme's vital areas if I knew where they were. Where should I deploy this force?"

"Supreme's vital areas are protected."

That gave Darzek pause, for it could easily have been true. Then he reminded himself that Supreme's protective devices would be useless against the Dark's subversion. Supreme had no way of knowing when a trusted servant had gone mad.

"Supreme," Darzek announced, "is a damned fool."

And left.

E-Wusk, looking a bit more shriveled, a bit. more faded, did not speak when Darzek entered. He unrolled a seemingly endless strip of inditing material and moved it past Darzek's face. Gradually the wavy lines straightened out, moved closer together, and in a final, jagged swoop, merged.

"I think I understand," Darzek said. "You're able to project these statistics of yours, and when the lines intersect the Dark should move. When will it be?"

"Yesterday," E-Wusk said hoarsely. "The Dark moved yesterday."

17

Gul Isc pointed a trembling finger. "There!" he said. His voice quavered with excitement.

A door.

Darzek wondered why he hadn't noticed it before, which was silly. He hadn't noticed it because he hadn't looked. He'd spent uncounted hours in the parks, but all of it had been directed at watching the natives, not at searching the transparent domes for an outmoded means of egression.

"There!" Gul Isc said, pointing again.

Between the park and the nearest building a strange structure slanted out of the ground, to terminate in a gaping opening.

"A ventilating system," Darzek said in an awed whisper. "I've always assumed that Supreme was underground. Let's have a look at it."

They rippled open the door and moved across a patch of sunlight to the opening. A strong current of hot air blew steadily into their faces as they strained to see down the dark, slanting tunnel.

"This is an exit vent," Darzek announced. "So somewhere there'll be an air intake. There may even be several of each."

"Several?" Gul Isc exclaimed, crestfallen. "Then even if we guarded this one, the natives could still—"

"Cheer up, my friend! You've done an excellent piece of work and given us the first break we've had. It doesn't matter how many ways the natives can get in, if only we can get in ahead of them."

"Ah!" Gul Isc squirmed with excitement. "Once we're inside, we can find those other ways and block them off."

"Right," Darzek said, peering into the gloom of the tunnel. "This looks like a job for Rhinzl's nocturnals. Would you pass the order for me? I want Rhinzl to bring both of his companies immediately. Tell Gul Kaln and Gul Meszk to place my entire force on alert and report to me here. As soon as Rhinzl arrives—but let's get away from this place before someone sees us."

They separated in the park's shrubbery, Gul Isc to deliver the orders and Darzek to pick his way to the opposite side, where Miss Schlupe and ursDwad were gazing about them in shocked disbelief.

The park thronged with agitators. They seemed to have materialized out of the air, so suddenly had they appeared, and the ferocity of their shrieking vituperation startled even Darzek, who had thought himself inured to their ranting.

Miss Schlupe looked on helplessly, shaking her head. ursDwad was watching them as a constrained cat might eye a scurrying horde of mice.

"Are you sure you don't want them picked up?" Miss Schlupe shouted.

"There are too many of them," Darzek shouted back. "It would take an army."

"So? You have an army."

Darzek nodded. "And I have something better for it to do—I think."

He could take some small measure of satisfaction from the fact that he *had* upset the Dark's schedule. The Dark had moved, the entire center of the galaxy had fallen, and Primores and its sister planets were still resisting. They were isolated islands of light in a sea of darkness; but the Dark had craftily thrown in its reserves, and its tide was running strongly. The end might come in a matter of hours.

Darzek beckoned ursDwad away and told him to keep an unobtrusive watch on the air vent. Then he went back to wait for Rhinzl.

Night had fallen before Rhinzl's nocturnals finally arrived. Darzek waited uncomplainingly; he could not fairly expect his makeshift army to perform with lightning reflexes, and in truth, the situation on Primores always seemed less critical under a comforting blanket of darkness. Most of the agitators subsided at sunset and went their separate ways, and the parks were quiet.

Rhinzl led Darzek down the sloping tunnel, guiding him with a hand's gentle touch. Ranks of nocturnals followed smartly, and as Darzek felt his way forward in total darkness he could hear only the measured thump of marching feet echoing behind him.

At the bottom they came upon a heavy grating, beyond which the tunnel made a vertical plunge to infinity, or at least beyond Rhinzl's sight. Rhinzl turned to one side, opened a door, and led Darzek through it. The dark passageway took an abrupt turn, and a long, red-lit tunnel lay before them.

"Wait!" Darzek snapped, as Rhinzl stepped forward. "I wouldn't want to walk through there unless Supreme itself invited me."

"Really? What would happen?"

"I don't know. I've experienced it twice when I *was* invited, and I don't remember either occasion with pleasure. I doubt if it would be worth the risk, because the tunnel will end at a transmitter that won't work if Supreme doesn't like you."

"Strange," Rhinzl mused. "If Supreme is so well protected, why are we to guard it?"

"There'll be natives who have Supreme's permission to come and go. When the mania of the Dark comes upon them they'll still have that permission."

"I understand. We are to prevent them from entering."

"You're to prevent anyone from entering, and you must take care to impress upon your troops that they aren't to enter, either."

"No one shall enter," Rhinzl said confidently. "I'll post a strong guard at the top of the tunnel, and another at the bottom."

"You won't need two companies for that. Your other noc-

turnals can start looking for more air vents. At dawn the rest of
the army will take over."

"Except in the tunnel?" Rhinzl suggested.

"Yes. You should organize shifts of nocturnals to guard the
tunnel."

"There may be many such vents."

"I'm afraid so. I'd hoped that we could reach all of them from
here, but obviously we can't. There are also the transmitter
connections with Supreme, and Supreme alone knows how many
of those there may be. This is a hopeless task, but we're bound to
do the best we can."

"We are bound to," Rhinzl agreed. He posted guards and led
the other nocturnals into the darkness to search for air vents.

At dawn Darzek received a staggering piece of news. Gul
Meszk, who had taken Darzek's admonition to look everywhere
literally, reported in from the opposite side of the planet. In
Primores's second city he had discovered another air vent. Darzek
inspected it, found the same type of slanting tunnel terminating
in a drop-off. Thoughtfully he posted a guard.

"I thought Supreme would be large," he told Miss Schlupe,
"but this is preposterous."

"Supreme has a good many different functions. They may be
located in different places."

"Obviously. One under every populated area, I suppose. Or
perhaps the populated areas grew up wherever Supreme was
located. This leaves me with the same problem I had in the
beginning: How can I guard a planet?"

"There's one slight difference. Time has run out on you. Have
you seen the parks today?"

Darzek shook his head.

"This is the day. If your army fights better when it has lines of
retreat, this may be your last chance to make the arrangements."

"I've already asked Gud Baxak to put every available ship in
orbit," Darzek said.

With ursDwad he began a circuit of the parks.

The agitators were out in full cry and overwhelming numbers, but Darzek had eyes only for the spectators. There were few of them, and they listened with the same stoic calm he'd been observing for so many days. The only emotion they betrayed was one of quiet puzzlement. They paused, listened indifferently, strolled on.

"Look!" ᴜʀsDwad exclaimed.

It was a foreigner, of a type Darzek had never seen before. Darzek watched dumbfounded as he waved spidery arms and added his chirping harangue to those of the native agitators.

"Why would they send foreigners to tell us to rise against foreigners?" ᴜʀsDwad demanded.

"It's the climax. Either that, or—" He turned to stare at ᴜʀsDwad. "Come on!" he snapped.

He led him on a reckless chase through park after park, searching for foreign agitators. They found hundreds of them, the pathetic accretion of the Dark's trek across the galaxy, all spewing their strange languages into the clamorous maelstrom of hate that swirled under the park domes. Most were unfamiliar types, but Darzek saw several Yorlqers and two of the ungainly, stalklike Quarmers, who seemed to turn up in sinister fashion whenever he contested with the Dark.

Finally they returned to Darzek's apartment. Miss Schlupe was there, talking quietly with Gul Meszk and Gul Kaln. ᴜʀsGwalus hovered patiently in the background, ready to resume his haunting the moment Darzek appeared.

"It's all over," Darzek announced. "The Dark has lost. All of its foreign agents have been turned out in a last, desperate attempt to move the natives, and the natives aren't having any of it. Supreme was right. Primores is not in danger. Supreme knows something that we don't know."

"Are you sober?" Miss Schlupe demanded.

"The Dark has only one move left," Darzek told Gul Meszk. "It can arm its agitators and foreign agents with the best weapons available and try to take control of Primores. We'd better start picking them up, and fast. I want you to seal off the parks, three or four at a time. Send the innocent natives home, and tell them to stay there. Take portable transmitters with you, and pack all of the agitators off to the ships. Put as many as you can into each passenger compartment, and then disconnect the compartment's transmitter. If they're feeling violent they can take it out on each other, and we'll sort through the pieces after they've quieted down."

"Right!" Meszk said happily. He and Gul Kaln hurried away.

"Are you sober?" Miss Schlupe asked again.

"I'm enjoying the heady intoxication of a momentous discovery, even though I can't begin to understand it. On every world where the Dark has been active, it induced madness in the natives and incited them against the foreigners. Why are the natives of Primores indifferent to it?"

uRsGwalus said apologetically, "If you will pardon me—"

"What is it now?"

"If you will pardon me, I venture to point out that Primores has no natives."

Darzek snorted. "What are they, then? Ghosts? They look substantial enough to me. uRsDwad, are you a ghost?"

"No, Sire."

"Aren't you a native of Primores?"

uRsDwad hesitated.

"Primores O has no natives," uRsGwalus said, "because Primores O is an artificial world! Why else would it bear the designation 'O'? It was built after the other Primores worlds had been numbered."

Darzek said blankly, "Primores O is *artificial?*"

"Primores O is Supreme, and Supreme is a world. Of course. No world would be large enough to contain it. It is so large that it must *be* a world."

"That can't be the whole answer," Darzek protested. "What about the other Primores worlds? Surely one of them has a native population."

"Primores II is the original home of those who populate this system."

"Then why didn't the natives of Primores II revolt? And those who live and work on Primores O must have been here long enough to consider themselves natives, artificial world or no. Why didn't they revolt?"

ᴜʀsGwalus made no answer.

"And what about the agitators?" Darzek went on. "Most of them have been Primorians."

"Their conduct is beyond my comprehension," ᴜʀsGwalus admitted. "It is beyond the comprehension of any of us. We Primorians dedicate our lives to the service of foreigners. They call us servants of Supreme, but we are not. We are servants of the galaxy. So is Supreme a servant of the galaxy. Why should we force the foreigners to leave? We welcome them. They are the reason for our existence."

"Yes," Darzek said slowly. "That might account for the Dark's failure to take Primores. It *must* account for it. And yet—"

"There were an awful lot of Primorian agitators," Miss Schlupe remarked.

Darzek nodded. "Any life form could be expected to have its fair share of paranoids and idiots, though. The question is why whole populations went paranoid on other worlds, but not on Primores. Could a mere sense of loyalty and duty be stronger than the Dark's weapon?"

Gul Meszk burst from the transmitter. "Gul Darr!" he gasped. "The *efa*—" He panted helplessly.

"Take your time," Darzek told him. "What about the *efa*?"

"Their command has gone mad. It is attacking Supreme."

They overtook the *efa*'s companies in the park near the air vent. The troops were shouting, shoving, swinging their pipe weapons wildly, fighting to be the next through the door. Brokefa circled them at a safe distance, pleading pathetically, and they laughed at him. Linhefa lay crumpled upon the grass, the victim of a swinging pipe.

Darzek drew his automatic. He fired over their heads, and so great was the din that he hardly heard the shot. He tried to force his way through them, and narrowly missed being felled himself. He could only holster his gun, and watch helplessly.

Then Gul Kaln arrived with reinforcements. Darzek formed them up, and they cleared the *efa's* troops away from the door with one determined rush.

Darzek leaped through. Perhaps fifty had already reached the tunnel, and they paused there, with their leaders looking down into the darkness, while from somewhere inside Rhinzl pleaded with them. His voice reached Darzek faintly, and was buried in a sudden, crashing shout as the troops charged into the tunnel.

Darzek, following closely, stumbled over Rhinzl. He had been knocked down and trampled. He got slowly to his feet, moaning with pain. "They wouldn't listen to me," he gasped. "What happened?"

"I don't know."

Meszk had caught up with him, with a company of loyal troops on his heels. Darzek dashed on ahead, plunging blindly into the darkness, and the limping Rhinzl kept pace with him, whimpering as he ran. From the bottom of the tunnel came the clash of battle as the nocturnal guards put up a valiant but vain resistance. They were overwhelmed before Darzek could reach them, and the *efa's* troops fumbled their way past the door and into the passageway beyond, and with a shout of triumph rushed into the red-lit tunnel that led to Supreme.

A shriek of hideous pain brought Darzek up short and left him cringing. Scream followed upon scream as strange sounds echoed through the tunnel and weirdly reflected flames bathed it in flickering light and grotesque shadow. Darzek was startled to find Miss Schlupe at his side, her head bowed, her hands clapped to her ears. ursDwad cowered nearby, and Rhinzl was huddled in a convulsive, unrecognizable mass. Darzek looked again, saw Rhinzl heave himself into a familiar shape, saw Meszk looking strangely pale in the red reflection, saw the looming shadows that came and went on the wall behind them.

The sounds died away, but the flickering light lingered. Darzek drew his automatic and announced to no one in particular, "It's the only way."

And shot Rhinzl.

He pulled the trigger again and again, oblivious to Miss Schlupe's scream and Meszk's baffled cry, until Rhinzl's body collapsed shapelessly in a sticky splash and slowly spread long filaments of ooze over the tunnel floor.

Then the light died away, and they were in darkness.

18

The beauty of Primores O had been ruined for Darzek. Those gleaming lakes were perhaps solar power intakes, the symmetrical hills existed only because they conformed to some humped requirement of Supreme, and the brilliant orange vegetation was a heat absorbent with the crucial mission of keeping Supreme's feet warm.

Even the rainbow atmosphere that hung about the planet like a shimmering halo had been appended as an afterthought. The domed parks were proof that the planet's surface had once been airless.

He turned away from the spaceship's viewing screen, and said to Gul Kaln, "I think there should be some smoke."

"Smoke?" Kaln echoed blankly.

"Colored smoke, with a whiff of exotic scent. Could you manage it?"

"The chamber would fill up with smoke," Kaln protested.

"The idea is to lend a touch of mystery, and also to screen the interior. Couldn't the doors be moved in, and smoke placed outside each end?"

"Yes. I could do that. How many chambers will you need?"

"No idea. Whatever it will take to pass a million million people through in a reasonable time."

Kaln shuddered. "Thousands. Maybe millions."

"Then that's how many we'll need. Get to work on it. You have unlimited solvency."

Kaln waved his arms despairingly and stepped into the transmitter.

E-Wusk stirred from a meditative tangle of arms and legs and remarked, "These are bitter times, my friend, and my mind is confused. The *thing* that you showed to me was not the Rhinzl that I knew."

"Supreme has confirmed that no such life form is known to this galaxy," Darzek said.

"I am sure that you acted wisely, but I cannot help regretting that you killed him. There is much that he could have told us."

"And nothing that he would have told us. I'm not so sure that what I did was wise, but it was necessary. I didn't know what weapons that tangle of living tissue concealed."

"Or what *powers?*" E-Wusk suggested. "Of course he had the power to make us see him differently from what he was."

"Yes. His true shape was so gruesome that even in a galaxy of gruesome shapes he would have been a thing apart, and therefore instantly suspect."

"And yet the Dark's mental weapon must be a different kind of power."

"Entirely different," Darzek agreed. "Primores may be safe for the moment, but unless we identify that power and learn how to contain it, the Dark will engulf the rest of the galaxy."

Miss Schlupe stumbled from the transmitter, and liquid sloshed over the brim of the goblet she was carrying and slowly settled to the deck. "Dratted transmitters!" she muttered.

Darzek took the goblet, tasted, licked his lips thoughtfully. "It's almost too good. I don't suppose you could make some that would be tasteless."

"I'm afraid not. How much do you need?"

"That depends on how susceptive the Primorians are to mass psychology. Make the stuff as fast as you can, and let's hope there'll be enough. Any news of my friends the proctors?"

"They're hueing and crying all over the planet. Five of them are still camped in our apartment. I told them I thought you'd done away with yourself in a fit of remorse, and they politely asked me where the body was."

E-Wusk said bewilderedly, "The proctors are searching for *you?*"

"Why did you think I was hiding out in space when there's so much work to be done? I got tired thinking up new identities for myself. 'Pardon, Sire, but I was wondering if you were the elusive Gul Darr, whom you most strongly resemble.' Certainly not. *My name is John Wellington Wells, I'm a dealer in magic and spells.* Bah! Every transmitting exchange, every park and public building is infested with proctors looking for me."

"But why?"

"I committed a dastardly crime: to wit, I caused the death of that eminent and widely respected trader, Gul Rhinzl. The proctors have also linked me with some Quarmers who were found dead under highly suspicious circumstances a long time back. They can be surprisingly efficient when they put their minds to it."

"But if you're really an agent of Supreme—"

"Don't mention Supreme to me. If I knew how, I'd blank out all of its memory circuits and make it start over, *cum tabula rasa.* No sooner did I report that I had disposed of Rhinzl, who was undeniably an agent of the Dark if not the Dark itself, when some remote transistor figuratively ran up a red flag and every proctor on the planet wanted me for that most horrible and rare of crimes, inflicting death. URsGwalus has been trying every way he can think of to convince Supreme that I acted in the line of duty, and Supreme absolves me of responsibility at the same time that it deputizes another army of proctors to track me down. Supreme needs someone to tell it what to do. That's why I wanted to see you."

"Excuse me," Miss Schlupe said. "I have fifty vats of beer cooking."

Darzek absently waved her away, and she tiptoed into the transmitter.

E-Wusk looked after her thoughtfully. "I feel sorry for Gula

Schlu. She was fond of Rhinzl. This must have been a painful shock to her."

"In a way. It pained her to realize that he wanted to marry her so he could find out what she and I were up to. She thinks I shouldn't have killed him, but only because that deprived her of the pleasure of kicking him to death."

E-Wusk managed a bewildered laugh.

"We desperately need a new Council of Supreme," Darzek said. "I think you should be one of the members. I'm going to tell Supreme to appoint you as the Council's expert in trade."

E-Wusk stared. "You couldn't! No one tells Supreme whom to appoint to the Council!"

"It's time someone did. Supreme's last choices didn't turn out well. I want a Council made up of members who are competent, trustworthy, receptive to new ideas, and willing to work."

"At least I qualify as to my willingness to work."

"I'll chance the rest of it," Darzek said. "I'll be in touch with you. And if the proctors come asking for Gul Darr, tell them this is the season when his kind goes into hibernation."

Miss Schlupe squared her shoulders, gazed down at the front of her new dress, and announced, "I look matronly."

"You look like yourself in a padded dress," Darzek said. "I still have my doubts about this."

"A little purgative never hurt anybody."

"I'm not worried about making a few people sick, though I wish we didn't have to. I'm afraid we'll be too successful and create a monster. There'd be small profit in saving people from the Dark by panicking them into destroying themselves."

"We'll keep it under control. Did anyone ever tell you that you'd make an excellent astrologer? The beard accentuates your classic profile, and the robes add just the right aura of mystery. The skull cap was a mistake, though. You need a pointed hat."

"I still think the beard would have been disguise enough."

"I still think you didn't have to come. Well—here goes."

She approached the next table, genuflected, and with her left hand held out a small medallion. Her right hand concealed a bulb, from which a tube ran up her sleeve and connected with the liquid-filled container that amplified her figure. Darzek hoped it wouldn't gurgle as it emptied.

"I found this near the transmitters," she said, waving the medallion. "Did you lose it?"

The diner, a gaunt Sqoffer, withdrew his proboscis from a goblet of liquid, scrutinized the medallion, and replied in the negative. "Have you ever seen it before?" Miss Schlupe persisted. "Do you know who could have lost it?"

Another negative. Miss Schlupe repeated the formula with his dining partner, and then moved to the next table. She left behind her two goblets generously laced with the synthetic rhubarb beer that she had manufactured from a Primores II herb.

The Sqoffers absently returned their proboscises to the goblets, and resumed their contemplation of the Primorian landscape. Darzek watched them tensely. The project turned on the question of how diluted the beer could be before it lost potency. The Sqoffers noticed nothing wrong with their drinks, which was favorable; but they were showing no ill effects, which was a pity.

Miss Schlupe was four tables away, and performing her routine with the practiced and engaging nonchalance of a hussy administering knockout drops. She zigzagged across the room, reached the far side, turned back. Darzek continued to watch the Sqoffers.

Someone screamed.

At the center of the room a native Primorian had lurched to his feet. He stood doubled up in agony, moaning softly. The diner who had screamed lay threshing on the floor nearby. The room was suddenly silent, except for moans and a widely scattered retching.

"I think it's time we got sick," Darzek said, as Miss Schlupe quietly returned to her chair. He clutched at his stomach and moaned, and Miss Schlupe, whose figure was now somewhat less matronly, produced a highly realistic abdominal spasm.

Abruptly the two Sqoffers made a break for the transmitters, proboscises flailing, gaping mouths spraying vomit. Others followed, and the departures became a stampede that swept Darzek and Miss Schlupe along with it.

Minutes later they were in another dining room, and Miss Schlupe, again with a matronly figure, approached the next table. "I found this near the transmitters. Did you lose it?"

The chief proctor's pallor was ghastly. Even his bulging hump was a pasty white. Through a stroke of sheer good fortune Miss Schlupe had encountered him a short time before in a transfer station dining room, and maliciously administered a double dose of beer.

"*Plague?*" he wheezed feebly. "A plague—on Primores?"

Darzek, smugly secure behind his artificial beard, said gravely, "I have seen the symptoms. I have experienced them myself. Earlier today, in a public dining room, I and many others were seized with violent illness."

"Such a thing has never happened on Primores," the chief proctor wheezed. "It couldn't happen on Primores. Who are you?"

"Gul Zek. Chief medical officer of the planet Gwaar. At your service."

The chief proctor slumped lower in his chair. "Then it's true? You couldn't possibly be mistaken?"

"I couldn't possibly be mistaken."

The chief proctor fluttered his hands helplessly, and then covered his face. with them. "A plague—on Primores!"

"This plague," Darzek said authoritatively, "is known in our local medical circles as Guaarer Disease, because it first appeared on my planet. It is characterized by sudden abdominal pains and cramps, nausea, constriction of the limbs, and perhaps a regrettable voiding of the stomach and digestive tract. It passes, and the victim—" Darzek gazed intently at the chief proctor. "The victim is left in a state of pallor, experiencing extreme weakness and lassitude and a loss of appetite. He soon recovers—"

The chief proctor brightened.

"—until the next attack, of course. The attacks continue, the victim is finally unable to retain food of any kind, and in the end he starves to death."

The chief proctor covered his face again and moaned softly. "What are we to do?"

"Fortunately the plague, or Guaarer Disease, is easily arrested. One has only to pass the population of the planet through purification chambers."

"Ah!"

"But the plague will return at once if its carriers are not identified and isolated."

"Carriers? *Plague* carriers?"

"Unfortunate individuals who harbor the plague germs. They may not be ill themselves, but they carry death wherever they go. They must be identified and isolated, or the population of Primores is doomed."

"How is this to be accomplished?"

"With the purification chambers. These purify the innocent victims and detect the carriers who are spreading the plague." Darzek gestured grandly. "I have saved five planets from Guaarer Disease, and I can save another. On my own responsibility I placed an initial order for purification chambers as soon as I identified the disease. You have only to put your chief medical officer under my orders, and I'll guarantee to arrest the plague promptly."

Miss Schlupe was incredulous. "He swallowed it? *All* of it? Didn't he even ask to see your credentials?"

"It was almost suspiciously easy," Darzek admitted. "You'd better keep making the rounds, just in case he changes his mind. How's the beer holding out?"

"I have a new batch almost ready."

Darzek strode to the nearest chair and sat down. "All right. Let's have it."

"Have what?" she asked innocently.

"You cannot keep a secret from me. Your nose twitches when you try. What's happened?"

"Nothing, really, except that Gud Baxak finally brought in that agent of the Dark that his captain picked up. Do you want to see him?"

"I suppose I'd better. Where is he?"

She opened the door to the next room and stepped aside, shaking with laughter. The agent of the Dark moved forward. Darzek stared, and then leaped to embrace him.

"Smith!"

Smith pulled free and backed away, and Darzek's first surge of delight faded quickly. He fixed his eyes on Smith's familiarly hideous face, and said to Miss Schlupe, "Is that what Smith is? An agent of the Dark?"

"Nonsense!" Smith said angrily. "I am supervising inspector of certification groups. I was making my scheduled inspection of uncertified worlds, when your captain—"

"What were you doing inspecting uncertified worlds in the Dark's territory?" Darzek demanded.

"The Dark has not molested the uncertified worlds. Our certification groups are still functioning on all of them, and of course they must be supplied and supervised."

"Sit down," Darzek said. "Talk."

"There is nothing to talk about," Smith protested.

"There's plenty to talk about. Why would the Dark bite off huge chunks of the galaxy and scrupulously avoid the uncertified worlds? Do you think the Dark would pay any attention to that silly quarantine of yours?"

"I know no more about the Dark than what I told you during your indoctrination," Smith answered stiffly. "I only know that the uncertified worlds are the responsibility of the certification groups, and the Dark has not molested them."

"That's very interesting. It might even be significant. As soon as I've purified a million million people, I'll look into it."

"May I return to my work now?" Smith asked.

"You may not. We've needed your help all along, and if you try to run away now we'll have you quarantined as a plague carrier. Come with me, and I'll tell you what's been happening."

Gul Kaln was setting up a row of purification chambers in the main transmitting exchange. Already there were Primorians waiting patiently in line, many of them marked with the pale ravages of an involuntary beer binge. The chief proctor hadn't wasted any time in getting his orders out, and he was waiting himself, at the head of the line.

"Monstrous!" Smith muttered. "And to think it was I who brought you from Earth!"

"Insult me all you like, but keep it in English."

Gul Kaln approached them cheerfully. "We're almost ready. Would you like to be first?"

"Come on, Smith. Let's get purified."

"I refuse to take part in such imbecile proceedings."

"Suit yourself. But in a very few days anyone on this planet who can't show a purification mark will be subject to instant incarceration."

Sputtering protests, Smith trailed after him.

Darzek stepped through a thin screen of rainbow smoke at one end of an enormous, rectangular box. A door dropped open before him, and he moved into the eerie blue half-light of the interior. Lights flashed in sequence, sending his shadow leaping in all directions. His bearded image leered back at him from reflecting walls. Finally a door dropped open at the far end, and he emerged through the second screen of smoke and extended his hand to receive the purification mark.

"Very nice," he said to Gul Kaln. "Perfect, in fact."

Smith stumbled out of the smoke, coughing and snarling, though he was careful to do the snarling in English. "What do you expect to accomplish with this hocus-pocus?" he demanded.

"Sssh!" Darzek wagged a finger. "The natives believe in it."

"Of course they believe in it! This isn't an uncertified world. They aren't accustomed to liars such as you, so they believe."

"You weren't here when the rabble-rousers were functioning, or you'd have heard these certified paragons doing an inordinate amount of lying themselves. But never mind. I have work to do."

"What *are* you trying to accomplish?"

"Rhinzl had the power to make us see him other than as he was," Darzek explained. "Fortunately it was a limited power, and he didn't fully trust it. He remained in darkness as much as possible, and he never became aware of shadows. Probably he couldn't see them himself. The scientists think his vision was somehow based upon infra-red light."

"Then you killed him because you saw his shadow?"

Darzek nodded. "That was the second time I'd seen it. The first time was on Yorlq, but there it passed so quickly, and I had so many other things on my mind, that I didn't realize what I'd seen. In the tunnel the sudden flash of light from Supreme's defenses took him by surprise. For a split second I saw the real Rhinzl. Then he exerted his power, and his appearance changed. His shadow didn't."

"I see." Smith gestured at the purification chamber. "Then this is really designed to reveal shadows?"

"Shadows and reflections, from every angle. Six attendants will be watching constantly, and if any of them sees anything vaguely suspicious he'll touch a control that will seal the chamber. You see—the Dark covered such a vast area that Rhinzl couldn't possibly have done it all by himself. There are other Rhinzls, and some of them may be here on Primores. We simply must catch them before they act again. We must make Primores absolutely secure, and then we can go to work on the rest of the galaxy."

"Scrutinizing the shadows and reflections of every intelligent being in the galaxy will take a long time," Smith said dryly.

"It'll take forever. Even if we catch all of the Rhinzls, there are more where they came from."

"Couldn't you manage it without this hocus-pocus?"

"Perhaps Supreme could, but Supreme can't make up its alleged mind about anything without precedents. Then there's another problem. These Rhinzls aren't stupid. If word got out that we were shadow hunting, they'd soon figure out why and go into hiding. On the other hand, they're bound to be apprehensive about this galaxy's diseases. If we make the plague convincing enough, they should be just as eager to be purified as the natives. I don't like it myself, but I can't think of a better way to get the job done quickly."

"It's unethical to terrorize an entire planet."

"Don't talk to me about ethics," Darzek snapped. "I've seen your ethical, certified businessmen refusing food to a starving world that couldn't pay."

They returned to Darzek's new headquarters. Miss Schlupe was still energetically spreading the plague, and every time she came for more beer Smith regarded her with horror.

"This must stop," he protested.

"We can't simulate a plague without making a few people sick," Darzek said.

"I've been asking myself what it is that you've accomplished. You've had ample time. You've expended a shocking amount of solvency. Your principal mission was to identify the Dark's weapon, and you haven't done that."

"No. We don't know why the natives revolt."

"Now you're poisoning the population of Primores, and when you finish, even if you catch any of these alleged agents, you still won't have identified that weapon. You haven't accomplished anything, and I can't see that you ever will."

"I caught Rhinzl."

"Yes. You say he was an agent of the Dark, but he's dead— murdered by you—and who will ever know what he really was?"

"His body was preserved for study. Go have a look at it. One look has convinced everyone who's seen it."

"We who work with the uncertified worlds aren't so easily convinced. We know the depths to which intelligent beings can sink. What you did to Rhinzl—"

"Take a nap, or something," Darzek said wearily. "I want to think."

He paced the floor silently, ignoring Smith.

Rhinzl. On the available evidence, one of a small group of freebooters who had set forth to conquer the next galaxy as a Cortez or a Pizarro had conquered an Indian empire. There were too few of them to hold the territory they won, or perhaps they hadn't tried to hold it because Supreme had been their objective from the moment they knew it existed. When the death of SIX frustrated their attempt to subvert the Council, they simply fell back on their tested method of interplanetary conquest and continued to move toward the center of the galaxy.

The solvency Rhinzl amassed with his astute trading had supported the Dark financially, but solvency seemed to play a surprisingly small part in its success. "The weapon's the thing," Darzek muttered. Smith was right. Until the weapon was identified, he would have accomplished nothing.

And he did not like the way the supervising inspector of certification groups was glowering at him. Darzek sent off a message to Gul Kaln, and shortly thereafter Smith found himself the subject of the unwavering attention of a squad of soldiers.

They waited, and nothing happened. Miss Schlupe continued to spread the plague to the unpurified; Gul Kaln set up purification chambers in every transmitting exchange and transfer station and began branching out into the parks and other public places. He operated them continuously, and the citizens of Primores marched through them by the thousand. A day passed, and another day, and nothing happened.

ursDwad burst from the transmitter in a soaring leap. "We've caught one!" he panted.

"A nocturnal? Another Rhinzl?"

"Yes!"

Darzek turned to Smith. "Come along. If a dead agent of the Dark won't convince you, have a look at a live one."

Darzek had never seen a transmitting exchange's nocturnal level. Normally he could have seen nothing there, for they were darkened according to the needs of the most light-sensitive life form likely to use them.

This one blazed with light. Gul Kaln already had a company of troops on hand, the chief proctor was there with a formidable force of proctors, and all were grouped curiously about the purification chamber.

Darzek shouted them away. "Do you want to catch the plague?" he demanded.

They fell over each other in their hasty retreat. Darzek activated a viewer, set the chamber's lights flashing, and said, "Well?"

Smith caught his breath. He said awesomely, "It looks closely related to several well-known life forms, but its shadow—"

The shadow loomed hugely, a pulsating mass with an infinite number of protuberances that abruptly flicked out filaments to probe every crevice of the chamber.

"Better stand back," Darzek said. "It may be armed."

"Rhinzl wasn't armed."

"Rhinzl was overconfident. This one won't be."

Smith moved away, and Darzek switched on a communicator. "Who are you?" he asked.

There was no reply, but the sensitive instrument picked up the shrill breathing of the captive, and a confused flutter of sound that could have been the throbbing of many hearts.

"Where do you come from?" Darzek demanded.

A voice said softly, "Gul Darr?"

Darzek said, "Yes—"

Then paralysis struck him.

His mind remained clear. He could see and hear, though he could not move his eyes. His breathing was a shallow, mechanical flutter within a rigid chest, and his attempted shout died in his throat. Slowly he tipped forward, until his head rested against the chamber.

The voice that boomed out of the communicator was seductive and melodious, like Rhinzl's voice. "This is the infamous Gul Darr, whom your proctors seek for causing the death of the trader Rhinzl. He is now attempting to cause the death of all of you with the sickness he calls a plague."

Darzek thought scornfully, "A fat chance you have of their believing you—*plague carrier.*"

But they did believe. He could hear the slap of sandals as the proctors edged toward him.

The beguiling voice was reciting the iniquities of Gul Darr. He had defied civil authority on the planet Yorlq and betrayed the world to the Dark. He had organized an army of misguided traders and brought it to Primores, intending to betray Supreme to the Dark, but fortunately he had failed. Now he was helpless, theirs for the taking, to be subjected to a just punishment if one severe enough could be devised.

And they were believing. They would believe anything. As Smith had said, they weren't accustomed to liars.

Rigid with paralysis, struggling to breathe through locked teeth, Darzek suddenly identified the Dark's mental weapon.

"It's the lie!" he wanted to scream at Smith. "The Dark's weapon is the lie! He's using it on you now. Don't you recognize it?"

"He will be helpless for some time," the voice purred. "Take him to a secure place and pass judgment on him before he recovers, or he will escape you. All of the power of the Dark is his to command. Let your judgment be swift and sure."

Hands seized Darzek.

"I am proud to have been of service to you," the voice went on. "And now—dim the lights, please. As you know, light is painful to a nocturnal. Dim the lights, and release me, and then destroy these chambers. They purify nothing. They are only another of Gul Darr's treacheries."

"If they release him," Darzek thought, "we'll never catch another one. He'll understand what we were trying to do, and so will all the other Rhinzls. The fools!"

The proctors hoisted him aloft. The lights began to fade, and as they turned Darzek's body he saw Gul Kaln himself opening the chamber doors.

Smith leaped forward. "Stop! He's a plague carrier! He must not escape!"

He tried to wrench Gul Kaln away, but the door was already open. A replica of Rhinzl moved swiftly across the room toward the transmitters. Darzek could only despairingly follow his progress at the periphery of his rigid sight.

Then a familiar figure moved to bar the way. Miss Schlupe. Darzek's shout of warning was an inarticulate moan. He would know who she was, and he would waste no lies on her. His weapon—

She moved her right hand, and a thin spray of liquid played over the creature, found his organs of sight, his crudely gaping mouth. He gasped, fell back with a shudder, and telescoped the weapon toward her. She leaped aside. Smith closed to grapple, struggled briefly, went rigid. The spray flashed again and again.

Abruptly the Rhinzl image faded. The repulsive thing lay on the floor, filaments flailing feebly, until Miss Schlupe prevailed upon Gul Kaln to have it dragged back into the chamber.

Her words sounded shrilly above the upwelling of amazed voices. "I didn't know what was wrong. I still don't know, but I knew he wasn't supposed to get away. Where's Gul Darr?"

Then the lights were turned up, and she saw Darzek. "What happened to him?" she wailed.

Darzek could not even thank her with his eyes. His only consolation was that he'd have plenty of time to rehearse all that he wanted to say to her before he was able to speak again.

19

"The lie?" Miss Schlupe echoed blankly. "The lie—a weapon?"

"Why not? We've seen it used often enough on Earth. Against a people conditioned to accept any statement as the absolute truth, it's the most devastating weapon imaginable. As you found out yourself, they don't even have a word for it. They can't disbelieve a lie, and if the conflict with the truth is drastic enough, it drives them mad."

"If you say so. It doesn't make sense to me."

"It wouldn't," Darzek said. "Not to inveterate liars like us. That's why the uncertified worlds were immune to the Dark. They have enough liars of their own to be able to recognize a blatant untruth when they hear it. In the rest of the galaxy, only the citizens connected with Smith's certification groups are capable of dealing with lies, and unfortunately none of the powers in Supreme's bureaucratic muddle thought to turn them loose on the Dark."

"For a people who have no concept of lying, the rabble-rousers did a pretty competent job of it."

"But they didn't! Not knowing that there was such a thing as a lie, they believed what the Dark's agents told them and repeated it as the truth."

"Why did it take us so long to figure this out?"

"That I'll never know," Darzek said soberly. "There were clues enough. The way they believed our own lies should have been clue enough, from my trading deals right down to our friend the chief proctor swallowing my hoax about the plague."

"The traders lied about the Dark."

"As E-Wusk said, they were wearing their fear. They were so terrified of the unknown power that they developed a mental block. Only Rhinzl practiced deceit in business. The difference should have been obvious to us."

"You didn't notice it because you were so busy practicing deceit yourself. But I'll buy it. The secret weapon was the lie, and the Rhinzls brought it to such perfection that they could set off revolutions almost simultaneously on thousands of worlds."

"Until they reached Primores," Darzek agreed. "When they failed on Primores they had no other weapon in reserve. They couldn't arouse the natives against foreigners, so they used their lies to arouse my foreign troops against the natives."

"What happens now?"

"Work," Darzek said wearily. "One of our first projects will be to correct certain deficiencies in the galactic languages. We need universal synonyms for 'lie' and 'liar.' We might toss in a few hate words, too, so the next invaders from outer space won't have to use their own, as I'm sure Rhinzl and his cohorts did with 'grilf.'"

"You need to do something about the uncertified worlds."

"Right. A little exposure to evil would be a healthy thing for the galaxy. People can't build up an immunity to it if they never experience it. That's for the future, though. We have to settle the Dark first, and since our captive hasn't talked—yet—we'll have to plan on doing it the hard way. Every certified world in the galaxy will have to be briefed and instructed—and purified."

"You'll need a lot of beer. I'll write out my recipe for you."

Darzek smiled. "If we have official support, I think we can manage it without making anyone sick."

"I can read you like a book," Miss Schlupe said scornfully. "A cheap comic book. I know what was in that message URsGwalus handed to you. Supreme wants you on the Council. What number did it offer?"

"ONE."

"Not bad."

"I think it's rather good. The first member of the Council of Supreme. Too bad it has to be secret. I could have designed some lovely calling cards."

"It's not bad for a hick from Earth. Who else is on the Council?"

"I won't know until we meet. I recommended E-Wusk and Smith. You needn't look surprised. Smith has potentialities I never realized. When a person who loathes lying the way he does is able to tell one when a crisis demands it, he's capable of growth. Then E-Wusk and I picked a dozen likely candidates from a list of worthy acquaintances of his, but Supreme probably did as it darn pleased."

"When do you meet?"

"Today. ᴜʀsGwalus is getting a temporary meeting place ready. Are you sure you won't change your mind? There'll be work for you to do, too."

She shook her head. "I miss my rocking chair. And my real rhubarb beer, and my confession magazines, and a lot of things you wouldn't understand. I haven't even been able to get any decent yarn for my knitting."

"We could make arrangements. Smith is going to keep me supplied with cigarettes."

"No. I want my confession magazines hot off the press. I want to be able to walk into a roomful of people without holding my breath—I know you've gotten used to the smells, but I can't. It's been wonderful fun, but I'm tired. I'm beginning to realize that I'm an old woman. Things bother me, like that—that *thing* touching me while I was squirting beer into it. I've taken a dozen baths, and I still feel slimy. Anyway, Smith has already made the only arrangements that interest me—to get me home. He's promised me an appointment to Earth's certification group, so I won't be completely out of touch, but being home is the important thing. I'm glad I saw the galaxy, but I want to die in Brooklyn."

"I suppose this is good-by, then. I owe you more than I can say, so I won't try to say it. I'll miss you, Schluppy."

"I'll miss you, too." Her voice faltered, and then she added brightly, "Anyway, I'll be taking one beautiful memory with me. I'll never forget what a handsome statue you made."

Darzek's first reaction to ONE's handsome official residence was a feeling of overwhelming loneliness. In all likelihood it would be his for the remainder of his life, and he could look forward only to more of the same, a loneliness that would grow and intensify with each passing period.

He could go back to Earth, of course. He'd have to, as soon as the most pressing matters were taken care of, to settle his affairs. But Earth could never be the same to him again, and Primores could never be his home. In a sense he was one of the masters of the galaxy, and he had no world of his own. With Miss Schlupe gone he would have no one to talk with, which was worse.

He dawdled over the notes he was making for the Council's agenda, deliberately waiting until the others had arrived so he could make an entrance. The delay would also give E-Wusk and Smith, if they were among the members, an opportunity to acquaint the others with the new ONE's sterling character and achievements.

"And if they don't give me a proper recommendation, I'll cashier both of them," Darzek muttered.

Finally he stepped through his private transmitter to the Hall of Deliberations. His vivid recollection of the place jolted him. It seemed only a moment before that he had left FIVE's oozing body here and despondently returned to EIGHT's residence and the sleeping Miss Schlupe.

FIVE's body had been removed, but otherwise the gloomy place was unchanged. Darzek hunched his shoulders against Supreme's stinging probes and slowly made his way through the red-lit tunnel.

Abruptly he stood in a dim hallway. From beyond an open door he heard voices, and E-Wusk's booming laugh. He composed himself and strode forward to meet the Council.

Printed in the United Kingdom
by Lightning Source UK Ltd.
9698600001B/68